T·H·E
COVENANT

T·H·E
COVENANT

HILDA STAHL

THOMAS NELSON PUBLISHERS
Nashville

Published in Nashville, Tennessee, by Thomas
Nelson, Inc.

Library of Congress Cataloging-in-Publication Data

Stahl, Hilda.
    The covenant / Hilda Stahl.
      p.   cm.
    ISBN 0-8407-3215-5 (pb)
    1. United States—History—Civil War, 1861-1865—Fiction.
  I. Title.
  PS3569.T312C68 1990
  813'.54—dc20   90-21809
                                         CIP

Printed in the United States of America
3 4 5 6 7 — 95 94 93

CHAPTER

1

♦ Jennet Cordell trembled with excitement and a touch of fear as she tucked the folded linen handkerchief that she'd hand stitched for Wexal Havlick in the frayed cuff of her brown serge work dress. She flipped her thick chestnut-brown braids back over her narrow shoulders. She was used to dressing in the dark, but this morning she'd felt all thumbs as she had buttoned the patched muslin petticoat at her narrow waist and slipped her dress down over her tall, hard-muscled body. She picked up her patched leather shoes, which she'd carefully stuck under the foot of the bed she shared with Marie. It was too dark to see the pegs on the wall where they hung their clothes or the chest or the three beds that almost filled the room.

The gentle snores of her six sisters told Jennet they were still asleep. She crept between the beds to the open stairs. Her heavy skirts swayed against her legs only inches below her knees. She'd tried to tell Ma that she'd grown too big for her dresses, that she needed a dress that covered her ankles since she was fourteen, soon to be fifteen, but Ma didn't hear. And when she'd tried to tell Pa he'd brushed her aside. Lois mumbled something, and Jennet jumped, then breathed a sigh of relief. Lois was talking in her sleep. She'd started doing it just after Ma had taken to her bed three months ago when Baby Vernon had died. Jennet bit her lip. Would Ma ever get over the death of her son? After seven girls she'd been pleased to present Pa with a boy, only to have him take sick and die when he was a month old.

Jennet stepped lightly down the stairs of the two-story cabin, avoiding the treads that creaked. It was almost dawn, and everyone would be up soon. For as far back as she could remember on every farm where Pa had worked, they'd all crawled out of bed at dawn, worked till dark, then fell into bed at night to sleep till dawn, except in the winter, when farm work let up some. Then she and her sisters, as each got old enough, sat at the kitchen table, and Ma taught them to read and write and do sums. Ma had planned to be a teacher before she'd married Pa and education was important to her.

This morning Jennet had to see Wexal before anyone was stirring here or over at the main house. She smiled. Her wide blue eyes sparkled at the very thought of Wexal Havlick.

As she reached the bottom step, the smell of the slop bucket next to the back door hit her and turned her stomach. She could barely make out the shapes in the room from the tiny glow of a heavy log smoldering in the huge stone fireplace. Chairs sat at both ends of the trestle table with a wooden bench at either side. Just beyond the table was the spinning wheel that Grandma Brison had given Ma as a wedding present sixteen years ago. A work table for preparing meals stood beside the cast-iron cookstove.

From the tiny space that Pa had partitioned off as a bedroom, Jennet heard Pa's loud snores and Ma's quieter ones, and she breathed easier. Since Baby Vernon's death, Pa had not slept well. It was still hard for Jennet to walk through the cabin and know that her little brother wasn't sleeping in his cradle but was, instead, in the wooden box Pa had made and buried in the frozen ground under an apple tree nearby.

Impatiently Jennet pushed aside thoughts of the baby. She'd see Wexal, then get the cows in before Pa had a chance to leave the cabin. He'd never know about her secret meeting with Wexal. Nor would Wexal's pa, she vowed silently.

Jennet slipped her shoes over her long wool socks and lifted the wooden latch of the heavy door. Chilly May air rushed in, and she shivered. She got her black wool work coat from a peg near the door and stepped into the predawn darkness. An owl screeched from the woodlot behind the barn. Granger ran to her, whining and wriggling with happiness. She knew he wouldn't bark. He'd been taught to bark only to warn the family or to herd the animals.

"Hello, Granger," she whispered, patting his thick neck and rubbing his pointed ears. "You stay put and wait for Pa."

Granger whined but sank to the ground near the back door.

Flinging her coat around her, Jennet ran lightly across the grass, bright green from April showers and now wet with dew, to the path that led past the two oak trees just budding. Pa had always said when the oak leaves were the size of a mouse's ears it was time to plant corn. He and the other workers on the Havlick farm were hurrying to get the fields ready to plant.

The entire farm had once been covered with hardwood trees and a few evergreen trees, but each year Roman Havlick cleared off more land to farm. He used some of the wood to build his buildings and to burn for firewood, then he piled up the rest of the timber and the tree roots and burned them to get them out of his way. Only the big woodlot remained. Jennet liked walking deep into the woods just to be alone with her thoughts, but she couldn't do it often.

Jennet ran along the barnyard fence toward the big red barn made from black walnut trees. She'd taken the same path many times during the past four years that Pa had worked for Roman Havlick. She glanced southeast of the barn toward the huge two-story farmhouse, but no light flickered in the windows. She knew that Kit, the hired girl, would soon be up to start the fires and cook breakfast for Roman, Lillian, Wexal, and Freeman when he was home. Jennet saw a tinge of light gray in the eastern sky and knew she had to hurry.

She raced along the last few feet of the board fence. Wexal would be waiting for her inside the barn, and she wanted as much time with him as possible. She knew he'd never forget their meeting. Her heart leaped, and she almost laughed aloud for gladness. She slowed as she reached the barn.

Suddenly a work-roughened hand closed over her arm and brought her up short. She stifled a scream, then giggled. "Wexal," she whispered. "You scared me out of a year's growth!"

"How'd you know it was me?" he asked with a low chuckle. "It could've been Free."

"Is your brother home again?"

"Came in last night." Wexal led Jennet inside the barn, closed the wide doors, and lit a lantern that cast a soft glow around them. For a moment the smell of sulfur covered the pungent odors of old hay and manure. The cooing of pigeons in the haymow floated through the early morning stillness. Wex hung the lantern on a peg in the huge hand-hewn support beam, then turned to Jennet. He was a few inches taller than she and lean with hard muscles from working the farm all his life. He wore dark heavy trousers with a gray collarless shirt buttoned to his throat. His head was bare, and he'd brushed his dark brown hair back off his narrow forehead. "Morning," he said softly.

She smiled and her blue eyes brightened. "Happy birthday, Wexal."

"Thank you, Jennet." He stepped closer to her but didn't touch her.

"I got a gift for you," she said breathlessly.

His dark eyes flashed and he chuckled. "Could it be a kiss?"

"No! You know not to ask for a kiss yet. When I'm sixteen, I'll give it some thought."

"That's not for two more years!"

"One year from next month!"

"Oh, so it is!" He grinned and reached for her, but she pushed him away.

"Do you want your gift or not?" she asked sharply.

"Yes." Wex flipped her chestnut-brown braid over her thin shoulder. "But I'd rather have a kiss."

She held out the handkerchief. "It's not much, but I stitched it myself. And look. I stitched a 'W' with white thread in the corner."

He ran his calloused finger over the fancy "W." "I'll treasure it forever, Jen."

Jennet gripped her coat tighter around her thin body. Two of the buttons were missing, and the collar was badly frayed. "You'll get better gifts from your family but not given with more affection. Oh, but I wish I could've given you more!"

"Having you remember is more than enough!" Wexal sighed. "This is just another work day to Pa. He won't remember it's my birthday. Ma won't make a special occasion of it unless Pa says she can." He hunched his broad shoulders, then smiled. "But Freeman brought me a knife and gave it to me last night. And Anne will remember, I'm sure. She'll drive over today unless the baby is cranky or she has another meeting to go to."

Jennet had heard the change in Wexal's voice when he

spoke of his sister's meeting. "I thought you were proud of the work she's doing."

"I am. But it's not right that she can go around making speeches to stop slavery and Pa won't even let me join the army." Wex's dark eyes flashed. "I want to be a Union soldier and help win this war!"

Jennet gripped his hand, and her blue eyes filled with sudden tears. "You know two of the Cross boys went and were killed in the swamps of Virginia! I don't want that to happen to you!"

"I don't either. But I don't want the South to win! Here it is the third of May, 1863, and the fighting is still going on! We all thought it would be over in '61! Nobody thought it would take so many men." Wex lifted his chin. "I don't want anyone to say that Michigan wouldn't fight to stop slavery."

"We've been saying we're against it for as long as I can remember, Wex."

"Saying is not doing! There's another call for Michigan men. I saw it in the Grand Rapids paper yesterday. I want to be one to go!"

Wex's voice rose and Jennet glanced around nervously. "Shh! If your pa heard us in here, he'd whip the daylights out of you."

Wexal's face hardened. "I wish I could be like Free! Pa wouldn't dare whip him."

"But he's twenty, not seventeen. And he doesn't live here like you do."

"I know. He lives in the woods." Wexal scowled. "Sometimes I think he should've been born sooner. He even dresses like the old woodsmen. He would've fit right in as a fur trader with Grandpa Havlick."

"Why's Free home now?"

"Money. He says he knows how he could make a fortune. But Pa is tight as skin on a hog."

"Forget about Free. Your Pa might let you quit early."

Wex rubbed his finger down the side of her face. "He won't," he said, shaking his head.

Roman Havlick owned the huge farm and had several workers, but he worked as hard as all of them. And he made sure his son did too.

"I don't guess my pa will remember my birthday next month what with Ma being how she is, and the spring planting." Jennet stepped closer to Wexal.

He caught her hand and held it. "Your pa would beat you if he knew you were meeting me, wouldn't he?"

Jennet didn't want to think about it. Lately Pa whipped her if she looked at him cross-eyed. She tugged her hand free. "I better get the cows in so he won't suspect I had this time with you."

All at once the barn door was thrown open. Roman Havlick stood framed in the doorway, his eyes blazing with anger.

Jennet wanted to run, but she couldn't move. She felt the tension build in Wex and she wanted to reach out to him, but she kept her hands at her sides. Blood pounded in her ears.

Wexal tried to act as if he wasn't frightened, but Jennet saw perspiration pop out on his upper lip, which was just showing signs of growing hair.

"I caught you two!" Roman unbuckled his wide black belt and jerked it off his thick middle. He folded it and slapped it against his leg with each step he took toward them. "I warned you to stay away from her! I warned you both!" Roman grabbed Wexal's arm, swung the belt, and struck Wexal hard across his backside.

Jennet caught at Roman's thick arm, but he brushed her aside as if she was a pesky fly. "Don't!" she cried. "I only brought him a birthday present!"

"Stop your lying tongue, girl!" growled Roman, his face red as he swung the belt again and struck Wexal a blow that almost sent him to his knees.

Wexal groaned but didn't cry out.

Finally Roman released Wexal and let him fall to the dirt floor. He turned to Jennet, his rage white-hot.

"We were only talking," whispered Jennet with a catch in her voice. "I gave him a birthday gift."

Roman grabbed Jennet's arm and raised the belt. "I told you to stay away from my son! I don't want the likes of you to entice him into sin!"

"I wasn't! I wouldn't do that!" Jennet struggled, but Roman's fingers bit unmercifully into her arm.

With an oath that burned Jennet's ears, Roman swung the belt and struck the top of her leg. Pain exploded inside her, and she cried out before she could stop herself.

Roman's loud, angry words filled the barn as he got ready to use the belt again.

Suddenly the belt was wrenched from Roman's hand. Through her scalding tears, Jennet saw Freeman toss the belt to the floor. A puff of dust rose around it. He pried Roman's fingers from Jennet's arm and pulled her tightly to his side. She smelled his buckskin shirt, heard his rough breathing, and felt the anger in him. Her leg was on fire, and she knew Roman had left a big welt on it.

"Don't strike her again, Pa!" Freeman's voice rang out with authority. He was tall and thin but as strong as the huge pine trees he always talked about. His skin was almost the same color as his leather shirt and breeches stitched together with rawhide. A long knife hung from the heavy black belt circling his lean hips. His dark eyes bored into Roman. "Leave her be! She's not yours to whip!"

"This is none of your affair, Free!" bellowed Roman, doubling his massive fists at his sides.

Jennet pressed closer to Freeman. Her heavy skirts brushed against the welt on her leg, and she almost cried out again. She glanced down at Wexal, who lay curled on his side. She wanted to go to him and comfort him, but she knew she'd better not move.

"I'm making it my business, Pa." Just seeing Pa raise a hand to the thin, frightened girl had sent Freeman's temper flaring. Pa was a hard man, but he had no call to whip a girl that wasn't even his to whip. "If you want to keep these two apart, let Wexal join the Union army like he wants."

"Never!" roared Roman. He kicked Wexal's heavy work shoe. "Not when I need him here." Roman pointed to Wex as he ordered, "Get your breakfast, then go finish plowing the oat field!"

Wexal scrambled to his feet and ran awkwardly from the barn without looking at Jennet or Freeman.

Roman watched Wexal until he was out of sight, then he glared at Jennet. "Your pa will hear about this."

"There's no need for that," snapped Freeman. He didn't want the girl to get yet another beating from Vernon Cordell. The man had always been too hard on her and, from what Wexal had said, was even harder now that his wife had slipped over the edge.

Jennet pulled away from Free, and he reluctantly let her go. She wanted to walk right up to Roman, look him square in the eye, and tell him what a fine son Wexal was to him and that he should appreciate him and trust him, but she couldn't find the courage. "I'll get the cows," she mumbled. Freeman's eyes locked with hers, and she blushed, ducked her head, and hurried from the barn. Perhaps later she could thank him for saving her.

The field hands who worked only during plowing, planting, and harvesting rode in on a wagon, stopped near the toolshed east of the barn, and jumped out to get the plows and horses. It was later than she'd thought.

Inside the barn Free took a step toward Roman. "Let that girl be, Pa. She works hard for you without pay. She and Wex are friends. No more than that." Freeman narrowed his dark eyes. But was that true? Maybe Pa should be concerned.

Roman buckled his belt around his thick middle as he

muttered, "How I treat that girl is *my* concern." Changing the subject, he said, "I thought you were leaving this morning."

"I need the money, Pa." Free hated to beg, but he was desperate. "I can get the land at a good price."

Roman's voice had a harsh edge. "You get that crazy lumbering notion out of your head. Work the farm. That's what you know to do. Not lumbering the white pine."

Free's jaw tightened. They'd had the same argument since Grandpa Havlick had told him of the money to be made off lumbering. "I will lumber the pines, Pa!"

"Not if you don't have money to work with." The reply was all-too-familiar to Free.

"I'll find a way to get it!" Free strode from the barn, anger churning inside him until he thought he'd explode. He'd been so sure that Grandpa had left money to him, but Pa had said different. "I'll get money," he vowed as he jerked open the back door of the house. He'd eat and then ride out. This time he'd not come back!

Several minutes later Jennet let the three cows in the back door of the barn, fed them grain, and milked them. Wincing from the pain in her leg, she carried each bucket of foamy milk to the milk house that stood almost in the shadow of the granary, strained it through the big strainer, lined in the bottom with cheesecloth, into several pans, and set it to cool on the wooden shelves chilled with a block of ice. Kit took most of the morning's milk to town to sell to special customers. Jennet skimmed the night's milk and set aside some of the cream; Kit or Lillian made the rest into butter. They made some of the skimmed milk into cottage cheese, and Jennet fed the rest to the hogs.

Finally Jennet washed the pails and lined them upside down on the wooden racks to dry. For the last three years this had been one of her jobs. Wexal had told her he'd had the job before her, Freeman before that, and their sister Anne before that.

Stepping outside the milk house, Jennet looked south across the rutted road to the hogpen, then east to the big farmhouse. Was Free inside with his mother, or had he already left?

The May sun felt pleasantly warm against her face and head as she walked toward the path leading between the granary and the barnyard. Her stomach growled with hunger. She knew her sisters would have breakfast waiting for her.

Jennet pushed back wisps of chestnut-brown hair that had escaped her braids. As she passed the barn on the way to the cabin, she relived the terrible happenings earlier. Had Roman told Pa yet? she wondered. She hoped Pa was already out in the field plowing.

Suddenly Pa came around the corner of the granary, and he stopped short at the sight of her. She wanted to run away from him and his anger, but she knew that would only make it worse for her when he caught her.

"Roman told me what you did!" roared Pa as he whipped off his thick black belt that kept his heavy red flannel shirt tucked into his patched trousers.

She looked down and plucked nervously at her dress. "I didn't do anything wrong, Pa," she said through a bone-dry throat.

"I heard different, girl!"

She tried to tell him of her innocent meeting with Wexal, but he cut her off.

"I won't listen to lies, Jennet! I told Roman I'd take care of you, and I aim to do just that!" Pa hauled her roughly out of sight of the men plowing the fields, sat on a stone, and turned her over his knee. She wanted to fight him, but she'd learned long ago not to or she'd be spanked harder. She closed her eyes and tried to pretend she was off by herself deep in the woodlot with birds singing above her.

Oh, where was Freeman now? If only he could stop Pa as he'd stopped Roman!

She felt the first whack of the belt and bit her lip to keep from crying aloud. Muttering angrily, Pa whipped her until she thought the skin on her backside would break and bleed. The pain was worse than when Roman had struck her, worse than the other times that Pa had whipped her. She tasted blood from biting her lip, but she didn't cry out. Yet she couldn't hold back the tears streaming down her ashen face. Finally he let her go, and she fell to the ground, unable to stand.

"That'll teach you to stay away from young Wex!" Pa almost shouted as he hooked his belt back in place. He straightened his hat and brushed at his thick beard and mustache. "Get the rest of your chores done. And don't you talk to Wexal again. If you do, Roman swears he'll turn us off his place. How would your ma feel if she had to leave little Vernon's grave? You think on that next time you're tempted to go against Roman's order."

Pa hauled her up, and she yelped from the pain of it. "Now get!" He walked away from her with long, angry strides.

Jennet's whole body ached. She knew she wouldn't be able to sit down very soon. Rage at Pa and Roman Havlick rose inside her, rage that would last long after her bruises and welts disappeared.

She walked slowly by the barn, her fists doubled at her sides. Just then she heard someone whisper her name. She stopped and looked around. Wexal stood just inside the barnyard. His eyes were red from crying, and he looked as angry as she felt.

"I'm sorry, Jen," he whispered as he pulled off his hat and worried the brim.

She lifted her chin and her eyes flashed. "We will always be friends! We promised we would—no matter what!"

"I heard your pa beating you. I wanted to stop him, but I couldn't."

"I know."

"Free's gone or he would've."

Her heart jerked. "Gone?"

Wexal rubbed an unsteady hand over his jaw. "I wanted to go with Free, but I couldn't."

"I know." She knew Wex was too frightened to leave. He couldn't make it on his own away from the farm. He wasn't like Freeman. "I'm real sorry your birthday turned out this way."

He nodded. "I better get to the field before Pa sees me."

"You better."

Jennet smiled and Wexal smiled back. She watched him trudge away.

A few minutes later she stepped into the two-story cabin that Free had told her they'd lived in until eight years ago when his pa had built a big, fancy home more befitting a wealthy farmer.

Smells of cooked food and coffee filled the room. Talking and laughing, the six girls still sat at the trestle table that Ma had insisted stay highly polished. Jennet knew with Pa out of the cabin they could do that. Three-year-old Evie was eating, but the others had finished. Ma wasn't there. Jennet knew Ma would be in her bed, staring up at the ceiling logs. She never heard what anyone said, and she spoke only to ask about Baby Vernon. At times she remembered he was dead.

Her braids bobbing, Marie jumped up and hurried to Jennet as she washed her hands in the basin. Marie was twelve and helped Lillian Havlick with meals when the field hands were there. "Are you all right, Jen?"

Jennet nodded, drying her hands on the damp towel. Her face, hands, and forearms were tanned bronze from hours of outdoor farm work.

Marie lowered her voice to keep Ma from hearing. "I heard Roman tell Pa what you did."

Jennet knotted her fists. "I only gave Wex a birthday gift!"

"I heard Pa say he'd beat you."

"He did," said Jennet grimly.

"I'm real sorry, Jen." Marie ran her hand down her patched, faded apron and fingered the end of her dark brown braid. "I kept your breakfast warm for you. Sit down and I'll bring it to you."

"I'll stand and eat it."

"Oh, Jen! Does it hurt that bad?"

Jennet nodded again. Marie handed her a plate filled with hashed brown potatoes, ham, eggs, applesauce, and two thick slices of homemade bread. Jennet wolfed down the food without tasting it. She drank two glasses of milk, then wiped her mouth with the back of her hand. "Shouldn't you be at the main house, Marie?"

"I'm on my way, but I wanted to see that you were all right before I left." Marie pulled off her apron and hung it on a peg. Lillian Havlick had a nice apron for her to wear.

Jennet set the heavy white plate on the work table. Five-year-old Ida and six-year-old Lois washed the dishes and cleaned the cabin. Nine-year-old Opal and eleven-year-old Nola cooked the meals, baked the bread, washed the clothes, carried the water, and chopped the wood. Jennet helped them if she finished early doing chores for the Havlicks.

Jennet glanced toward Ma's room. "How is she today?"

Marie shrugged. "The same. She wouldn't let me wash her or change her sheet."

Jennet sighed. She had to slop the hogs, feed the chickens, gather the eggs, then clean and sort them so Kit could sell them in town. When those chores were done, it would be time for dinner. After that she'd clean the barns and do evening chores, eat supper, and fall into bed.

With heavy steps Jennet followed Marie out the door.

CHAPTER

2

♦ Freeman Havlick left his hired horse at the livery in Big Pine and strode down the plank walk past the blacksmith and across the sawdust-covered street. As his eyes swept the area, he could see stumps of white pine trees beyond the buildings and the giant pine the town was named for. The pine was about five feet across and reached, arrow straight, at least a hundred and fifty feet into the sky with long sweeping green branches low enough for Free to touch. The needles were over four inches long with five in a blue-green bundle. The gray bark was thick and deeply furrowed into narrow scaly ridges. Once the whole area was covered with giant pine trees, but George Meeker had lumbered them off, making a small fortune. Many a man made his fortune from the trees.

Free knew Grandpa Clay would want him to invest in lumber just as Grandpa had invested in fur trading. They were one blood, born to explore and take chances and fight to survive in the Michigan wilderness. Pa, Ma, and Wex took to farming and Anne to town living. Freeman shook his head. Not him. He wanted life in the wilderness.

A leather sheath on his belt held the knife Grandpa had

given him years ago and had taught him to use in the woods for survival. Although the woodsmen didn't carry guns or knives, defending themselves instead with their feet and hands, Free couldn't give up his knife. It was a frequent reminder of his special times with Grandpa.

For the last two winters Free had chopped down the giant white pines for two different lumbermen. Last summer he'd helped set up camp, but this summer he had a chance to work with Willie Thorne, timber walker, also called a cruiser by some, a man who walked the woods, looking for the timber to cut that would provide the most board feet. Willie had said there was a good chance Free could work with him for George Meeker. But Free didn't want to work for a lumberman. He wanted to be one! Pa should've lent him money to buy timberland, but he wouldn't.

"You stay on the farm where it's a sure living," Pa had said in his gruff way. "Don't get wandering feet like your Grandpa Clay had."

"I thought Grandpa left me money," said Free. Studying Pa carefully, Free wondered, *Would Pa even tell me if he did?*

Pa had pulled his hat lower over his forehead and snapped, "You think I wouldn't tell you if he had left you anything? You think I'm that kind of man?"

Impatiently Freeman forced back thoughts of Pa and watched two men go into the boarding house, a two-story white clapboard building with a peaked cedar-shingled roof. It looked about three times bigger than Pa's house. Off-white muslin curtains hung at the row of windows on the second story. The wide front window on the first story shone as if it had been freshly washed.

The noon sun burned down on Free, making his dark brown hair wet with sweat under his hat. He recalled his first year as a shanty boy in the lumbercamp. One of the men had demanded that he sing a song or tell a story or they'd put him up. He didn't know that putting a man up meant throwing him over the big beam that supported the building they all bunked in while one man held down his feet, another held his head, and yet another pounded his backside with a bootjack. After that he'd gladly told a story or burst into song when asked. He got so he liked the sound of his own voice and sang even if he wasn't asked.

Horses pulling buggies and wagons clip-clopped past him. Big Pine was a small but growing town, busy during the fall and winter when the shanty boys were cutting down trees and during the spring when the river hogs, men wearing high-laced boots with hobnails on the soles to give them a better grip on the logs, floated the logs downriver. Already the river hogs had floated the logs away from Big Pine and on to Grand Haven. It was somewhat quiet during the summer when only the local sawmill was busy and the men setting up camp for the coming winter were around.

Free stepped into the crowded dining room, took off his hat, and rubbed his damp hair. Inside were two long tables with backless benches, and several small round tables with banister-back chairs pushed up to them. All the tables were covered with white tablecloths that looked freshly laundered. Most of the tables were jammed with roaring, swearing, sweating, laughing shanty boys with their red sashes, river hogs whose hobnail boots marked the puncheon floor, and mill workers coated with sawdust. Freeman had made plans yesterday to have dinner and a talk with Willie Thorne. His hat in his hand, Free looked around for Willie.

During a lull, silverware clattered against thick china plates. Smells of coffee, roast pork, and fresh baked bread made Free's stomach growl with hunger. He hadn't realized he was hungry. Since he'd walked away from Pa two days ago, he'd been too angry to think about eating more than a handful of dried corn and some fatback he carried in his pack.

The image of Pa bringing his belt down on Jen flashed

across his mind, and he bit back a groan. He'd wanted to save her from Pa, but he knew he couldn't do more than stop the whipping. Wex should've stood up to Pa and put a stop to the beating. Wex was a fine boy but too scared of Pa. Wex said he loved the girl, but he didn't do anything to protect her. *How could that be love?* Free wondered.

Abruptly Free switched to thinking about his own situation. He had to find a way to make money so that he could buy the sections of timber he wanted to lumber.

Just then he spotted Willie's bright red head. Free made his way through the crowded room to Willie Thorne, seated at the long table. In his late twenties, free as a bird and the best timber walker around, Willie could tell the cash value and board feet of a tract of timber within pennies of the real value. George Meeker paid him well. But Willie had said it was his last year when Free had talked to him yesterday. He wanted to get married and settle in one place to raise a family. He said he'd teach Free everything he knew. Free already knew a lot about timber, and he was willing to learn more.

"How do, Free," said Willie as Freeman sat down. "I already ordered today's special and it'll be here directly."

"Thanks, Willie."

Willie's brown eyes flashed as he smiled. His skin was tanned to a fine teak. His red hair was parted in the middle and combed back on either side of the part. "I talked to George Meeker. You got the job if you want it. It don't pay much, since you're mostly along for the walk. But when you take over from me, it'll pay a whole sight better."

A big-boned woman brought two heavy plates loaded with food and set them down before Willie and Free. They did not speak while they ate. The noise of the place pressed against Free, and he longed to be in the supreme silence of the woods. After finishing two big mugs of coffee and half an apple pie each, they strolled outdoors to the pleasant spring afternoon. Free let the breeze blow through his hair for a minute, then clamped his hat in place. He and Willie crossed the street to the dock where several small boats and canoes were tied.

"Abel Witherspoon is trying to take over some of the property George Meeker wants," said Willie in a low voice for Free's ears alone. "It might get to court, I hear. Meeker wants us to nose around a bit and put a stop to it."

Free trembled with suppressed excitement. He knew how bad some of the fights could get, and the way he was feeling right now he wanted to be in the middle of a big one. It just might help get rid of some of his anger and frustration toward Pa. "What'll we do?" he asked, making sure he didn't sound too eager.

Willie stopped at the water's edge. "I went in this morning and filed. Witherspoon said his timber cruiser filed before me and the clerk wasn't paying close attention."

"Then it's your word against Witherspoon's timber walker," said Free as he watched the water rush along and listened to the frogs sing.

"What he don't know is I always keep two records. The one I file at the clerk's office and the other one with Meeker's lawyer Justin Bracken. If he sold out to Witherspoon, I'll know it. And if it's not him, it's the clerk getting paid off by Witherspoon." Willie pulled out his pocket watch, studied the big face, and finally dropped it back in his pocket. "Mr. Bracken should be in his office. Let's go have a confab with him."

The newly constructed courthouse still smelled of sawed lumber. A man standing in an office doorway puffed at a stubby cigar and nodded slightly as Free and Willie passed him. A sign hung on the wall just inside the wide doors for all to see: HOBNAIL BOOTS NOT ALLOWED. In the silence of the building their boots sounded loud against the wooden floor polished to such a high sheen that Free could see his reflection as they walked down the wide hallway to the third door on the left.

Justin Bracken had his name etched into the glass on the door. Willie pushed it open without knocking, and Free followed him into the large office with walls of wide walnut boards.

Bracken looked up with a scowl. He had a heavy dark beard and mustache and thick hair that reached just below the collar of his suit coat. The room smelled of the pipe that hung from the corner of Bracken's mouth. "What're you doing here, Willie?"

"Witherspoon's timber walker said he already filed on that section Meeker wanted," Willie replied.

"You don't say!" Bracken paused. "When did he file?"

Free saw the lawyer's dark eyes staring intently at Willie.

"This morning when the clerk opened for business."

"Then you filed last night just as the clerk closed for business," Bracken stated flatly.

Willie grinned and nodded. "Right."

Free stiffened. He felt as if someone had hit him in the stomach.

Bracken looked Free over, then turned back to Willie. "Who's that?"

"Free Havlick. Going timber walking with me."

Free moved restlessly from one foot to the other.

Bracken locked eyes with Free. "You closemouthed?"

Free's mouth was so dry he couldn't answer. He shrugged.

"You better be." Bracken pushed himself up and walked around his big desk. "This is a dangerous business, Havlick." Bracken's forehead wrinkled as he thought a minute. "Havlick. Hmmm. Havlick. Ever hear of Clay Havlick?"

"My grandpa."

"You don't say!"

Free nodded.

"You in charge of his tracts of timber?"

Free hadn't heard about the tracts, but he didn't want

Bracken or Willie to think he was stupid about business matters. "My pa is."

"Too bad. We could've worked something out with George Meeker. He's buying timberland as fast as Willie here can find it and claim it. But maybe your pa would want to sell."

Free finally found his voice. "I doubt it. He hangs on tight to what he's got."

Willie laughed and slapped Free on the back. "That's why Free here has to work. He wants to be a lumberman, not a timber walker."

Bracken rubbed his smooth, pale hands together. "I'd like to get a hold of that lumber on Clay's land."

Free didn't want Bracken to approach Pa about any lumber business.

Willie cleared his throat. "Time's a wasting. Let's get on over to the file clerk."

Bracken picked up his pen, dipped it in black ink, and wrote in a ledger. He blew on the ink, blotted it, snapped the ledger closed, and tucked it under his arm. "Ready."

The clerk's office was just down the hall. Three men waited in line at the clerk's window, but Bracken pushed open a gate and walked around to where the clerk stood in front of a huge map.

Free watched them talk quietly. Bracken showed the clerk the ledger, and the clerk nodded. He wrote out a paper and gave it to Bracken.

"I'll get word to Witherspoon that I made an error," Free heard the clerk say as he dabbed sweat off his forehead with a big sweat-stained hankie.

"You do that," said Bracken, chuckling.

Free nudged Willie. "You see what he did?"

Willie frowned at Free. "Keep your thoughts to yourself."

"But he cheated."

"You want a tree to fall on you when you're not looking?

Don't say another word about this deal. I thought you understood how it worked."

Free could hardly believe all he had witnessed. They were cheating Witherspoon! Something told him he should walk away and forget about timber walking with Willie Thorne.

"Don't let Bracken know you're squeamish about cheating," whispered Willie gruffly.

Bracken walked back to Willie and pushed the paper into his hand. "There's your claim deed."

Sweat pricked Free's skin. Pa and Grandpa had taught him to be honest. He scowled. Being honest didn't get him the cash he needed, though. He had to have money. He hadn't done anything wrong; Willie and the lawyer had. He'd keep his mouth shut and he'd go with Willie.

Outdoors several minutes later Willie lifted his pack on his back and checked Free's to see that it was secure. "Get ready to learn how to be a cruiser, Free. The pay is good if you can stay alive and if you can beat the other walkers to the clerk's office."

Free grunted an answer as he walked with Willie toward the trail leading through the stumps into the deep timber. He was going to make money to buy timberland, and right now he didn't care how he did it.

CHAPTER

3

♦ On her fifteenth birthday, June 12, 1863, Jennet stood outside the barn and watched Roman and Lillian Havlick drive onto the dirt road that led to Grand Rapids. Their matched team of grays stepped cautiously, and the buggy bumped along over the ruts. Jennet knew they'd be gone until dark, and she forced back a cheer of freedom. Yesterday when Wexal had whispered that they could meet she'd almost flung her arms about him. This time they could spend time together without getting caught. Even Pa was gone for the day to pick up the gravestone for Baby Vernon.

Jennet felt the warm morning sun on her head and shoulders. Her brown serge work dress felt heavy and hot against her. Her stockings, bloomers, and petticoat were damp with perspiration. Suddenly it didn't matter. Today was her fifteenth birthday! She was practically a grown woman. Maybe now Pa wouldn't take his belt to her if she made him mad.

She watched the daisies along the fence row sway in the gentle breeze that blew the smell of the hogs across the fields and away from the yard. The windmill squeaked as it pumped water into a tank for the horses and cattle. Chickens clucked and scratched in the yard. A rooster crowed, then crowed again.

"Jennet," said Wexal from behind her.

She spun around, smiling. "Wex!" He stood just outside the barn with his hands resting lightly on his lean hips. His blue collarless shirt was buttoned to his chin and the cuffs rolled up on his forearms.

Her braids bobbing, Jennet ran to him. He caught her hand and pulled her inside the barn away from the prying eyes of Kit, the house maid, or any of Jennet's sisters who might be outdoors working.

The barn seemed pitch-dark to Jennet after the bright glare of the sunlight. She closed her eyes tightly, then opened them and was able to see the shadowy stalls and the huge support beams.

Wexal held her work-roughened hands. "Happy birthday, Jen!"

"Thank you! Marie is the only one who remembered." Jennet threw back her head and laughed, and the sound rang to the rafters of the barn. "But I don't care a whit! I remembered and you remembered! And I'm but a year from being sixteen."

Wexal dropped her hands and stepped even deeper into the barn's darkness. "I have news."

She froze at the tone in his voice. The neckline of her dress suddenly seemed too tight. "News?"

"Anne helped me."

"Your sister helped you do what?"

"Enlist. In the Union army."

"No!" The cry tore from her body, and she flung herself against him. She pressed her face into the sweaty front of his rough shirt and gripped his arms with calloused hands. She felt the thud of his heart and heard the sharp intake of his breath. "You can't go, Wex! You can't!" she cried against his chest.

"I must!"

"No! I read the list of the dead in Pa's newspaper yesterday! So many have died in the past two years! And always President Lincoln says the fighting won't last much longer!"

"I am going, Jen."

She lifted her face and saw the set of his jaw. He looked much like Freeman at his most stubborn.

"I'll write to you, Jen. Anne said I could send the letters to her in Grand Rapids and she'd see that you got them."

"I can't let you go! You'll be killed!"

"I must go." Gently he held her from him and looked down into her ashen face. "The president has sent out another call for men. They need me. And I can't stay here any longer to have Pa beat me if I even look at you."

"But what of me? I can't live without you!"

He pulled a folded bit of linen from his pocket. "Take this handkerchief that you stitched for me and keep it close to your heart. It's my promise that I'll come back to you."

"Oh, Wex!" She pressed the folded hankie to her lips and tears filled her wide blue eyes.

"I have more news," he whispered. "This is about you."

Trying to calm herself, she tugged at the high collar of her work dress and pushed damp wisps of hair back against her braids.

"Anne knows a woman in Grand Rapids who is looking for someone to take care of her three children. I said you would want the job."

"But how can I leave my family with Ma the way she is?"

"Marie is a fine, big girl. She can manage."

Jennet finally nodded. "Yes. Yes, she can."

"I told Anne that you'd take the position."

Jennet closed her eyes for just a moment, her head

whirling at the daring thought, then she opened her eyes and said, "Yes. Yes, I'll do it!"

"Good." Wex trailed a finger down her sun-browned cheek. "I'll miss you, Jen."

"Oh, Wex!"

"I leave two days hence, and I will take you to Grand Rapids with me. Anne will see that you get to the family she knows."

Jennet's heart almost burst. "Two days!"

"You can be ready."

She looked at him uncertainly. "I can't picture how it will be not to work the farm!"

"Anne said you will have time to read and to sew. You'll have one day off a week, and your wage is very generous." He named the sum and she gasped, her head spinning at the thought of such wealth.

"I've never had my own money," she said.

"Anne said they provide your clothing and your room and board. Your money will be yours to use in any way you choose."

Jennet sank back against a stall. A barn cat rubbed against her ankle, mewed, and ambled off toward the open door of the tack room. Dust particles floated in the air around her. A barn swallow swooped in, around the great rafters, then out. "Money of my own! Is it a dream?"

Wex caught her hand and held it to his heart. "When I return, I want you as my wife."

"Your wife!"

"I love you, Jen. You know I do. I signed up for three years, but talk is that the war will be over before 1863 draws to an end. When I return, we'll be wed."

She tugged her hand free. "What of your pa?"

Wexal's face drained of color, but he lifted his chin a fraction. "He'll not be able to stop me."

"He will," she whispered.

Wex hung his head.

Jennet rubbed his hankie against her cheek. "I'll keep this with me always. When you return, we'll see."

"But you will wait for me? You won't marry another?"

She laughed breathlessly. "Who would I marry?"

"When you live in town, you'll meet available men, men who will see your beauty and charm."

She flushed. "Beauty? Charm?" She didn't know she had either.

He laughed and pulled her to him. "Since I might not be with you on your sixteenth birthday, may I have a kiss now?"

Her lips tingled with the thought, but something held her back. She laughed shakily and pushed away from him. "You are too bold, Wexal."

"Only one kiss, Jen."

She shook her head.

Anger flashed in his eyes and she thought he would take a kiss, but the anger faded and he smiled and shrugged. "I will wait."

He led her to the wooden bench in the tack room where he'd sat many times to oil and repair harnesses. He held her hand as he talked of the war and how he planned to fight. "I will make Michigan proud! I will make you proud, Jen." He smiled and looked off into space. "And even Pa."

"I will indeed be proud of you," Jennet whispered. She couldn't imagine traveling so far away. She'd lived her whole life in Michigan on farms in the Grand Rapids area. Pa had worked on several farms, and the last four years on Roman Havlick's, one of the largest farms around.

They sat in silence a long time, and finally she asked him more about what the woman would expect of her. He told her all that Anne had told him. Butterflies fluttered in Jennet's stomach.

"I will meet you Sunday morn in the woodlot behind

your cabin," said Wexal as he traced a scratch up the back of her hand to her rolled-up frayed cuff. "Have your things ready, so you can go with me."

"Oh, do I dare?"

"You must! I want a better life for you. I don't want your pa to beat you ever again." Wexal gently squeezed her hand.

Right then she decided that she would give him a good-bye kiss. She would not wait until she was sixteen and old enough to wed! The daring thought almost took her breath away. She smiled a slow, secret smile. He would take her kiss with him to war as her promise to him. He would have it just as she had his handkerchief.

For the rest of that day and the next, Jennet smiled each time she thought of her bold decision. Once Marie asked her if she had a secret, but she wouldn't tell. Oh, but Marie noticed too much!

On Sunday evening Jennet returned to the cabin for supper. Granger ran to meet her, wagging his tail. She patted his head and started to speak to him, then stopped when she saw a horse and buggy hitched to the rail.

Just then Pa and another man walked into sight from behind the cabin. "Uncle Tait," she muttered. He'd probably come to collect the money Pa had owed him for over a year now. She knew he wouldn't get it this time either, for Pa had used it to buy the gravestone for Baby Vernon.

"Jen," called Pa. "See to Tait's horse."

Jen wanted to refuse, but she didn't dare. She hated being near Uncle Tait.

Tait pulled his pipe from his mouth and grinned. "Hello, Jen." He was almost forty, three years older than Pa. They looked alike with the same dark unkempt beard and mustache. But they dressed differently. Tait owned a store in Prickett, a settlement in the pines north of Grand Rapids. His white shirt and dark suit showed that he was a well-to-do merchant.

He eyed Jennet up and down, then slapped his thigh. "I swear, Jen, you growed more since last I saw you."

"I am fifteen now," she said.

"You don't say!"

Jennet quickly unhitched the horse and led it to the small barn where Pa kept his horse and wagon. She took as long as she could feeding and watering the horse. Leaving the barn, she looked at the woodlot where she was to meet Wexal at dawn. In the morning her new life would start! Finally she walked to the cabin, her steps a little lighter.

Jennet hesitated at the door. Maybe she could go right upstairs to bed without eating so that she wouldn't have to see Tait. But her stomach reminded her of how hungry she was.

She pushed open the door and went in. Tait's pipe tobacco smoke clouded the room. Supper was on, and the girls sat at the table along with Tait and Pa. The girls ate in silence while the men talked about the war and how they'd both go if they were younger and didn't have responsibilities. Jennet slid into her spot and filled her plate with a thick slab of roast beef, several chunks of potatoes covered with rich gravy, and a mess of dandelion greens. She buttered two slices of bread and filled her cup with milk. Several times she caught Marie looking oddly at her. Marie couldn't know that she was leaving with Wexal before dawn, could she?

Suddenly Jennet realized that Tait would be sleeping the night on a pallet near the fireplace. Could she leave without waking him? What would she say if she was caught with her bundle of clothes? Oh, she was too tired to think! Come dawn she'd know what to do.

The next morning Jennet crept around the beds in the darkness. She'd decided to leave her things. Marie could have them. Thoughts of sneaking past Tait pushed aside the terrible feeling of leaving her family. Later she'd find a way to write to them about her wonderful job and her life in town.

At the top of the steps, Jennet stopped dead. The sound of low voices told her Pa and Tait were already up! She went down a step or two until she could see Tait in Pa's chair and Pa on a bench, his right arm snaked across its back.

Jennet's heart hammered hard against her rib cage, and her tongue clung to the roof of her dry mouth. What could she do? Her head spun as she tried to think.

Maybe she could go outdoors as if she was headed to the outhouse. Maybe they wouldn't give her a thought.

She breathed easier as she walked down the steps. She knew the lamplight was too dim for them to read the fear on her face.

Jennet immediately sensed the tension in the room. She turned to run back upstairs, but Pa looked up and spoke her name. Trembling, she approached the long trestle table where they sat.

"Good morning," she said stiffly. Oh, she had to get to Wexal! Would he leave if she didn't meet him before sunrise?

Tait turned to Pa. "You want to tell her?"

"Tell me what?" asked Jennet, suddenly too frightened to stand. As she sank to the empty bench, she heard a sound overhead and knew the girls were dressing. She glanced frantically toward the door. Wexal would be wondering where she was.

Pa rubbed a large hand over his mustache and beard. "Jen, you're going with Tait to work for him."

Her mouth dropped open, but she snapped it shut as she shook her head in disbelief.

"It's all settled," said Tait. He jabbed Pa's arm. "Vern, I'll put it in writing that your debt is settled."

"Pa?" she said with a questioning look.

He scowled at her. "This'll keep Roman from throwing

us out, and it'll settle my bill with Tait. You work for him until the bill is paid."

"But I can't!"

"Mighty sassy girl there, Vern."

Pa reached across the table and grabbed Jennet's arm. "You watch your mouth, girl! This very day you will belong to Tait."

"Belong to him?" she whispered.

"Indentured slave," said Tait. He prided himself on knowing all kinds of facts.

"A slave? But Michigan won't allow slaves," she said.

"This is different," snapped Tait.

But Jennet couldn't see how.

"I own you until the debt is paid. You can't leave me until then." His eyes hardened. "If you try, you'll be sorry. It's legal to beat indentured servants who don't obey their masters."

Jennet looked helplessly at Pa, hoping for a sign that would show her he wasn't serious. But he kept his eyes on the papers in front of Tait.

Pa cleared his throat. "You write it down there that Jen works for you only three years. And no more than that! I won't have you work her all her life."

Tait chuckled. "So be it, Vernon." He scribbled on one paper and pushed it toward Pa. "Sign it and date it."

A bitter taste rose in Jennet's mouth and her stomach rolled. "What about Ma? What will she say about me being gone?" asked Jennet.

"She won't notice," said Pa bitterly.

Jennet glanced toward Ma's room, then back at Pa. "When do I go?" she asked hoarsely.

"Now!" announced Tait.

"Now?" she said in agony.

"Let the girl eat first," said Pa.

Tait pulled out his gold pocket watch, then shrugged his broad shoulders. "I could use some food too."

"What about my chores?" asked Jennet weakly.

"Marie will do them," said Pa.

Jennet locked her icy hands behind her back. Pa had all the answers. Oh, what was to become of her?

Pa strode to the stairway and called, "Girls, get down here and get breakfast on the table." He turned to Jennet. "Gather your belongings so you'll be ready to go when you're done eating."

Jennet looked at him, her eyes wide in horror. Could her pa actually sell her? Did he hate her that much? She left the table. The girls scurried into the room and she stopped Marie with a look.

"I heard," whispered Marie, close to tears.

"Tell Wexal," whispered Jennet.

"I will."

"Tell him now. He's in the woodlot."

Marie cocked a dark brow, but Jennet didn't answer her unspoken question. Marie nodded and whispered, "I'll tell him."

"Thank you!"

"I'll miss you, Jen."

"I'll miss you. Try to get Ma out of bed."

"I will." A tear ran down Marie's cheek, and she quickly brushed it away.

Upstairs Jennet tied her change of clothes into a gray shawl that she used on chilly days. She pulled Wexal's hand-stitched handkerchief from inside her bodice and held it to her face. Would Marie find Wexal to tell him what had taken place? Had he seen the light in their cabin and left without her? The morning that had held such promise had turned into a nightmare.

Jennet tucked the hankie against her heart and picked up her bundle. Back downstairs the others sat around the table eating. She looked longingly at the door. Could she make a run for it? She and Wexal could ride away where neither Tait nor Pa could find her.

Marie nodded slightly when Jennet caught her eye, then left the table and went outside. Maybe after Wexal heard what was to become of her he'd rush to her rescue.

Her shoulders slumped. Wexal was not Freeman. She couldn't escape, and she might as well stop thinking about it.

She tiptoed into Ma's room and sat on the edge of the bed. Morning light already shone through the window. Ma didn't look at her but kept her glazed eyes on the ceiling. Her chestnut-brown hair hung in tangles, and the room smelled of sweat and body odor. Jennet picked up Ma's lifeless hand and held it firmly. "Ma, I'm going away," she said softly. "Pa sold me to Uncle Tait." Her voice broke. "I must stay with Uncle Tait for three years and work off Pa's debt. Oh, Ma, please hear me! Stop Pa from doing this!"

But Ma wouldn't hear, and Jennet finally leaned over and kissed the pale face. "Good-bye, Ma."

Jennet joined the others and ate without talking. The girls silently watched her. Pa and Tait discussed the war and how much the government was pushing to get more Michigan men to join the army. Jennet thought unhappily of Wexal's being one of those men.

A few minutes later Jennet forced back her tears and told her sisters good-bye while Tait went to hitch the horse to the buggy. The girls cried a little, but Pa hushed them with a hard look and harsh words.

Pa followed Jennet out the door. She glanced around for Marie. Probably Wexal was long gone, but had Marie seen him before he left?

"I want to say good-bye to Marie, Pa," said Jennet.

"I'll say it for you," Pa said coldly without looking at her.

Her heart sank. How she wanted to cry and scream and refuse to leave! Instead she climbed up beside Tait in the buggy. He grinned broadly and sat with his shoulders square, a tall beaver hat on his head. He was proud of having become prosperous.

"So long, Vern," said Tait, laughing. "I was beginning to think you'd never be out of my debt."

Pa turned away without answering him.

Jennet's eyes filled with tears, but she wouldn't let them fall as the buggy rolled away from the cabin and out to the dirt road. Oh, how she wanted to leap out and run where Tait couldn't find her!

"Buggy's too rough," Tait declared. "River is my way of traveling." He gripped the reins tight as if he wasn't used to the feel of them in his hands. "I'll leave the buggy when we get to the Thornapple River. We'll take a canoe up the Thornapple to the Grand to Prickett."

Tait rode in silence by the grain fields and around a tree-covered hill. He passed the turn-off that led to Irving where Kit sold milk and eggs. Then he cleared his throat and said, "Your pa says you can read and write and do sums."

"I can," she managed to say as they rode into the shade of several tall oaks.

"You can help with the books as well as keep the store clean. We work long days."

Jennet was used to that, but she wasn't used to working indoors or being away from home. When Tait turned off on the road that led to the Thornapple River, she asked, "Where will I live?"

"Alone in a room in back of the store."

How would it feel to have an entire room to herself? She'd always shared a room with her sisters. "Where do you live?" Her voice sounded strained even to her ears.

"I have a place," he said, looking sharply at her from the corner of his eyes.

Pa had said that he lived with a Pottawatomie squaw, but Jennet didn't ask about that.

"I have a dress for you, one that don't smell like a cow barn."

Jennet's jaw tightened. She hadn't realized she smelled.

She didn't like his sweaty body odor or the stench of his pipe, but she didn't tell him.

Within an hour Jennet saw other buggies and wagons near the bank of the Thornapple River. Farmers stood talking and laughing outside a general store that looked cluttered on the inside as well as the outside. Jennet wrinkled her nose at the fishy smell of the river. Along the opposite shore mallard ducks caught her attention.

After returning the hired buggy to an old man leaning against a wooden fence to the left of the store, Tait spoke to a couple of men inside the store. They came out and loaded his supplies in a wide birchbark canoe. Two Indians were ready to paddle them to their destination.

The canoe swayed as Jennet stepped in, and water slapped against its sides. She moved easily with the pitch of it and carefully sat on the middle seat. Boxes covered the floor in front of and behind her, situated just right for balance. Tait sat beside Jennet without a word to her. He talked to the Indians as they pushed off. They answered back with short, gruff sentences.

Jennet held back the cries of despair that rose in her as the canoe shot through the water, taking her further away from her family and the only way of life she knew. She heard the birds singing in the trees lining the river, but she didn't look at them. She kept her eyes glued to the Indian's back.

The day felt like one long painful blur. She barely noticed when they left the Thornapple to go into the Grand River.

Just after midday the Indians docked between two boats at Prickett. Across the rutted street a big wood frame building painted white displayed a huge sign above the door: TAIT'S PLACE. Farm implements stood on one side of the building. A large white warehouse occupied a lot on the other side. Through the store's open door, Jennet saw an old man talking to a woman with a basket on her arm. Goods of all kinds lined shelves and were stacked in the wide front windows that badly needed washing. Down the street on the same side as the store, another building was labeled TAIT'S SHOE FACTORY. Several yards away from the docked boats a stone building bore the sign TAIT'S GRISTMILL. Jennet frowned. Uncle Tait owned much more than she thought. There were other buildings, but they didn't carry his name.

Tait stepped to the dock and said to the Indians, "Unload the supplies and take them across to the store. Old Gabe will pay you in supplies."

Jennet carefully climbed from the canoe, her bundle in her hand. She felt as if she were still swaying in the water, but she soon found her legs and crossed the street with Tait.

They went around to the back of the building. A small barn and an outhouse were just beyond the back door of the store. Tait led her into a room that smelled closed in and dusty. Jennet saw a small greasy cast-iron cookstove, a cot, a dresser, one chair, and a small wooden table scarred with scratches and burns crammed into the tiny space.

"The man who worked for me slept here," Tait said.

"Where'd he go?"

"Killed by a bear. Left me shorthanded."

His matter-of-fact tone made Jennet look at him uneasily. Just as she dropped her bundle on the cot, a mouse zipped across the room and into a hole in the wall.

Tait ignored the fleeing creature. He pointed to her bundle. "Those clothes clean?"

"Yes."

"Put 'em on so you don't smell the place up." He looked down at her feet. "Got shoes without manure on 'em?"

"Only these."

He peered down at them, taking the measurement with his eyes. "I have a pair you can wear, but that'll be added to your bill. Anything you cost me will be added on to your time here."

Jennet bit back a response. He really was going to treat her like a slave!

Tait opened the connecting door to his store. "I'll get your shoes," he said and walked away.

Her head down and her eyes wet with scalding tears, Jennet thought, *What is to become of me? If only I'd been able to go to Grand Rapids with Wexal!*

In a few minutes Tait came back with a pair of black shoes and a gray dress of a lightweight fabric. He dropped them on the cot beside her bundle.

"I'll be out there working," Tait said, jabbing his thumb toward the connecting door. "You come in as soon as you change. And make it snappy."

Jennet barely nodded.

Tait closed the door behind him, and she stood alone in the room that reeked of tobacco and liquor and dirt.

She sank to the chair and moaned desolately. She pulled Wexal's hankie out and ran her finger over the "W" she had stitched. Tears again filled her eyes and slipped down her cheeks. A spider dangled from its web near her face and she swatted it away, sending the web and spider flying across the room.

Finally she closed the outside door, shutting out sounds of the water slapping against the dock and the men shouting at one another on the boats. She found fresh water in a pitcher, washed, changed her clothes and slipped on her new shoes. They felt strange on her feet but fit fine. The high-necked dress tucked in at her narrow waist, then billowed out to hang almost to the floor. She touched the black piping that went around the neck and down either side of the row of black buttons. She glanced down at her feet and noticed that her ankles were covered. She brushed out her hair, rebraided it, and pinned the braids across the back of her head instead of leaving them hanging over her shoulders. She patted Wexal's hankie that she'd tucked in her bodice. Suddenly she remembered that she'd never had the chance to give Wexal her kiss. He had nothing of hers to see him through the war.

"Oh, Wexal," she whispered brokenly.

She took a deep steadying breath and with a heavy heart entered Tait's store.

CHAPTER

4

♦ Jennet walked uncertainly down the crowded aisle toward the front of the store where Tait was talking with the man he'd called Old Gabe. The strange combinations of smells of the fabrics, leather goods, tools, and the black licorice sticks in the jar near the cash register made Jennet's stomach turn.

"Well, well," said Tait, eyeing Jennet up and down. "You clean up real good." He turned to the white-haired man beside him. "Old Gabe, this is my niece, Jen. She'll be working for me for some time to come. You get on back to the mill. Tell Park I'll be there before closing."

Old Gabe grinned a toothless grin at Jennet and limped out without a word. Wide gray suspenders kept his heavy baggy trousers up high on his skinny hips and his faded blue shirt tucked in. He stuck a floppy-brimmed hat on his balding head.

Tait pulled out a big gray and white feather duster from behind the counter the brass cash register sat on. He shoved it toward Jennet. "Run this over the shelves, and then you can walk down the street to the boarding house and get yourself some supper."

"I never ate anyplace but home," she said as she gripped the feather duster.

"Nothing to it!" Tait spread his hands wide. His whiskers moved as he talked. "You walk in, sit down, and somebody will ask you what you want to eat. You tell 'em and they bring it to you. You eat it and pay for it and walk out."

"Pay for it?"

He reached in his pocket, pulled out a coin, and flipped it to her. She caught it easily and looked down at it, wondering how anyone could spend so much on a plate of food.

"Get to work. And be quick about it! One thing I can't stomach is a dawdler." Tait turned away to open one of the wooden boxes that he'd brought on the canoe.

Jennet laid the coin on the counter. She started at the end of the first aisle that held piles of men's shirts and trousers and brushed the feather duster over the exposed wood of the shelf and across the top items. She climbed up a ladder to reach the top shelf nailed to the back wall and dusted kerosene lamps of various sizes, glass flower vases, and decorative cans to use in a pantry for foodstuff to keep out the bugs and mice. "This is not like cleaning a barn," she muttered to herself.

From her high perch Jennet glanced around. The main room was a little bigger than Pa's cabin. Tait's office was even smaller than the room he had given her to live in. The store walls were wide boards and had aged to a deep brown. A potbellied stove stood in the center of the room with a rocking chair and a short bench beside it. The stovepipe ran up through the ceiling to a brick chimney. Counters with shelves reaching the ceiling lined the walls, breaking only for the doors. An L-shaped shelving unit stood between the front door and the stove. Could she survive working here for three years after being so used to outdoor work?

Jennet swallowed hard as she climbed down the ladder. She had no choice. She had to survive.

Canned goods, jars, tools, rifles, axes of different sizes,

knives, crockery, cooking pots and other utensils, shoes and boots, folded shirts, ladies' clothes, yard goods, and items Jennet couldn't begin to name—everything was coated with dust, and cobwebs hung from the ceiling. Several times she stepped out on the plank walk to shake the dust off the big feathers. The man who'd been killed by a bear must not have dusted in a long time.

When she finished, she stuck the duster back under the counter and said just above a hoarse whisper, "I'm done."

Without looking up from his bookwork in his office, Tait said, "Don't dawdle over your food either."

"I won't." She wondered when he'd eat, or if he'd even take the time. Would his squaw have supper waiting for him?

Outside the store Jennet looked up and down the street. A man on horseback rode silently past, a muzzleloader resting across his legs. A bulldog in front of the gristmill rose to its feet, watched the rider, then settled back in the sunlight. The river splashed against the dock, rocking the boats. Over the sound of the water Jennet heard children laughing and shouting, but she couldn't see them. Would she meet someone her age? She frowned. Tait wouldn't let her take time to make friends, so why even think about it?

She headed toward the weathered frame boarding house on the far side of the shoe factory. A warm breeze blew smells of the river and the pines to her. Suddenly she stopped and looked helplessly back at the store.

"Ma, why did you let this happen to me?" Jennet chocked back a sob. "Pa, how could you sell me?" The day's events tumbled through her mind. Just then a man and a woman walked out of the boarding house, letting the screendoor close with a sharp bang. The noise jarred Jennet from her thoughts. She knew she better hurry up and get a meal.

Inside the boarding house several woodsmen sat along one side of a long table. Two middle-aged women encased in big white aprons waited on them. Ladder-back chairs were turned upside down on the small square tables along the wall. A stone fireplace covered the far end of the room, the hearth blackened from use. The wide wooden boards of the floor were scarred with bootmarks but seemed clean. Pencil drawings of a lumbercamp and of trees were framed and hung on the unpainted wide boards of the walls. Smells of ham, beans, bread, and coffee made Jennet's stomach growl and her mouth water. But she wasn't sure where she should sit and her face burned with embarrassment.

"Look at that purdy girl!" cried one of the men no older than Free.

Jennet looked around for the girl he was talking about, but she couldn't see one. She glanced at the man to find him staring at her. He'd called her pretty! How strange!

The man walked right up to her. "How about sittin' with me, purdy girl?"

The smell of whiskey on his breath turned her stomach as she jerked back. "Get away from me," she whispered.

"Leave her be, Pike," said an older man.

"Not till I get her to sit with me." His black hair was cut short, making his ears seem extra big. He hiked up his gray trousers as his dark eyes sparkled with laughter. He pushed his face up to hers, and she jumped back to get away from him. When he caught her arm and pulled her toward him, she doubled her fist and punched him square in the nose. Blood spurted, and he yelped and covered his nose.

The other men cheered. One man yelled, "A real wildcat! That Tait's one lucky man."

Jennet's face flamed. "I am his niece," she said as calmly as she could. "And I work for him!"

"That's sure good to know," said a man with bright red suspenders. "We thought you was his woman. Can I come calling?"

Jennet scowled at him. "I am promised to a man off fighting to set the slaves free," she said. It wasn't exactly the truth, but close enough.

"Don't tease the girl," said a tall man with blond hair and a scar running from the corner of his right eye down to his jaw.

Smiling, one of the women walked up to Jennet. She had gray hair and wrinkles lined her face. "My name is Midge Dooley. Don't mind these men. They're not around unattached females much. They don't remember their manners at times. Sit right down and I'll get something for you to eat."

The kind voice brought tears to Jennet's eyes. She ducked her head and blinked them quickly away, then sat at one end of the long table away from the rowdy men.

The ham, beans, bread, and milk took away her hunger, but she couldn't enjoy the food with the men watching her every move. She turned down the cookies, paid for the meal, and walked out. The sun was low in the sky. Would Tait think she'd dawdled?

When she walked into the store and around the aisle, Tait glared at her. How she wanted to turn and run from him!

"News travels fast around here, girl." Tait slapped a piece of leather strap against his leg. "I heard you bloodied Pike's nose. Made a real spectacle of yourself. I won't stand for that."

"He wouldn't leave me alone!"

"Don't sass me, Jen Cordell!"

She saw the anger in his eyes, and she turned away without another word.

"Don't you turn away from me before I'm done talking to you! Your pa might've spoiled you, but not me! You don't back talk me and you don't walk away from me till I give you leave!" Tait swung the leather strap and caught Jennet on the backside. She cried out in pain and backed away from him until she bumped into a counter of material. Tait slapped the strap against his hand. "That's only a warning. Next time it'll be worse."

Jennet moaned as she thought of three years of Uncle Tait. Maybe she should run away into the wilderness and try to survive there, despite the wild animals. But she knew she wouldn't. She and Wex were just alike. Neither of them had the courage to stand up and fight or to run away. But Wex had found the courage to join the army.

Had he really gone, or had his pa learned his plans in time to stop him?

"Unload them boxes onto them shelves and be quick about it," said Tait as he motioned to the boxes.

Jennet stacked canned goods on the shelves and worked until it was dark out.

"I put together some groceries for you so you don't have to spend time or money at the boarding house," said Tait as he carried a box to her room. "Don't go eating it all in one day. What I gave you has to last a week."

That night after she'd used the outhouse and carried in a bucket of water from the well, she sank to the edge of her cot. The lamp cast a soft glow around the room. She'd locked both doors, but still she felt afraid. It was so quiet! Were her sisters already sound asleep for the night? Could she sleep without hearing them nearby?

Tears trickled down her face as she slipped into her nightdress. She washed with the cold water and dried with a towel that Tait had given her.

Jennet heard a dog bark and a man yell at it. She looked at the lone window covered with shutters. "I can't stay here," she whispered. "I can't! Not for three long years! Not even for three days!"

She crawled between the scratchy blankets on the cot and rested her head against the pillow. How different the cot felt! Oh, how could she sleep without Marie beside her?

After a long time Jennet drifted into an uneasy sleep and

woke the next morning with a start. She thought she'd overslept and Pa would beat her for not milking the cows on time. She sat up and realized she was at Tait's store, not the Havlick farm. Her heart sank. "No! It's not a bad dream!"

She lit the lamp, started the fire, quickly boiled a pot of water, and made cornmeal mush that she ate with maple sugar. It was a far cry from the breakfasts her sisters fixed for her.

She had just finished washing and dressing when someone knocked lightly and a little hesitantly on her back door. Who could that be? Cautiously she opened the door a crack. It was light out already, but the sun wasn't up yet. An Indian woman younger than Ma stood there with a basket in her hands. She was dressed as a white woman, but her straight black hair hung to her shoulders and a headband was tied around her forehead. Jennet stared at her in surprise.

"Don't be afraid of me," the woman said.

"What do you want?" asked Jennet uncertainly.

"I brought you milk and bread and butter," said the woman in a soft, pleasant voice.

"Why?"

"I knew you'd need them."

Jennet stepped aside for the woman to enter.

"I am Eve," said the woman. Her dark eyes sparkled as she smiled.

"Eve?"

"A white woman's name, I know. But I am called Eve because I am a follower of Jesus Christ. I am Tait's wife."

Jennet gasped in surprise. "His wife?"

"He calls me his squaw because he is ashamed that he married a Pottawatomie." She talked as she set the jar of milk, a loaf of bread, and a large chunk of butter onto the table. "He said you came back with him. I was afraid he wouldn't take good care of you. I brought you this while he is still asleep. It would be better if he does not know what I did."

"Thank you very much." Jennet rubbed a hand down her dress. "I'm sorry if I seemed rude, but you took me by surprise."

"I know," said Eve. "We live in a cabin a short walk from here. If you need me, I will be there."

"Thank you."

"But don't tell Tait that we have met. He likes to think that I spend my days in his house away from people." She laughed, and Jennet found herself liking this gentle woman.

Jennet smiled. "I'm glad you came."

"I must get back and milk the cow before it's time to make breakfast."

Jennet didn't want to see her leave. "Will you come again?"

Eve nodded. "Each morning just after dawn."

"Thank you! I am so lonely!"

Eve wrapped her arms around Jennet and held her close.

Jennet stiffened, but it felt so good to be held that she relaxed. It had been a long time since Ma had hugged her.

Eve smoothed Jennet's hair and gently patted her back. "May you learn to lean on Jesus my Lord. He will take away your loneliness and your pain."

Jennet had read Ma's Bible, but she didn't know that Jesus could take away loneliness or pain. "I have no Bible to read to learn about Jesus."

Eve stepped back from Jennet but caught her hands and held them tightly. "The preacher gave me one, but I can't read. I will share it with you."

"Thank you."

"You are very welcome." Eve smiled, pulled her shawl tighter around her slender shoulders, and walked away with the empty basket.

Jennet watched until Eve was out of sight, then quickly

sliced off a great hunk of bread, buttered it, and ate it. The crust was crunchy and delicious, the inside soft and yeasty. The butter was sweet and lightly salted, as good as any she'd tasted at home. She drank all the milk because she had no place to keep it cool during the day. Now, she felt as if she'd had enough for breakfast. She tucked the bread and butter away so that Tait wouldn't see it if he entered her room. She'd eat it before she went to bed.

A few minutes later she started to work in the store. She'd try not to do anything that would make Tait angry enough to whip her. He'd said he'd show her how to work the cash register and wait on customers. Once she'd learned that, he wanted to teach her to keep the books for the store, the shoe factory, and the mill.

Jennet thought of what he'd do to her if she couldn't learn as quickly as he wanted her to and she groaned. She unlocked the front door and looked at the quiet river. Not a boat or a canoe was in sight. "Wex, come get me," she whispered.

She turned away with her head down and her eyes burning with unshed tears. Wex wouldn't get her. Not even Free could save her this time.

CHAPTER

5

♦ His heart hammering, Free ducked around a giant pine out of sight of Driscoll's timber walker Keith Kirkwood. If Willie Thorne knew that Kirkwood was marking off the same section as they were, he'd see that a heavy branch fell on him and pinned him down for a while or maybe even for good.

Free pulled off his hat and wiped sweat from his forehead and hair. His shirt felt too tight and his trousers too hot. And it had nothing to do with the steamy September weather. During the summer, he'd learned how far Willie went to get land for George Meeker.

Willie just might be desperate enough to kill Kirkwood. Free's jaw tightened. He didn't want any part of murder. He wanted money in a bad way—but not that bad. A few times he'd thought of leaving Willie, but he couldn't seem to do it. He frowned. He had to admit that fear was part of it, and he didn't want to lose the money he'd earned for the summer's work even though it was only twenty dollars.

Mosquitoes buzzed around Free, but he ignored them as he pulled out his compass and carefully charted the direction. If he walked to the creek and went northwest, he could meet up with Willie to lead him away from the section Kirkwood was marking, then they could head for Big Pine to file before Kirkwood did. As payment Willie Thorne received a quarter of the land he found for George Meeker. Willie had told Free he wanted as much as he could get so he could live in comfort for the rest of his days. Free wanted to make that kind of money, too, and more, but not if he had to kill and steal for it.

Squirrels chattered from high in the pines. A blue jay scolded, then flew away. Usual smells of the woods were covered by the heavy aroma of pine.

Free slipped from one giant tree to the next until he was too far away from Kirkwood to be spotted. In an hour he reached the riverbank where he and Willie were camped. Free lifted his brows in surprise to find Willie already there.

Seeing Free, Willie hoisted his pack on his back. His red hair stood on end and looked bright against the dark bark of the trees. "Get a move on, Free. We got to hotfoot it to Big Pine now. We can't wait till morning like we planned."

"What's happening?" asked Free as he gathered his things. He kept his face carefully masked to keep Willie from reading anything in it.

"I caught sight of Witherspoon's timber walker not more than an hour ago. I got this gut feeling that he plans to claim them sections upriver that we marked three days ago. They're the best we saw yet and I want 'em."

Free kept his mouth shut about Driscoll's timber walker, Keith Kirkwood, as he fell into step beside Willie. There was no need for Willie Thorne to know about Kirkwood.

Pigeons by the score rose from the trees and almost blocked out the sun. Many times at home Free had gone out at night with a long pole to knock the pigeons out of the trees to feed them to the pigs. That made him think of Pa and Wex and even Jen. What was happening with them? Maybe he should write home just to let Ma know he was still alive.

Free frowned as he jumped over a stream swollen from last week's rain. Let them think he was dead! They didn't care anyway. But Wex did, he knew. And so did Ma. Maybe he would write when he got to Big Pine.

Just then Free saw movement several feet away. Was it Witherspoon's walker? Or maybe Kirkwood had seen him and decided to race them to Big Pine. Last month Free had seen two timber walkers racing to file. When they saw they'd reached town at the same time, they fell on each other in the street outside the courthouse and beat each other to a bloody mass, figuring the winner would file. While they rolled on the ground in combat, Willie Thorne walked right in and filed those tracts of land. He still had a good laugh over that one.

Suddenly Willie stopped short and motioned for Free to do the same. Willie gestured toward his left where Free had seen the movement. "Bear," mouthed Willie.

Free's stomach tightened. He was more afraid of bears than wolves. Once, three years ago, he'd come up on a black bear that had attacked him when he'd walked too close to her cub. He still had a scar on his shoulder from it. A stranger had suddenly appeared and chased the bear away.

Willie crept forward with Free close behind. The bear rooted at the base of a tree and didn't seem to notice them as they passed. Free breathed easier, then his breath caught in his throat as a man stepped into sight, a .50 caliber muzzleloader aimed right at Willie. The man had dark matted hair, which hung low on his wide forehead. His dark eyes flashed as he looked from Willie to Free. His big gnarled hands were encrusted with dirt. A ragged gray shirt hung on the man's big frame and over leather breeches. He wore beaded moccasins and had a pack on his back.

Free heard the sharp intake of Willie's breath as the man pulled back the hammer of his muzzleloader. The click seemed to echo through the trees.

"I told you, Willie Thorne, never to set foot in these here woods," said the man in a gruff voice with an accent that Free could barely understand.

Willie shook his head and laughed, but sweat popped out on his upper lip. "I heard you was dead, Jig."

"Not dead. Close to. But not dead. Not dead even from your knife, Willie Thorne." Jig turned his eyes from Willie to study Free from under matted brows. "You I have not seen before."

"Freeman Havlick," said Free.

"Havlick. Clay Havlick?"

"My grandfather."

"Ah! So, what is Clay Havlick's grandson doing with this man who kills?"

Free shot a startled look at Willie before he turned his attention to the old man. "Did you know my grandpa?"

"I was a young man when Clay Havlick's name was a legend among the fur traders and trappers. For many months I shared his camp and his food. I am Dag Bjoerling from Sweden, but Jig I am called." The wrinkles in Jig's face deepened. "Clay Havlick would hurt deep in his heart if he knew you walked the same trail with this one." Jig nodded his head toward Willie.

"He's a man who can make up his own mind," snapped Willie. "He wants money, and I gave him a chance to get it."

"What does Clay Havlick's grandson need of money made the way this one makes it?"

"To become a lumberman," said Free. Jig's piercing look made him uneasy. It was the same look that Grandpa had given him each time he'd told a lie or let fly a swear word.

"What of Clay Havlick's land?" asked Jig, frowning slightly.

Free's hand trembled as he gripped the strap of his backpack. This was the second man who'd mentioned Grandpa's land. Maybe Pa hadn't told him the truth. "Where is my grandpa's land?" asked Free in a tight voice.

"North and east of here." Jig motioned with his head.

Free felt as if he'd been kicked in the stomach with hobnail boots. Was it possible that Grandpa had left him land instead of money? But wouldn't Pa have told him? Free frowned. Pa wanted to keep him on the farm, so he might've kept the information to himself. "I don't know about any land," said Free, "but I'll check into it."

"George Meeker will pay big for it, Free," said Willie, sounding eager. "We'll make you a fair offer."

"Never!" barked Jig as fire shot from his dark eyes.

"You're as crazy as ever, Jig." Willie brushed his red hair back, then settled his hat in place. "Free, let's get away from him. He don't know his right hand from his left."

"What about the land, Willie?" asked Free.

"He's telling a tall tale," said Willie. "Ain't that right, Jig?"

Jig hunched his shoulders.

"You see, Free?" Willie took a step forward. "Time's a wasting!"

Free started to follow Willie, but Jig stopped him with a look.

"Stay, Clay Havlick's grandson!" Jig turned his eyes on Willie. "Because of Clay Havlick I will let you, Willie Thorne, go on your way. But, Willie Thorne, if you walk where I walk again, I'll fill you with lead." Jig eased back on the hammer but kept the muzzleloader aimed at Willie's heart. "Walk away and don't return."

Willie wiped sweat from his brow. "This is my last season, you old scoundrel, so don't think you're chasing me off."

"Your pride is false pride, Willie Thorne, but claim it if you must to keep from seeing a true image of yourself."

Willie swore under his breath as he walked away. Free nodded to Jig and started after Willie only to have Jig pull him up short again.

"Clay Havlick's grandson will not walk where Willie Thorne walks," said Jig. "You will walk with me."

"But I won't get paid if I don't go with Willie," said Free.

Jig shook his head. "So, what of pay? Can it buy you pride in yourself? Can it meet your heart's cry?" Jig thumped Free's chest and shook his head again. "Clay Havlick's grandson will walk where I walk. He must keep his pride."

Willie called over his shoulder, "Come on, Free. Don't let that crazy old wolf-bait fill you with lies."

Jig squared his broad shoulders. "Jig does not lie."

"Jig, I have to go with Willie," said Free.

"Clay Havlick's grandson cannot choose. He will walk with me. Clay Havlick would want that."

Free could see in the man's eyes that he wouldn't let him follow Willie. "What do you want of me?" Free asked hoarsely.

"You will stay with me for a spell. You will rid yourself of Willie Thorne and his bad ways."

"And if I don't want to?"

"You cannot choose," said Jig in a deadly calm voice. "From this day forward you will not walk where Willie Thorne walks."

"Get a move on, Free," urged Willie. He had stopped about twenty yards away to wait on Free.

Free sighed heavily. He had to go with Jig if for no other reason than to learn what the old man knew about Grandpa's land. "Willie, I'm going with Jig," called Free.

Willie's face darkened with anger. "Don't expect no pay from me or from George Meeker if you don't come with me now."

"I won't," said Free. He hated to lose the money, but he couldn't see a way around it.

"Clay Havlick's grandson does not need money," said Jig.

Willie strode away, muttering angrily to himself.

"Come," said Jig, motioning with his head to Free.

Free walked with him in silence. For the first time in the months since he'd joined up with Willie Thorne, Free felt like his old self, the man Grandpa Clay would've been proud of.

Jig led Free to an Indian trail that was about six inches deeper than the other part of the ground, three feet wide, and covered with pine needles clumped together five in a bundle.

Over an hour later Jig stopped in a clearing near a stream to look in on an old friend, he said. A tiny shack nestled in the giant trees. The Indian trail took up again on the far side of the stream. A smell so bad that Free's stomach turned rose up around the shack.

Jig laughed and slapped Free on the back. "Clay Havlick's grandson gets sick from the smell of my friend Old Windy's work."

"What is it?" asked Free. He wanted to cover his nose and mouth against the smell, but pride kept his hands at his sides.

Jig showed Free the carcasses of freshly skinned animals that lay on the ground near partly gnawed piles of bones. A wolf inside an iron cage bared its teeth. "Old Windy's a trapper. He uses the she wolf as bait to draw he wolves. He kills 'em and skins 'em and gives the animal in the cage the carcasses." Jig jabbed a dirty thumb toward the red-eyed slavering wolf. "Then he sells the pelts and collects ten dollars' bounty on each pair of ears. Keeps him from having to set traps and walk a trap line. It's a far cry from the fur trading Clay Havlick did, but it's a living for an old man." Jig walked to the door of the shack and stuck his head inside. "You here, Windy?"

There was no answer, so Jig closed the door. "Must be he got over the chills. I look in on him regular like until they pass."

"I have to get away from the smell," said Free, fighting against the bile that burned in his mouth.

"Not yet," said Jig as he clamped a gnarled hand on Free's shoulder as they walked away. "You learn this, Clay Havlick's grandson. The sins of man are a stench in God's nostrils. Each man must choose who and what he is. If Willie Thorne and George Meeker gave off smells for what they did, they'd be worse smells than this." Jig tapped Free's arm. "The same smell would cover you if you walked longer with Willie Thorne. Clay Havlick would be ashamed. Sin God hates, but you, Clay Havlick's grandson, God loves."

In the back corners of Free's memory he could hear Grandpa telling him how important it was to walk upright and honest before God and man. During the past few years, he'd been so angry with Pa and so determined to become a lumberman that he'd set aside much of what Grandpa had taught him.

Walking and listening to Jig brought back the longing ache for Grandpa that Free had thought was gone for good. It had been five years since Grandpa had died, five long, lonely years.

Suddenly, without warning, Willie Thorne leaped from behind a tree and with a bloodcurdling yell swung a thick branch at Jig's head. Reacting almost instinctively, Free fell against Jig and knocked him to the ground just in time to escape a bashed-in skull. Free rolled away from Jig and leaped up just as Willie swung the branch at him. Free sprang aside. Willie's face turned red with rage.

"Is this the way you want it, Free?" roared Willie. He stood with his feet apart and his knees bent as he held the branch ready to swing.

Free's eyes locked with Willie's. "Back off, Willie. Go on your way and leave us be."

Willie swung again, barely missing Free's skull. Free jumped at Willie just as he swung again. Free ducked, and the branch snagged a strand of his hair and jerked it out. Free heard Jig shout something just as he jumped high and kicked Willie in the chest with both feet. Willie's breath whooshed from his lungs and he fell backward in a bed of pine needles. Free landed with a thud near him, but in the flash of an eye bounded to his feet and stood over Willie.

"You got him now," said Jig with a low chuckle.

Groaning, Willie moved and opened his eyes. Free stuck his right foot on Willie's chest and leaned down. He smelled his own and Willie's sweat and blood.

"Willie, get on to Big Pine and leave us be."

Willie fought for air and finally gasped, "You'll never work as a timber walker in these parts, Free Havlick. I'll see to that."

"You, Willie Thorne, will not threaten Clay Havlick's grandson," said Jig as he pulled the hammer back on his muzzleloader. The sound sent a chill down Free's spine.

"Don't shoot him, Jig," said Free firmly.

"I will shoot him if he tries again to kill me. Or you."

Free lifted his foot off Willie's chest and stepped back a few paces. "Get up and be on your way."

Willie pushed himself up and swayed weakly. "I won't forget this, Havlick."

"See that you don't," said Free gruffly.

Willie glared at them, then turned and stumbled away.

"Willie Thorne is a dangerous enemy," said Jig.

"I'll watch out for him," said Free. He turned to Jig. "Are you all right?"

"It would take more than Willie Thorne to put me under." Jig chuckled as he straightened his pack. "Come with me. I have something else to show you."

Much later Jig stopped at the bank of a clear sparkling stream that rushed over rocks. He pointed across it at a stand of virgin white pines such as Free hadn't seen before in all of his days as a woodsman or even in the miles of travel away from the Grand River and along the Muskegon River to the shores of Lake Michigan during the summer as a timber walker with Willie.

"See the beauty of it," said Jig just above a whisper.

Free nodded as he looked up, up the rough bark of the tree trunks that had to be at least five feet across, to the dark green pine needles. Just in themselves the trees were magnificent, but calculated to board feet they meant thousands of dollars to the owner.

Jig stepped closer to Free and said softly, "God sees greater beauty when He looks on a man with a pure heart."

Free asked solemnly, "Is there a man with a pure heart? There is no man without sin." It was as close as he could come to admitting that he had not led a pure life and he knew it.

Jig rested his muzzleloader against a tree and dropped his backpack beside it. "When a man asks Jesus to forgive him of his sin, then God looks at that man in all his beauty, a beauty of more value than the timber you see."

Free eased his pack off, then sank to the ground beside Jig to feast his eyes on the timber as he thought about what Jig had said.

"Now, you are free to go, Clay Havlick's grandson."

Free looked deep into the old man's eyes. "I will never go back to work for Willie or for George."

Jig smiled, slowly stood, then waved his arm wide to take in the pines. "All of this is Clay Havlick's land," said Jig.

Free shot to his feet. "Can it be?"

Jig nodded. "Ten sections."

"Ten!" A section was 640 acres. Free saw the fortune in the trees, and his heart beat so hard he was sure Jig could hear it even over the call of the birds and the rushing of the water in the stream.

Had Grandpa left the land to him? If he asked Pa about it, would he tell him the truth? Probably not.

Free jumped across the stream to measure a tree. From what he'd learned from Willie Thorne, Free knew just that one tree would have well over 10,000 board feet. All of them together boggled his mind. "I have to see if this is my land and if these are my trees!" he cried.

Free thought of Grandpa's lawyer, Lem Azack. He'd talk to him and learn the truth just as soon as he could get to Grand Rapids. By river he could make it in a couple of days. His head spun with the fortune that might be his. He turned to call to Jig. But Jig, his pack, and his rifle were gone.

"That's strange," said Free as he looked around for Jig. "Where'd he get to? Jig! Where are you? I need to ask you more about Grandpa."

Free waited several minutes for Jig to return but finally had to admit he wasn't coming back. Free pulled out his compass to find his way to the nearest settlement so that he could hire a boat to take him to Grand Rapids.

In Grand Rapids, Free hesitated as he walked past the newspaper office on the way to the barber. Maybe he should stop in and ask Tunis Bowker what he knew about Grandpa's will. Tunis and Grandpa had been good friends for years. Free scowled. Today he couldn't put up with Tunis trying to get him to understand and be patient with Pa.

Free strode into the barbershop, got a shave, paid for a bath, and changed into a clean tan shirt and dark brown pants, then walked to the courthouse. A muscle jumped in his jaw as he walked down the quiet hall, into Lem Azack's office, and right up to the heavy walnut desk where a big white-haired man in his fifties sat. He wore a dark suit that stretched tight across his shoulders and arms, a white shirt and collar that seemed too tight around his thick neck, and a short black tie.

"I'm Freeman Havlick," said Free, fighting to keep his voice from shaking. "I came to hear about Clay Havlick's will."

"Have a seat," said Lem Azack with a broad smile and a flash of interest in his blue eyes. "I figured you'd be in here sooner or later to see about Clay's will."

Free sat down on the edge of an oak armchair. Blood pounded in his ears.

Lem Azack pulled out Clay's will from an oak file cabinet and scanned it as he sat back down. He found the place that pertained to Freeman, then grinned across the desk at Free. "Here we go. I have it here in legal terms, but I'll just say outright what is yours." Lem Azack cleared his throat and Free grabbed the arms of the chair. "Clay left you fifty thousand dollars, a house here in town, and land."

All the strength flowed from Free's body. Fifty thousand dollars! It was too much to comprehend. A house in town! "Where is the land?" he asked weakly.

"North of Big Pine near the Muskegon River," Lem Azack told him, then showed him on a map that he pulled from a drawer. It was the very place that Jig had showed Free!

"Does Pa know about this?" asked Free, his muscles tighter than the chain wrapped around logs on a skid.

Lem Azack nodded. "Told him just after Clay died."

"That's been five years! And he never told me!" Anger rushed through Free until he thought he'd explode. How dare Pa keep the money and the property from him? "How soon can I get the money and the deed to the property?"

"That could be a problem, Free," said Lem.

"Why?"

"Clay didn't exactly leave the timber to you."

Free leaned forward. "What do you mean?"

"He left it to your wife."

"My wife?" Free snapped.

Lem cleared his throat. "And you can't get the money until you're twenty-five or until you marry, whichever comes first."

Free's jaw tightened. "I'm almost twenty-one! And I have no wife and have no intention of getting one! I need the money now to timber off the land! Isn't there a way around the will?"

Lem shook his white head. "Sorry, Free. Clay wanted you to know your own mind. He didn't want anyone to take advantage of you."

Free shot from his chair and towered over Lem at his desk. "I thought Grandpa cared about me!"

"He loved you, Free. He talked about you often to me."

"Then why did he tie up my money?"

Lem folded his hands over the will. "Clay never realized how important his family was to him until his wife died and his son didn't want anything to do with him. He spent twenty years of his life fur trading. Roman was about your age when Clay finally settled down. He'd missed all those important years with his own son." Lem shook his head, his blue eyes sad. "Clay knew you didn't know the importance of family because of how he was and how Roman is. You told him often enough that you never wanted to marry and have a family. But Clay wanted you to have a wife and children and be a part of their lives. Love them and enjoy them, that's what he said." Lem paused. "When you do have a child, you inherit this section of land here." Lem pointed out several more tracts of timberland north of Big Pine, adjoining the land Jig had showed him.

Free's head spun. He'd wondered why that land hadn't been lumbered off already. It belonged to him! After he married. After he had a child.

"There's no getting around the will, Free," said Lem softly.

Anger churned inside Free. How could Grandpa have done this to him? Free knotted his fists at his sides. "I don't need Grandpa's money or his timberland! I'll make my own money to buy my own timber. I will become a lumberman in any way I can!" He strode from the office with Lem Azack's plea to calm himself ringing in his ears.

CHAPTER

6

♦ Shivering with cold, Jennet bent over Tait's books on her scarred table and carefully printed the amounts coming in and going out for the month of January, 1864. Her back ached from a day spent cleaning and stocking shelves. The old year was gone and a new one was beginning. The days and months since she'd left home had become dark blurs.

Jennet laid aside her pen and suddenly realized just how cold it was. She jumped up and pushed wood that she'd split earlier into the small stove. She yawned as she sat back down to the books. She'd brought them to her room so that she wouldn't have to work in Tait's unheated office. He wouldn't allow her to build a fire in the store's stove after closing time.

It was very late at night, but she had to finish the books before she could go to sleep. Her hair fell in dirty tangles around her shoulders, and her navy blue dress hung on her too-thin body. By the end of her first week with him, Tait had taught her how to keep the books for his three businesses. She'd been doing it on her own for over four months now. If she was late or did something wrong, he whipped her. So, she'd learned to finish on time and to do it right.

Jennet rubbed her eyes and knew she had dark circles under them. Tait had one looking glass in the store, and she used it to fix her hair each morning before he came to work. In that looking glass she'd watched her healthy glow turn to a sickly pallor.

At times Tait was kind to her. At times he even teased her to try to make her laugh. He was a hard worker and an honest businessman, she had to give him that.

At last Jennet closed the book and stood, her hands pressed to the small of her back. Her stomach growled with hunger, but she was too tired to find something to eat. She'd already finished the daily supply of bread and milk that Eve had brought at dawn.

"Wex," she whispered, then frowned. Just when had she taken to talking to Wex? She shrugged. Talking to him sometimes pushed back the terrible loneliness. "Wex, where are you tonight? I am waiting, longing for the day when you'll come for me." She bit her lip and closed her eyes. "Oh, Wex! I will marry you! I will give you all the kisses you want! Just come take me away from here! Will you come tonight? Please!"

Jen opened her bloodshot eyes and looked around the small room that smelled of wood smoke. Wex wouldn't come tonight, just as he hadn't last night or the night before or the night before that.

Every week she'd carefully read the list of casualties that Tait posted beside the front door of the store, holding her breath until she was sure Wex wasn't listed. She didn't know where he was fighting or what regiment he was with. Each time customers talked about the fighting she listened intently as she went about her work.

With a heavy sigh Jennet picked up the books, then lifted the lamp to light her way through the dark store to the cubbyhole Tait called an office. She sat the lamp on his desk and opened the drawer to lay the books inside, then realized she'd opened the wrong drawer. Just as she started to close it, she caught a glimpse of her name in handwriting she recognized. Marie's! Frowning slightly, Jennet gingerly picked up the envelope only to find three others with it. Marie had written to her, and Tait had not given her the letters! All along she'd thought no one from home had remembered her or even cared about her. She'd written letter after letter to them, and when they hadn't answered, she'd thought Pa had refused to let anyone write. But they had written, and Tait had kept the letters from her! Oh, what a cruel, cruel thing to do to her!

Jennet held the letters to her racing heart, then sank to the stool and placed them near the lamp to see them better. They were still sealed! She started to rip one envelope open but stopped short. If she opened them, Tait would know that she'd been in his desk and he'd whip her. She laid the letters back in the drawer. Tears burned her eyes as she stared down at them. She *had* to read them!

Quickly Jennet slipped the books in place, grabbed up the precious letters and the lamp, and carried them to her room before she lost her nerve. Tait wouldn't come back again tonight, not with the wind howling and the snow falling so heavily. He was all settled in his own place.

The silence pressed against her but no longer frightened her as it had the first several weeks after she'd arrived. Jennet was glad for quiet after the hours during the day of listening to customers and Tait, who couldn't find anything good to say about her work. Yet he continued to pile it on. The rage inside her had built until at times she wanted to take one of the guns from the case and shoot him. It was a horrible thought that she knew she'd never act on because Ma had taught her not to harm other people, not in word or in deed. Oh, but she wanted to forget what Ma had said and act on her feelings!

Jennet held Marie's letters, closed her eyes, and tried to

call up the sounds of her sisters in the two-story cabin. Off in the far reaches of her mind she heard them, and gradually the sounds returned until she could almost pretend that she was right there with them, talking and laughing. Even Ma's voice rang out in laughter as she told one of her funny stories. But Ma hadn't laughed or told a funny story since before Baby Vernon was born. She'd been too weak and too sick.

Jennet opened her eyes and kissed the top letter. Her cold hands shook as she carefully broke the seal so that she could reseal it to keep Tait from learning she'd read it. She saw the date: December 10, 1863. She whimpered as she realized the letter had been hidden over a month while the terrible loneliness had grown inside her until she thought she'd lose her mind.

Lovingly she spread out the letter, but before she would allow herself to read it, she opened the others and put them in order according to the dates written in Marie's neat hand. The first one was dated June 25, not long after she'd left. The second one, August 12; the third, October 24; and the last, December 10.

Tears welled up in her eyes and slowly overflowed to slide down her pale cheeks, which once had been rosy red from good health and fresh air. Now, the only time she was outdoors was to chop the wood, carry in the water, or walk to the boarding house for an occasional meal.

Impatiently Jennet brushed away her tears. She must get control of herself and not waste her valuable time crying. Taking a deep, ragged breath she started to read.

> *Dear Jen,*
>
> *It is so strange here without you. Ma is the same. I tried to get her out of bed like you said to do, but she wouldn't budge. The girls don't laugh as much as they once did. Pa never laughs at all. But you already know he hasn't since Baby Vernon died. He never*

yells at us anymore, and he hasn't lifted a hand to
strike any of us since you rode away with Uncle Tait.
I know Pa is sorry that he let Uncle take you, but he
never says anything about Tait or about you. He
won't let us talk about you or even speak your
name when he's around.

I know you're anxious for word of Wex. I did meet
him in the woodlot. He was so upset about you that he
wanted to steal you right away from Uncle, but he
decided he couldn't do that. I told him that I would
write to him. We talked for a few minutes. He was
excited about going to war, but he was scared too. I
tried to make him feel better. He rode away, sad about
you, but excited about the life ahead for him. Roman
was in a rage when he learned that Wex had joined
the fight, and Lillian cried for days. Roman said
Anne can't come to the house because she helped Wex.
That made Lillian feel even worse. When Roman
isn't around, she talks to me about Wex. Finally I
told her about seeing him the day he rode off. Every
chance she gets she begs me to tell her every detail of
our meeting. I feel so sorry for her.

I did your chores for a while, but Lillian said she
couldn't get along without me up at the house, so
Roman hired a boy named Tim to do them. He sleeps
and has his meals up at the main house. He's nice.
You'd like him. Roman tried to take his belt to him
once for spilling a pail of milk, and Tim said he'd
walk out if Roman even dared touch him. I was
surprised, but Roman backed right down. Sometimes
I wonder if he's sorry for being so hard on his boys.
And on you. He won't ever talk about you or Wex or
Free. He looks older every time I see him. And he's
sad. He works himself even harder than he did before.
I'd feel sorry for him if it wasn't partly his fault for
your being gone.

It's different here without you and Wex.
I miss you a lot and so do the girls. I hope Uncle
is treating you well.

Your loving sister Marie

Jennet read the letter again. Would Ma ever get better? If she did, what would she do when she realized Pa had indentured her to Tait?

Pa! Oh, but she hated him! She hoped he never laughed again as long as he lived. He and Roman could work themselves into the ground for all she cared.

Wex had wanted to steal her away from Tait! "Oh, Wex, why didn't you?" she whispered hoarsely.

Finally she put the letter aside and read the next one dated August 12.

My dear sister Jen,
I have heard twice from Wex. He is in Tennessee.
He says it's very different there. He almost killed a
Confederate. He said he was glad he missed. He
wants to come home, but he won't. He asked about
you. I told him I haven't heard from you. Oh, Jen,
when will you write? We long for word from you!
Ma has come to the table twice in the past week.
She even let me wash and brush her hair. She held
Evie for a while, then went right back to her bed. She
won't go look at the gravestone Pa bought for Baby
Vernon. That big, fancy angel cost a lot of money.
The little girls say the angel is watching over Baby
Vernon. I wonder if that's true.
Pa has really taken to the hired boy Tim. He makes
Pa smile and that sure helps around here. Pa usually
walks around with a sad face. I learned that Tim is
fourteen and has no family. Pa brings him home for
supper most nights. The girls love Tim. He always
teases them and tells them great stories. He gives

*Evie, Ida, and Lois piggyback rides and they like
that. Opal wishes she wasn't already ten and too big
for a ride. But Tim takes time for her in other ways.
Nola and I have been teaching him to read and write.
He's slow, but he is learning. In the winter we'll have
more time to teach him.*

*Why haven't you written, Jen? Won't Uncle even let
you write home? I asked Pa, but he got so angry that
I never asked him again.*

*I have grown so much that I'm as tall as you by
now. Unless you grew more, that is. Did you? I miss
you, Jen! Please, please write!*

Your loving sister Marie

Jennet groaned. She had written a letter a week, and Tait
had said he'd send them. Had he hidden them away somewhere in the store? Or had they gotten lost between Prickett and home? She'd hunt around his office and the store for
them.

She read the letter again, savoring every word as she
pictured Marie talking right to her.

Jennet laid the letter on top of the first one and picked up
the one dated October 24.

Dear Jen,
*Pa said he was going to town, so he said for me
to write a quick note for him to mail. That sure
surprised me because he still won't let us talk
about you when he can hear.*

*Pa wanted you to know that Ma is better at last.
She talked to all of us today. She even walked out to
see Baby Vernon's gravestone. Jen, it made me cry to
see her kneeling at his grave, tears pouring down her
cheeks. When she came inside, she asked about you
and Pa said that you'd agreed to go help Uncle Tait,
but he didn't tell her that you're indentured to Uncle*

for three years to pay off his debt. He doesn't think we know, but we all do. I told the girls not to tell Ma because it might make her sick again. When she is well, I'll tell her and maybe she'll make Pa get you back from Uncle.

I got another letter from Wex. He killed three boys and he said he cried when he did, but he had to kill them before they killed him. I cried, too, knowing how much it hurt Wex to take a life. He wants to come home. He said it's better to be home, even though his pa beats him, than to be there. He never has enough to eat, and he has to share a blanket with another boy. It hurts me to think of him being cold and hungry. I write to him every day.

Why don't you write, Jen? Are you angry? Please, please, please write!

Marie

Moaning, Jennet touched the letter and rocked back and forth, back and forth. Pa had told Marie to write to her!

She knotted her fist beside the letter. It was way too late for him to be sorry!

As she read the letter again, jealousy stabbed her when she reached the part about Wex writing to Marie and her writing back. "Wex, did you ever write to me? Do you remember that you want to marry me? Do you remember you said you loved me? I think of your words all the time and it keeps me going."

Finally Jennet picked up the last letter dated December 10.

Dear sister Jen,

Christmas is coming soon and we want you home. Pa says there's no way for you to come home, but Ma told him to find a way. I wish he could!

Ma has some bad days, but most of the time she's

*all right. She is too thin and we've been trying to get
her to eat more. She gets tired when she does even a
little work. She sure does like Tim. I think it helps
her forget about Baby Vernon to have Tim around. He
loves Ma a lot. I think he pretends that she's his ma.*

*In three days Nola will be twelve. She looks very
grown up, and she says she's in love with Tim and
will marry him as soon as Pa will let her. I think
Tim likes her too. He treats her special. It sounds
funny to have Nola talk about getting married.*

*Did you think of me on my birthday last month? I
am thirteen as you know. Wex sent me red and yellow
ribbons for my hair. Pa let the girls bake me a cake.
It was a fine birthday, but I wanted you here to share
it.*

*Wex says he can't wait to come home to see me. I
can't wait to see him either. He says there is a chance
he'll come home in the summer. I hope he can.*

*Pa says the war is going to last a whole lot longer
than anybody thinks because of those men in the
White House. I heard him tell Ma about some
runaway slaves that he helped hide on their way
to Canada. I didn't know Pa would do that,
but I'm glad he did.*

*I miss you, Jen. Why don't you ever write? Please
don't be so mad at Pa that you forget about the rest of
us. If you can't come home for Christmas, Merry
Christmas from all of your family!*

Your sister Marie

Jennet covered her face with hands now blue with cold
and cried because Nola was big enough to talk about marrying Tim, Wex had bought Marie ribbons for her birthday,
Ma was better, and Pa had helped free slaves even while
she was a slave to Tait. She cried because on Christmas
Day she'd worked just as hard as any other day only there

hadn't been customers. She'd worked the whole day doing bookwork, cleaning, and stocking shelves without seeing anyone or talking to anyone. Finally she'd pretended Wex came to see her, and she'd talked to him about their wedding and about how happy they'd be. Tait hadn't given her money to eat at the boarding house, so she'd eaten food that she'd heated on the stove. Eve wasn't able to get away from home and bring her even bread and milk. That night Jennet had cried herself to sleep.

After a while Jennet read each letter again, then smoothed them lovingly as if she was rubbing Ma's cheek.

Oh, she couldn't part with the letters! But she couldn't keep them or Tait would know. What could she do?

Suddenly she jumped up. "I'll copy them!" Her words rang across the room, startling her. She ran to Tait's office to find paper that he wouldn't notice was missing, and in a careful hand she copied each letter so that she'd be able to read them anytime she wanted to. She tucked them inside her pillowcase where they'd be safe from Tait's prying eyes. Then she carefully resealed Marie's letters and stuck them back in Tait's drawer. She searched for the letters that she'd written home but couldn't find them. Maybe Tait had burned them, or maybe he'd taken them to his house.

Anger rushed through Jennet. She wanted to tell Tait that she knew about the letters, but she knew she'd never dare tell him or show her anger.

Jen went back to her room, got ready for bed, blew out her lamp, and sank exhausted to her cot. The crinkle of the letters comforted her aching heart. Somehow she'd find a way to send a letter to her family without Tait's learning about it. Sighing heavily, she closed her eyes and fell into a deep, deep sleep.

The next morning she was awakened by a knock at her door. She peeked out to see that Eve was standing in the snow with the basket she brought each morning. She was shivering even with her big coat on. Snow covered the roof of the barn and the outhouse. Jennet threw open the door and Eve stepped inside, bringing icy air with her. Chunks of snow from her booted feet dropped onto the floor.

"I overslept, Eve!" cried Jennet.

"Are you sick? You look pale, and there are dark rings under your eyes."

Jennet wanted to tell Eve about Marie's letters, but she couldn't take the chance. "I'm fine, Eve," she said as she shook the grate in the old potbellied stove and quickly started the fire.

"I had to circle around to get here so Tait wouldn't see where my footprints led."

"Oh, but you take too much of a chance!"

Eve smiled and shook her head. "Did you learn another Scripture to tell me?"

"No. I'm sorry." In the past few months Jennet had read the Bible Eve had given her, then quoted a Scripture to Eve each morning and helped her memorize it. "I'll have one for you tomorrow."

"Thank you. I must hurry back," said Eve as she quickly unloaded her basket and walked to the door. "I, too, am late this morning. But I could not leave you without food."

"Thank you!" Jennet hugged Eve close and kissed her cold cheek. "Tomorrow I'll walk to your house to get the food."

"No! Tait might see you, and he would beat us both."

Jennet signed heavily. "Why do you stay with him?"

"He is my husband."

"And I am his slave," Jennet added. "We both are, it seems. If I could, I'd take you and run away."

"That is foolish talk, Jen."

Jennet kissed Eve good-bye, then quickly dressed in a warm dark green dress with black piping around the collar and the cuffs and down the front to the waist.

Later just as Jennet unlocked the front door of the store she saw Tait coming up the snow-covered walk toward her.

She thought of the letters he'd hidden from her. How she hated him!

Forcing her hands to stay steady, Jennet twisted her uncombed hair into a bun and quickly pinned it in place before Tait stepped through the door. "Good morning, Jen," he said, sounding cheerful for once.

"Good morning, Uncle." She wanted to spit in his face, but she kept her voice pleasant so that he wouldn't slap her for being sassy or rude.

"I'm going to Grand Rapids today."

Jen bit her lip to keep from begging to go along with him to see her family.

"I just might go see your pa and tell him how you're getting along."

Words welled up inside her, but Jennet forced them back. Maybe if she acted like she wasn't interested, he might take her along. "Have a pleasant trip," she said, almost choking on her politeness.

"Do you have a message for them?" he asked, eyeing her carefully as he stroked his beard.

Her heart raced and she lifted her chin a fraction. "Give them my love." But not Pa! Tell him I will never love him and never forgive him!

Tait laughed and slapped his leg. "And I'll tell them I made you into a fine woman with good manners." He looked around the store. "Where's the heat?"

"It's taking a little longer to warm up in here."

"Shake down the ashes and fix the fire," Tait said with a scowl.

Jen hurried to the black cast-iron stove, shook down the ashes with the shaker handle, and opened the door. Flames licked up the sides of the stove as she pushed a few chunks of wood inside. She didn't dare tell Uncle that she'd been late starting the fire. He liked it warm when he came so he could stand with his back close to it while he gave her orders for the day.

Tait hung his coat and hat on the hooks just inside his office, then walked to stand with his back to the stove. "I'm going with Rusty Zimmer on his sleigh. He figures with his team and sleigh he can make it through the snow. If Pete Stillman comes in while I'm gone, you tell him to pay his bill. Don't give him more credit till he does."

Jennet nodded.

"I have money in my desk. Get it for me."

Jen started toward his office, but he stopped her.

"Never mind. I'll get it myself."

Jennet knew he remembered the letters and knew she'd see them. He'd forbidden her even to open the desk drawers except for the one holding the books. Why hadn't he burned her letters? Did he have a conscience after all? If he did, he kept it well hidden.

After telling her a list of things to do and things to remember, Tait checked over the books. Finally, he closed them and pushed them back in place. "I'll be gone three—maybe four—days. You keep things going while I'm away and don't try to pull a fast one on me. If the men come in from the lumbercamp, you see that they pay with cash. No credit. None!"

Jennet nodded, immediately feeling her spirit lift. Three or four days without him! What wonderful freedom! It almost made staying behind worthwhile.

Just then the front door opened and a man named Kelso walked in. He was short and squat and wore a heavy bearskin coat that reached below his knees. He pulled off his bearskin cap, revealing a shiny bald pink head, and stopped in front of Tait near the counter. Kelso shook his thick finger at Tait and roared, "I tell you it was John Morgan that kilt the most people when he cut a sweep through Kentucky, Indiana, and Ohio with about 2,500 mounted cavalry."

Jennet rolled her eyes. The arguments about the war between Kelso and Tait were a daily ritual.

Before Tait could speak, Kelso bellowed, "It could be

that one of these days some of them raiders will make it right up here to Michigan." Kelso brought his fist down hard on the counter. "Lee's army is boasting about moving north to fight on northern soil!"

Jennet shivered at the horrifying thought as she picked up a man's work shirt and refolded it.

"Idle threat!" cried Tait, his beard moving in agitation.

"So you say," muttered Kelso.

"I read about William Quantrill again in last week's paper. He's an ugly son-of-a-gun!" barked Tait as he tugged at his beard. "He killed folks in Kansas and Missouri like they was flies!"

A shirt clutched to her chest, Jennet bit back a cry of alarm. Was Wex near Kansas or Missouri?

"You'd think all them Michigan boys that went to fight would make a difference," said Kelso.

"Maybe you and me should go show 'em how to fight." Tait laughed and slapped Kelso's thick shoulder.

Jennet didn't think the war was anything to joke about, but she kept her thoughts to herself, as usual.

"I'm ready to sign up when you are!" Kelso tipped back his shiny pink head and laughed hard.

"I'm in a hurry, Kelso, so you be on your way now. Talk to me when I get back."

Kelso tugged his bearskin hat down over his head and walked out the door without another word.

Tait pulled on his coat and cap and strode out into the brisk winter morning toward the mill. Jennett longed to call after him to take her along, but she clamped her hand over her mouth to keep back the words. If he did take her along to see her family, it would be too painful to leave them again.

About an hour later Jennet stood in the doorway and watched Tait ride away with Rusty Zimmer in a sleigh pulled by two powerful chestnut draft horses. Their harnesses jangled and bells on the harnesses jingled.

Jennet closed the door against a fierce blast of icy air. She suddenly felt as light as a feather on the duster she used daily. Tait was gone! A smile tried to break through, but it faded before it reached her lips.

All day she worked as if Tait was there, but after she closed the store in the evening, she slipped on a heavy coat and hat and walked out the back door and through the trees to Tait's house to see Eve. The bitter cold had reddened Jennet's pale face by the time she reached the front gate.

Tait lived in a one-story white frame house with a white wooden fence around it. A barn and an outhouse were in back. Two tall pines stood in the front yard and several behind the house on the far side of the fence.

Jennet knocked on the door and finally it opened a crack. "It's me, Eve," said Jennet softly.

"Jen! Come in!" Eve opened the door wider, smiling in surprise and happiness. "Tait said not to let anyone in while he was gone. But you, I let in."

Jennet stepped into the cozy room and stood beside the mirrored hall tree, which held coats, umbrellas, and boots. A fire crackled in the stone fireplace, sending a glow over the brick hearth and onto the maple rocking chair next to it. A horsehair couch sat against a wall between two windows covered with ruffled muslin curtains with the kitchen area beyond that. Jennet smiled at Eve. For the first time since fall had turned into winter she saw Eve without a coat. "Eve, I didn't realize you were this close to having your baby," said Jennet.

Eve smiled and nodded. "He will be born tonight."

"Tonight?" cried Jennet in alarm.

"Yes. But don't be frightened. I'm not. I've helped many women birth their babies. And the pain is not too bad."

"What a terrible day for Tait to be gone!"

"No." Eve closed her eyes for a minute and pressed her hand to her stomach. Finally she smiled again. "It will be soon. That is why Tait went away. He was very angry to learn about the baby. When I told him this was the day for the birth, he found a way to be gone. But I'm glad!" Eve sucked in air and closed her eyes tightly again. When she opened her eyes, she said, "If you don't want to witness the birth, leave now."

"No! You shouldn't be alone!" Jennet hung her coat on a hook on the hall tree and dropped her hat on the seat. She could tell that Eve's pains were very close together. "I've been around birthing of Ma's babies and the animals on the farm. I'll stay."

In the kitchen area Eve perched on the edge of a chair at the table and waved for Jennet to sit down. "I can do this alone, but I am happy you are here with me. Did you bring a Scripture for me?"

"Yes. I wrote it out for you." Jennet hurried to her coat and pulled the paper out of her pocket. She'd written the Scripture for Eve to help her when Tait was mean to her, but now it seemed to suit even better. "Psalm 32:7. You are my hiding place; You shall preserve me from trouble; You shall surround me with songs of deliverance."

Between the obvious labor pains, Eve repeated it after Jennet. Right in the middle of saying the verse alone Eve stopped and gasped. "The baby is coming now," she said softly.

Jennet waited for her to go to the bedroom and give birth on the bed the way Ma always had, but Eve went to a spot in the kitchen where she'd fixed a special pallet of blankets with a white muslin sheet over them. She pulled off her dress and slipped on a gown. She squatted near the pallet, and with low groans and a mighty push she delivered the baby on the pallet.

"I'll cut the cord," said Jennet as she looked at the dark baby lying on the blood-and-water-covered sheet.

"I will do it," said Eve. Without Jennet's help Eve cut and tied the umbilical cord. "It is a boy," said Eve proudly.

She lifted the baby by his tiny feet and held him upside down. He gasped and cried, then cried louder. Eve held him out to Jennet.

"He sounds healthy," said Jennet as she wrapped a soft blanket around him. "You take him while I clean up the afterbirth."

"I will do it," said Eve. "You take care of the baby."

Jennet held the baby close to her heart while Eve cleaned up the afterbirth and dropped the pallet in a tub of cold water, then took care of herself.

"You lie down while I bathe him," said Jennet.

"Yes, I will rest now," said Eve, smiling. "You bathe him. I am tired."

Jennet looked at the tiny red-faced baby who was part of Tait. For just a minute hatred rose in her but just as quickly vanished as the baby squirmed in her arms.

Several minutes later Jennet sat at the edge of the bed while Eve cuddled the baby to her breast.

"His name is Joshua, and he will be a man full of God's strength and love."

"What about Tait?" asked Jennet hesitantly.

Eve's face hardened. "If Tait raises a hand to beat Joshua, I will leave him. That I promise myself and my baby."

Jennet nodded. She knew Eve didn't mean a spanking to discipline, but the kind of beating that Tait gave her. "I'll help you leave," said Jennet as a solemn vow. She would do all in her power to keep the baby safe from Tait, but maybe he'd look at Joshua and love him like he'd never loved anyone before, like Pa had Baby Vernon.

Jennet glanced around the small bedroom at the bed, chest of drawers, commode, and looking glass made of oak. The headboard of the bed was hand carved with swirls and leaves and acorns. She looked back at Eve to find that she and the baby had fallen asleep.

Jennet went back to the kitchen, fixed the fire, and banked it for the night. She found a bright block-work quilt and feather pillow in a chest beside the bedroom door and curled up on the horsehair couch and fell asleep.

CHAPTER

7

♦ Jennet carefully wrote June 11, 1864, on Tait's books, then gasped. Tomorrow would be her sixteenth birthday! Almost a whole year had passed since she'd been indentured to Tait. How could that be? But she knew how it had happened. She'd worked long, hard hours without a letup, and time had slipped away before she had even known it. Months had passed since Tait had whipped her. He was happy to think he'd turned her into the type of woman she should be, hardworking, submissive, and silent.

Jennet thought of the stolen moments with Eve and Joshua, and she smiled grimly. A couple of times she'd slipped off into the very edge of the woods just to absorb the serenity there. Tait would be surprised to find that a different kind of woman was developing behind that submissive facade. She did whatever she wanted after store hours.

The warm afternoon breeze blew in the open door of the store, bringing with it the smell of the river and the dust from the mill. Men's voices floated in from across the street at the dock. Jen heard Tait's voice above the others, and she peeked through the window to see who was making him angry. A trapper walked past the window and blocked her view. Quickly she turned back to her work to finish it before Tait returned.

When Tait walked in with a man following, Jennet pushed the finished work in the drawer and closed it. She touched her braids, which had fallen over her shoulders, and brushed dust from her gray summer dress. She walked to the counter in case Tait wanted her to wait on the customer. Jen glanced past Tait to the man behind him.

Her heart jerked to a stop, then leaped into life, hammering so hard against her rib cage that it hurt. The man was Freeman Havlick! Instead of the leather shirt and pants that he'd worn the last time she'd seen him, he wore a lightweight gray shirt buttoned to his chin and tucked inside heavy blue trousers. His face was clean shaven, and a hat covered his dark hair and shaded his brown eyes.

Jennet sagged weakly against the counter, her icy hands limp at her sides. Freeman Havlick stood only a few feet from her! But maybe it was her imagination since she desperately wanted to be rescued from Tait.

When Freeman saw the woman behind the counter, he frowned slightly at the intensity of her stare, then his eyes widened in shock. Could the thin, pale woman be Jen? But what would she be doing here? This woman looked much too old and tired to be the farm girl he knew with flushed rosy cheeks and flashing blue eyes. But it was Jen! Had she run away when Wex went off to fight?

Jennet wanted to cry out to Free, but her voice was locked behind the tightness in her throat. Finally he pulled his gaze away from her without saying a word to her.

Turning to speak to the man who'd brought the canoeload of supplies, Tait scowled at the way he and Jennet were staring at each other. Tait didn't want to lose Jen to any man who took a shine to her. He needed her at the store, and he wasn't about to see her marry and leave him. He shot a look at Jennet and said sternly, "Get on back to your room."

Jennet hesitated, not wanting to leave in case Free vanished, but crept away before Tait could snap at her again. She wanted to beg Free to take her with him, but she slipped inside her room and left the door open so she could hear them.

"Who is she?" asked Free, looking past the cold potbellied stove toward the open door.

Tait knew he couldn't be too rude to the man. He owed him money and right now cash money was tight. "Jen Cordell. My niece. She works for me."

"Cordell." With a great effort Free kept his anger hidden from Tait. "Her pa, Vernon Cordell, works for Roman Havlick."

Tait lifted his brows in surprise. "You're right. You know them?"

Freeman nodded, but he didn't want to go into his private life with this man he'd instantly disliked. Tait knew him only as Free. He'd been forced to take on different kinds of jobs, the latest being to sell supplies along the river to any business that would buy them. He'd brought a load of supplies to Prickett to earn more cash on his way to an area where he was checking on a job as a timber walker. So far Willie Thorne had made sure no one hired him as a cruiser, but he kept trying. Not everyone could be influenced by Willie Thorne. Free pushed his hat to the back of his head. He glanced toward the door Jen had walked through, then back at Tait. Free wanted to call Jen out to talk to her, to make sure she was all right, but he didn't have time for her or her problems. He shrugged impatiently. "It's getting late. I'll take my money and head out."

Tait cleared his throat and pulled at his thick beard. "Thing is, Free, you caught me at a low time. Short of cash money."

Free's response was curt. "Then I'll take the supplies and sell them to someone who has money." He turned to go.

"Just hold on." Tait couldn't let Free leave. He needed the supplies. He strode toward the back of the store and barked, "Jen, get out here now!"

Jennet took a deep breath and walked on unsteady legs through the connecting door. Oh, she hated for Free to see her looking so haggard and old!

Free saw her whipped dog look and balled his fists at his sides. Tait was probably as quick to beat her as her pa had been.

Jennet didn't look at Free but kept a wary eye on Tait. "Yes, Uncle."

"You get them books figured?"

"Yes." Jennet heard Free move, but still she couldn't look at him.

"And?"

Jennet hesitated. She knew he wanted her to tell him that the books were wrong and that they did have money coming in soon. "The same," she whispered.

Free could feel the fury building in Tait and see the fear on Jennet's face. Free took a step toward Jennet but stopped. This was not his affair.

Tait glared at Jennet, and she shrank back. Anger shot through Free as he watched Jennet cringe away from Tait. From the look of him the uncle might be worse than Jen's pa.

Tait stepped toward Jennet, his fists doubled. He needed the blankets and clothing and the stock of food that Free had brought. Finally he turned back to Freeman. "You'll get your money, but not today. Come back in a couple of weeks."

Freeman needed his money now. "I can't wait. I'll take the stuff to Deerhop. Gene Littleton will pay cash for it." He started for the door, and Jennet's heart sank to her toes.

"I'll trade for the stuff," said Tait, sounding desperate.

Free turned and eyed Tait. "Trade what?"

Tait thought fast. What would Gene Littleton be short of that he had? "I need what you brought and could be Littleton needs things that I got." Tait looked around, his head spinning. "Jen, name off some things that Littleton could use."

Jennet looked helplessly at Tait. Her mind wouldn't function with Free looking as if he'd walk out and leave her behind. "Traps? Tools?"

Without warning Tait slapped her hard across the face and the sound rang through the room.

Jennet fell back against the counter, her hand at her burning cheek.

Freeman leaped forward and caught Tait's arm before he could strike Jennet again. Free forced himself to hold Tait's arm steady and not jerk it back and up to break it. "You got no cause to hit her," said Free in a voice he managed to keep dead calm.

Jennet stared at Free, remembering the other times he'd rescued her. A glimmer of hope flickered inside her.

"She's my business," snapped Tait. "Indentured to me. I can do what I please with her."

Fire shot from Freeman's dark eyes. Indentured! "Just how much money is owing?"

"None of your concern." Tait gave each word equal emphasis.

Jennet eased away from Tait until she was out of his reach. She wanted to hide in her room, but she couldn't bear the thought of being away from Free.

"I'm making it my concern," said Free in a cold, hard voice. Suddenly seeing to Jen was more important than making money. The thought surprised him. "How much time does she have left?"

"Two more years," said Tait gruffly.

Hearing that Jennet was supposed to be with the quick-tempered store-owner for two more years turned Freeman's blood cold. How had Wex let her get in such a fix?

Free's mind whirred with ideas, but he knew only one would work. "You take your supplies, Tait, and I'll take the girl."

Jennet gasped, her hand to her heart. Maybe she'd be home soon where she could wait for Wex to be discharged from the army, then they could be married.

Tait shook his head. He knew he couldn't get along without Jen. She worked harder than any man he'd ever had, harder even than he himself worked. "She's not for trade," said Tait sharply.

"Then I'm off," said Freeman. He walked toward the door, his back straight. He'd learned how to read a man, and he was sure he'd read Tait correctly.

Jennet's breast rose and fell as if she'd run ten miles without stopping. Blood pounded in her ears, and she had a sick taste in her mouth. Would Free just walk away without her?

"Wait!" cried Tait.

Freeman turned slowly, his brow cocked.

Jennet bit her bottom lip. Free wouldn't leave her after all. She could see that Tait had more than met his match.

"Leave the supplies and come back in one week, and I'll pay you," said Tait desperately.

Freeman turned and walked out the door.

Jennett sagged weakly against the counter. Freedom had been so close!

On the board sidewalk outside Tait's store the warm wind blew against Free, who listened for Tait's next move. Free's stomach knotted, and for a minute he wondered if Tait would let him walk away. He knew he couldn't leave Jen, no matter what Tait did.

Feeling defeated, Tait ran after Free. "Bring in the supplies."

Free said, "You'll trade?"

Tait nodded. "I can always get Old Gabe to help me a while."

Her nerves as tight as a snagged fishline, Jennet stood in the doorway of the store. Her legs trembled, and she almost dropped in a heap to the floor she'd kept swept and scrubbed every day for the past year.

Free glanced at Jennet. Hopeful anticipation shone in her wide blue eyes. The desire to help her grew even stronger, and Free turned back to Tait. "Sign her over to me and I'll unload the boat."

Tait reentered the store and stormed toward his office. As Jennet ducked out of his way, she saw a pleased look cross Free's face before he masked it.

Free followed Tait inside and waited near the front counter. He stood there wondering what he would do with Jen. He couldn't send her home to be overworked by his pa and beaten by her pa. Wex was still off fighting the war. And he couldn't leave her with Anne even if she'd agree to it. With Anne's work in the underground railroad anyone near her would be in grave danger.

Tait struggled with the hard spot he was in. Finally he grabbed Jennet's paper from a drawer in his desk and signed her over to Free. Then Tait walked to the counter and told Free, "You're making a bad deal."

Free looked over the paper and tucked it inside his shirt. "Get your things, Jen," Free said to her without taking his eyes off Tait.

Jennet could hardly believe what was happening. Her life was taking yet another turn. But this time it was for the better. This time she'd be happy.

Jennet darted a look at Tait, saw his rage, then sped to her room. With jerky movements she gathered up the letters from Marie, the Bible Eve had given her, and her few clothes.

Eve! How could she leave Eve and Joshua without saying good-bye? She couldn't leave a note because Eve couldn't read. Would she dare ask Free to let her see Eve one last time?

Jen peeked out to see Free and Tait unloading the supplies. Taking a deep breath, she crept out the back door and raced to Tait's house. She burst in without knocking and found Eve washing the noon meal dishes.

"What is wrong?" asked Eve in alarm as she grabbed a towel for her hands.

"I'm leaving," said Jennet, rubbing her sleeve over her sweaty face. "Right now!" In as few words as possible she told Eve what had transpired. She hugged Eve close. "I hope to see you and Joshua again someday. I will never forget your kindness to me."

"I will never forget your love and your help," said Eve as tears welled up in her eyes. She kissed Jennet, then scooped up Joshua from his cradle, and thrust him into Jennet's arms.

Jennet held him close and kissed his flushed cheeks. His dark eyes sparkled, and he plucked at her hair with his fat little fist. Reluctantly she held him out to Eve.

"Go with God," whispered Eve.

"Good-bye," said Jennet around the lump in her throat. She hugged Eve one last time, then ran out the door, past the tall pines, and along the path to the store.

A few minutes later she stood beside the canoe while Free and Tait finished unloading the supplies. She watched Free's shirt tighten against the muscles in his arms as he worked. She was afraid to take her eyes off him in case he vanished in a puff of her imagination.

Once the men had cleared the canoe, Tait stopped in front of Jennet, his dark eyes narrowed, and shook his finger at her. "Your pa will hear about this, Jen," said Tait menacingly.

Before Jennet could say a word, Freeman replied, "The debt her pa owed you is paid. The girl is mine now. You tell her pa that."

Tait glared at Free. "Just what do you plan to do with her?"

"She's my property now, and I don't have to answer to you!" Free dropped Jennet's bundle in the canoe, then turned to Jennet.

Jennet froze. His property? What did he mean?

Free felt Jennet's hesitation, and he frowned. Didn't she want to leave with him after all? He held his hand out to her, and she immediately slipped her hand in his. A tingle ran over him from her touch. He handed her into the canoe, waited until she sat on the middle seat, then he took his place. Quickly he lifted the paddle and pushed away from the dock.

Freeman didn't speak until they were out of sight of the Prickett landing. Instead of heading toward Deerhop he turned toward Grand Rapids. He saw the droop of Jennet's shoulders. Just what was he going to do with her? "Are you all right?" he asked.

Jennet shrugged slightly. She wanted to ask Free what he meant when he'd said she belonged to him now, but she couldn't force the words out.

"Did you want to stay with him?"

Jennet shook her head hard enough to make her braids flip, but she didn't speak. She watched a duck fly up from the water and disappear in the bright summer sky. The fishy smell of the river and a faint smell of smoke from the chimney of a cabin nestled in the trees near the riverbank filled her nostrils.

Free frowned out across the water as he paddled along the shaded side of the river. When he'd left Grand Rapids this morning at dawn, he'd expected to return with money in his pocket. He needed it to add to his nest egg so he could pay for the tract of timber he was buying. What would he do now? Suddenly he thought of Grandpa's will. Freeman felt as if he'd been kicked in the stomach by a river hog's hobnail boots. If he married, he'd inherit money enough to buy many tracts of land. He could marry Jen. But should he marry her? What of Wex? The

91

last Free had heard, Wex had planned to marry her.

Jennet felt Free's eyes on her back. He seemed different than the times she'd talked with him while he still lived at home.

His head spinning, Free watched a great blue heron fly away from the river. He focused his attention on the water and where he was going. If he paddled too close to shore, he knew he'd hit a snag. Almost against his will he looked at Jennet again. Here was his chance to become a big lumber baron. Why should he consider Wexal's feelings? Or Jennet's?

Jen sat quietly as he paddled down the Grand River. They rode past a landing where boys were fishing. The boys waved and shouted, and Free waved back. Jennet managed to lift her hand. What did Free expect of her?

Just before dark Free paddled past the Grand Rapids dock where a row of fishing boats, steamships, a dugout canoe, and a few birchbark canoes were tied up. Men talked and laughed and shouted to one another as they unloaded a huge steamship. Horse-drawn buggies, drays, and carts rolled along the sawdust-covered street beside the dock. A group of rowdy barefoot boys ran past, shouting and laughing.

Jennet watched Free tie the canoe to a tree at a landing near the livery. Her mind was a jumble of thoughts. *Will he just leave me stranded in Grand Rapids? If he does, I can walk home in the morning even though it will take hours. What will Pa say if I suddenly turn up?* Now that Ma was better she might be able to convince Pa to keep her. It had been almost five months since she'd gotten a letter from Marie. And still Marie begged to hear from her, so somehow the letters that she'd sneaked past Tait hadn't reached home.

What if Free planned to keep her to work off her two years? Just what was he going to do with her? He'd saved her life. Surely he wouldn't harm her. Maybe he would let her go home. She'd wait for Wex and then they'd get married. She bit back a sigh, then, her legs trembling, she stepped to the sandy ground.

Freeman took Jennet's bundle from her and his hand brushed hers, sending sparks through him. Could he tell her his plan?

"I don't know if Pa will pay for me," said Jennet with a catch in her voice.

Her pa? How could she want to return to him after the way he'd treated her? "I won't give him a chance," replied Free evenly.

Jennet bit her bottom lip as she followed Free up the hill to the livery. Horses nickered in a wooden pen outside the building. A wagon drawn by draft horses rumbled past, leaving a cloud of dust behind it. The smell of the river below and the horses manure from the livery above mingled in the air. Jennet waited to speak until she reached the top of the hill. "I don't have any money. I can't pay you," she said weakly.

Free couldn't look at her in case the agony in her blue eyes made him change his mind. He watched a coon dog settle down on the porch of the old blue frame house beside the livery. "You can," he said gruffly.

Her stomach knotted. "How?"

His mouth was so dry that it was hard to speak. He gripped her bundle tighter. "Marry me."

Jennet stopped short and stared at him. Had she heard him right? "What?" she whispered in alarm, her eyes wide in her ashen face.

Free looked into her eyes and almost lost his nerve. "Marry me."

"Do you want to marry me?" she asked in surprise.

"No! I don't *want* to marry you. But I need a wife."

She touched the hankie near her heart. "What of Wex?"

"What of him?" Free looked angrily away from her just as a rider stopped outside the livery door and called to the owner. Free looked back down at Jennet. "Wex didn't do anything to help you. He's off fighting to free slaves and left you just as bad off as a slave!"

"I promised I'd wait for him," whispered Jennet.

"It's a promise you'll have to break," snapped Free.

"Don't make me," she whispered as she pressed her hands to her cheeks and stared at him fearfully.

"Don't look at me like that!"

"How can you force me to marry you?"

Yes, how could he? He looked away from her and said bluntly, "I need a wife."

Freeman walked her toward a clump of maple trees where they could have privacy and told her quickly about his grandfather's will. "I'd give you a place to live."

"I can't," Jennet whispered hoarsely.

Freeman's stomach knotted. Was his dream going to slip through his fingers again? In frustration he pulled the paper from his shirt front and shook it at her. "This paper says you belong to me. You marry me, or I'll take you straight back to your uncle."

The look of horror on her face tore at his heart, but Free clamped his mouth shut and waited for her to give in.

Jennet groaned, but what little fight was left in her vanished when she saw the set of Free's jaw and the anger on his face. She didn't have the energy or strength to fight him. Besides, he owned her.

At last Jennet tipped her head in agreement.

"I won't ever beat you," Free told her.

"Does it matter?" A tear spilled down her cheek, and she let it drop to the sandy ground.

"We'll get married and see Grandpa's lawyer and get it settled this night."

Jen backed away from him, stumbled, and he caught her arm to steady her, then quickly released her.

"We'll hire a buggy and be on our way."

Jennet couldn't move.

"Let's go!" Free walked toward the livery. Finally she hurried to catch up to him.

At the livery Jennet stood near the wide door while Free paid for a horse and buggy. In silence Free drove to a church that he'd attended a couple of times with his sister Anne. The minister lived in the house next door, and Jennet stiffly waited on the church steps as Free knocked on the door to get the minister.

A few minutes later, with shaking legs, Jennet stood before the minister and in a blur listened to the words he spoke over them. Her dress was dirty and sweat stained, her hair in tangles. Could this really be her wedding day?

At one point Free almost backed out, but he hardened his resolve and let the man finish the short ceremony.

After Jennet signed her name under Freeman's, he took the certificate of marriage and tucked it away in his shirt with her indenture paper.

Next Free drove them several blocks away to Lem Azack's home because his office was closed on Sunday. Jennet hung back, but Freeman took her arm and they followed the maid across the wide room to a half-open doorway.

Freeman and Jennet Havlick stepped into a large study lit by several lamps. Overstuffed leather chairs, a huge mahogany desk, and a leather sofa were arranged around the room, which was bigger than Tait's store. Jennet trembled, and Free's grip on her arm tightened. A white-haired man sat in a high-backed red leather armchair behind the carved desk. As they walked across the highly polished hardwood floor, Lem Azack hoisted his dangling wide black suspenders back up on his broad shoulders and pushed himself up.

"Hello, Mr. Azack." Free dropped his hand from Jen's arm and cleared his throat so his sudden attack of nerves would not show in his voice. He felt Jennet beside him, but he couldn't look at her for fear of backing out even at this late date.

"Free," said Lem Azack as he held out a hand that was white and soft from working indoors all his life. "What a pleasant surprise." He smiled, then turned his attention to Jennet.

Jennet felt dirty and ragged and wanted to run from the man's steady gaze.

"Mr. Azack, this is my wife, Jennet." Free's voice trembled slightly, but he forced himself to continue. "I came to claim my inheritance." He handed the certificate of marriage to the lawyer.

Lem took it, glanced over it, his eyes stopping to reread the date, and then handed it back to Free. Lem held out a big hand to Jennet and reluctantly she held her small one out to him. "Hello, Jennet. I am pleased to meet you."

The older man's kind voice eased the pain around Jen's heart just a little. She couldn't find her voice to answer him back the way Ma had taught her a lifetime ago, so she only nodded.

"Please, sit down," said Lem, motioning toward the dark red leather sofa against a wall covered with family pictures.

Jennet perched on the edge of the sofa and locked her trembling hands in her lap. Free sat beside her but far enough away that they didn't touch. She could smell his sweat as well as the leather of the sofa.

Lem sat on a matching leather chair beside an occasional table that held a coal oil lamp with flowers painted on the glass bowl and globe. "So, you got married."

Free nodded and Jennet bit back a moan.

Lem ran his finger under his collar and smoothed back his white hair. "Free, I'll meet you at the bank in the morning at nine and see that the money is turned over to you."

"I'll be there."

"Your house is furnished and stocked with canned food if you choose to go there tonight."

Free shrugged. The house was nothing to him. The money and the land were all-important.

Lem smiled at Jennet. "Free's grandfather left a house here in town on Grove Street for the two of you, Jennet. It's small but pleasant and has a stable with a horse and buggy. A woman keeps it aired and dusted to be ready at a moment's notice. I'll get the key." Lem went to his desk, looked through a drawer, and finally held up a long brass key. He handed it to Free as he told him where the house was located.

Jennet's head spun and for a minute she thought she'd faint dead away, but she managed to hold on and listen to the rest of the men's conversation.

Later, in the buggy Jennet locked her hands in her lap and kept her eyes down as Free drove away from the attorney's house and down the darkened street. After a few blocks a horrible smell made her nauseated.

"It's the tannery," Free said, turning onto Monroe Street. "It takes getting used to." But the few times he'd smelled the stinking rot of animal skins and carcasses he'd never gotten used to it.

Lights shone from the huge three-story brick house that Galen Norcross had built for his Dutch wife six years ago. At Grove Street, Free turned left, drove past five large houses with wide, sweeping lawns, past a stand of hardwood trees, and pulled into the driveway of a small white house. Suddenly he realized that Grandpa's friends Tunis and Nina Bowker lived close by. In the dark he couldn't tell which house was theirs.

Free stopped beside the barn and just sat there. He heard Jennet's gentle breathing and the wild thud of his heart. Jen was his wife and this was his home. Suddenly his hands dampened with sweat. His wife! His home!

Free stepped from the buggy, and it moved under his weight. Wordlessly he helped Jen to the dirt driveway. The moon was bright enough that they could see their way to the front door. Freeman unlocked the door, found a lamp, and lit it, leaving a smell of sulfur that soon disappeared.

The front room was pleasant and held the fragrance of wild roses.

"I've never been here before," said Free as if he was talking to himself. He lifted the lamp high to show a brick fireplace with a wide wooden mantel, an oak rocking chair, comfortable cushioned chairs, and a deep blue sofa at the side of a wide window with heavy brocade drapes. "Let's look at the rest of it," said Free in a voice that didn't sound like his.

Jennet hesitantly followed him through the front room and into the dining room that held a long oval walnut table with six banister-back chairs pushed up to it. A long hutch full of dishes stood against a flowered wallpapered wall with a matching corner hutch built into the wall next to a window. The beauty of the room took Jennet's breath away.

Reluctantly she followed Free into a big kitchen that had a hand pump built right into a counter, a cookstove, table and chairs, and more cupboards than she'd ever seen in a house. A kerosene lamp sat in the middle of the round table. They opened a door that led to a pantry and another that led to a back shed where split wood was stacked. From the shed door they saw the outhouse and the barn with the hired buggy sitting beside it. A horse nickered and the hired horse answered. From a neighbor's yard a dog barked.

Suddenly Jennet yawned, then yawned again. "I'm sorry," she said, flushing with embarrassment.

"You're worn right out, aren't you?" asked Free.

Jen ducked her head. "I am tired."

"You get right to bed." Possessively he took her arm and led her down the hallway behind the kitchen, past two small bedrooms, one on either side of the hall, to a large bedroom with a canopy bed. He found a lamp on the dresser and lit it. It cast a soft glow over a portion of the room, showing a humpbacked trunk against the wall beside a dresser and a dark pink chaise. "We can talk in the morning after you've rested," Free said gently.

Helplessly Jennet looked at him. "Are you leaving?"

He nodded, wondering if he could walk away from her. She was his wife, and he had every right to stay! "I want to take the buggy back, and I have to check out a few things."

Dare she ask him his plans for her? Jennet tried to stop the frightened beat of her heart. "Will you be back tonight?" Oh, she wished she knew what to expect of him!

"I plan to."

"Oh."

Free saw her fear and a muscle jumped in his jaw. "I won't wake you. I'll sleep in another room."

He walked to the door. "See you in the morning," he said without smiling.

Jennet nodded and watched him leave. Before she could move, the door opened and he handed her bundle to her. Their hands brushed and sparks leaped between them.

"Try to rest," he said hoarsely.

She looked at him, trying to take in all the events of their day together.

"Good night," he said just above a whisper.

"Good night," she mouthed, unable to bring up even a whisper. She could barely breathe as Freeman Havlick walked out, closing the door behind him.

CHAPTER

8

♦ Jennet sat bolt upright. She'd overslept! Tait would beat her until she couldn't move. Sunlight already shone through the three partly open windows. A warm breeze puffed at the muslin curtains. She glanced around and frowned at the unfamiliar sight of the canopy bed, the chaise lounge, and the chiffonrobe against the wall to the left of the bed. With a start she remembered that she was in a house that belonged to Freeman Havlick. She was no longer Jennet Cordell, but Jennet Havlick!

Shivering even though the breeze was pleasantly warm, Jen swung her legs over the side of the bed, expecting her feet to touch the floor. The bed was not close to the floor like the narrow cot at the store. She'd become so used to the cot she'd slept on only a small part of the bed last night. Jennet picked up Wex's hankie off the pillow next to hers where she'd laid it last night and rubbed it over her cheek. "Wex, I married your brother. What will you do when you find that out? I know I said I'd wait for you, but I couldn't." Jennet's voice broke.

She slid off the bed and stood up. The carpet felt soft under her feet, and she couldn't help smiling as she traced around the design of a large cabbage rose with her bare toe. In awe she touched the pink muslin canopy that matched the pink ruffled curtains at the three tall windows. Never had she slept in such a room! The cream-colored wallpaper was covered with small pink-and-red rosebuds intertwined with rich green English ivy. She ran her fingers across the mahogany commode beside the bed and looked around at the matching chest, quilt rack, and dresser, and then gasped at the sight of a framed full-length looking glass standing on a carved base. She saw her bare feet and the ragged hem of her once-white nightdress that hung around her ankles. She tilted the glass to show her thin body and her pale face. Her braids had come loose in the night and tangled chestnut-brown hair hung limply to her thin shoulders. She pushed strands of it from her forehead, then met her wide blue eyes in the mirror. Oh, but she was ugly!

Jennet turned away and sank to the edge of the chaise lounge.

Just then Free knocked on the closed door and said, "Jen."

Jennet leaped back in bed and pulled the cover to her chin. "What?" she answered.

Freeman opened the door and walked in. He wore a dark blue suit and white shirt. His stomach tightened at the frightened look on her face. Why, she was as afraid of him as she had been of her pa and uncle! The thought made him want to beg her forgiveness for forcing her to marry him. Abruptly he pushed the thought aside and said, "I'll be gone most of the day, so you'll be on your own."

On her own for a whole day with nothing to do! Never had she had a day to herself!

Jennet's relief hurt him and that surprised him. "You'll find a tub in the kitchen beside the stove. I put water on to heat for your bath."

A bath with water that she hadn't carried and heated! A bath that she didn't have to hurry through!

"There's food for you too." Freeman turned away, then said over his shoulder, "I'm using the horse and buggy today, but otherwise it'll be for your use."

Jennet could only stare at him. Was this a dream? Could she walk out the door and hitch up her own horse to her own buggy and go to a place of her choice? "Could I see my family tomorrow?" she asked in a weak voice.

Free hesitated. Did he want her to see her family? They might find a way to get her out of the marriage and back with them. He had to talk to Lem Azack to see if there were any loopholes in the marriage. "We'll talk about it when I get back." He walked to the door and once again turned back. "I left a bundle of clothes for you on the kitchen table."

Clothes!

"If they don't fit, I'll return them." Free walked out, closing the door quietly behind him. He stood outside her door. What had he done? Jen was frightened of him and probably hated him. But could he blame her? He'd forced her into this marriage.

Free lifted his chin defiantly. She was certainly better off with him than with Tait or with Vernon Cordell! She wasn't capable of taking care of herself.

Jennet waited until she heard the outer door close, then she scurried down the hall to the large kitchen. A copper boiler full of hot water bubbled on the cast-iron range, and a round galvanized washtub sat on the floor in front of the stove. Three open windows with white ruffled curtains and green tiebacks kept the kitchen from being too hot for comfort. The wooden cupboards built into a wall between two of the windows and against the wall between the kitchen and dining room were stained a pleasant green. A big round table with four chairs pushed up under it stood almost in the middle of the room.

With a low laugh Jennet touched the red-handled pump.

She'd never seen a pump in the house before. How much time and backbreaking work it would save! She pumped cold water into a five-gallon bucket that she'd found beside the counter and poured it into the washtub. She added hot water from the boiler until the tub water felt comfortably warm. She filled the large bucket with warm water and hung a dipper on the side, then knelt beside the tub and washed her hair. She wrapped a small towel around her head, added a little more hot water to the tub, stepped in, and thankfully sank down in the water.

Several minutes later Jennet stood beside the table with a big white towel wrapped around herself and looked through the bundle of clothes that Free had left for her. She blushed scarlet as she found pantaloons, a soft cotton chemise, and two full gathered underskirts that he should never have looked at, but quickly she slipped them on, then pulled the blue cotton dress over her head and let it fall down over her, almost to touch the floor. She buttoned the long line of hidden buttons up the front, making the dress nip in at her narrow waist. The bodice fit snugly against her instead of hanging loose like her other dresses had. The small collar and the narrow cuffs were ruffled. She almost ran to the bedroom to look in the looking glass.

Oh, the dress was beautiful, just the blue of her eyes! The two underskirts made it bell out at the bottom becomingly. With shoes on, it would be the perfect length. Jen brushed her hair, which suddenly looked soft and luxurious, then tied it back with a blue ribbon that had been in the bundle. She stared at herself in the mirror for a long time, then finally whispered, "I *do* look pretty! Oh, Wex, I wish you could see me now. You'd be surprised, but happy."

Next Jennet emptied the tub, a bucketful at a time, on the ground beside the barn. As she walked back toward the house, she heard a sound behind her. She spun around to see a slender woman with graying hair, kind blue eyes, and a warm smile walking across the wide expanse of lawn. The older woman wore a light gray dress with darker gray piping and a high collar and a cameo at her throat.

"Hello! Mrs. Havlick?"

Mrs. Havlick! Jennet barely nodded. "I'm Jennet . . . Havlick." She felt awkward, fixed all fancy as if she were somebody important.

"Don't be frightened. I'm Nina Bowker, a friend of Free's, and I live next door," she said, pointing to the white frame house to the west. "I saw you and Free come last night, and I saw Free leave earlier. I wanted to make sure you were comfortable and see if I could help you."

"Help me do what?" asked Jennet in a weak voice as she set the bucket down.

"Get used to your new home and new surroundings."

"Oh." Jennet couldn't imagine anyone helping her. "Do you know Freeman?"

Nina smiled. "Yes. For years. My husband Tunis and I were best friends with Free's Grandpa Clay and Grandma Sarah. We made a promise to Clay before he died that we'd always watch out for his grandchildren. Clay bought this house next door to us for Free so we could do just that."

Jennet locked her fingers together. She'd never had anyone watch out for her since she was five years old. Just what did it entail? "I've never lived in town before," said Jennet.

Nina laughed with delight. "Then I'll show you around. Where to buy vegetables and meat. Clothes. Just everything!"

Jennet nodded.

Nina patted Jennet's arm. "But not today, dear. You'll want today to yourself, I'm sure. Today you rest and enjoy your new home and your new husband."

Jennet was at a loss for words. "It's all very different," she finally managed to say.

Nina Bowker smiled as they walked to a wooden bench

beside the back door of the house and sat down. "Tell me about yourself, dear."

Jennet hesitated. She didn't want to tell a stranger what had happened in her life, but she didn't know how to tell her that. As quickly as she could Jennet told about her family and about working for Tait. She did not tell Nina that she'd been beaten or indentured to Tait. She went into detail about Eve and Joshua, then skimmed over the part where she had married Free.

"You are a very remarkable young woman," said Nina.

The praise warmed Jennet's heart. "Thank you."

"I shall call you Jennet and you call me Nina. I hope we'll become close friends."

Jennet smiled. She felt the same kindness in Nina that she'd felt in Eve. "I hope so too. Mr. Azack said someone took care of the house. Was that you?"

"I had my housekeeper dust and keep it aired out. My gardener took care of your yard, the barn, and the horse."

"Will they keep doing it?"

"Only if you want them to. It's your decision."

Her decision! The thought was heady. "I'll take care of it myself then," she said.

"I'll tell them," said Nina. "But if you ever want their help, let me know."

"Thank you. I will." But why would she need help taking care of such a small place? One horse, one barn, one house, one yard. She could do that and still have time left in a day. "I don't see a garden."

"There's a spot for one on the far side of the barn. It's a little late to put one in this year, but you could plan for next."

Jennet's stomach tightened. She hadn't thought that far into the future. Would she be here next year?

"I'm going back home now so you can get on with exploring your new place." Smiling, Nina caught Jennet's hand and squeezed it. She walked back to her yard and the large house surrounded by several maples and oaks. A large barn stood behind the house with a wooden fence around the barnyard.

Jennet looked all around. She smelled the roses she saw climbing on a trellis at the side of the house and heard birds singing in the trees around her place and those of the neighbors on either side as well as across the street. All the houses were far enough apart to have room for barns and barnyards for their horses. A breeze ruffled Jennet's hair and pressed her skirts against her legs. No one was here to tell her what to do or beat her if she didn't work!

Jennet ran to her barn and pushed open the heavy door. Dust particles danced in the sunlight. A calico cat stretched, ambled over, and rubbed against her ankle. She lifted the cat in her arms and held it close. It purred and snuggled against her. "You're a nice cat. Do you have a name?" The cat purred louder.

The barn was clean and empty except for the cat. She saw the spot for the buggy and the stall the horse had been in. She peeked in the tack room and saw a wooden bench in the middle of the floor and pegs on the wall for harnesses. A saddle was flung over a special rack, and a bridle hung from a peg beside it. Jennet walked to the back door of the barn. A tank filled with water stood next to the barn, and a wooden fence enclosed the lush grassy barnyard. Trees shaded part of the barnyard and wild flowers grew here and there, dotting the green with bright blue, yellow, and orange.

With the cat in her arms Jennet walked all around the outside of her house. Before she went back inside, she put the cat down with a pat. She inspected each room again. The lawyer had called the house small, but to Jennet, it seemed gigantic for only two people. Could this entire house belong to her to do with as she wanted? It was too strange to be true.

Then she thought of Freeman. She was married to him

and had to do what he told her. She wasn't as free as she'd thought.

Jennet sank to a rocking chair near the front window. She rocked back and forth and tried to stop the wild beat of her heart.

Frowning, Free stopped outside the newspaper office. GRAND RAPIDS NEWS was printed in black block lettering on the dirt-streaked window. Should he go in and talk with Tunis Bowker? Free brushed dust off his arm as he glanced toward the barbershop where he'd had his hair cut. Maybe he should get another haircut and forget about talking to Tunis. Could he face Tune after his angry outburst the last time they'd met? Tune was always trying to get Free and Roman to understand each other. He said he'd promised Grandpa Clay. Free scanned the street as horse-drawn buggies, carts, drays, and wagons passed by, harnesses rattling. A small dog barked at the heels of a barefoot boy running down the sidewalk.

Free looked in the wide window of the newspaper office. Maybe he should walk away. But now that he lived right next door to Tune and Nina he couldn't just ignore them. He missed the special talks he and Tune used to have. He almost filled the empty place that Grandpa Clay had left when he died. Finally Free made up his mind.

As he pushed open the heavy door, the smell of printer's ink hit him. The noise of the printing press, which almost filled the room, made his ears ring. A man wearing an ink-stained apron stood watching paper pass through the giant machine. The scarred plank floor was covered with scattered newsprint. Another man sat at a high counter facing the wall as he proofread the pages in front of him. Signs and advertisements hung on the bare wood walls.

His hat in his hand, Free walked through the front room and back to Tunis Bowker's office. Tune sat in his shirtsleeves behind his big desk. Gray hair on his balding head stood on end as if he'd rubbed his fingers through it and hadn't smoothed it back in place. He looked up from his work and, on seeing Free, smiled warmly, got up, and strode around to hug Free. The smells of ink and sweat, which he had always associated with Tune, surrounded Free as surely as the older man's arms.

"I'm glad you came, Free," Tunis said in his deep voice.

Free twisted the brim of his hat as he sat down. "I was very rude to you the last time we talked."

Tunis sank back against his desk and crossed his ankles. His baggy gray pants hung on his long frame. "It's over and done."

"I am sorry."

Tunis smiled and spread his big hands wide. "Forgiven and forgotten!"

"Thank you." Free sighed heavily. "I was so angry with anyone connected with my father. You and he are friends, and in my mind that made us enemies."

Tune leaned forward, his brow cocked. "But now you've decided differently?"

"Yes. I guess I grew up some."

"So has your father."

Free frowned.

"He's sorry for forcing you out of his life. And I think he's beginning to understand that you want a different life than he has. And that it's okay."

For the past eight years that Tune had been part of their lives, he'd tried to help Roman understand that he needed to let his children choose their own destiny. He'd also tried to help Roman understand and love Clay while he was still alive. It hadn't worked. Clay had died with Roman still angry and resentful.

"So, he listened to you at long last?" asked Free.

Tunis shrugged. "Somewhat." He smiled slightly, walked around his desk, and sat back down. "Your father has a lot of anger to work through. But I think he's doing it."

Free didn't believe that, but he didn't say so. "Tune, the reason I stopped by. . . ." Free's voice faded away.

"Out with it, Free. I love you, boy, and I'll do anything I can to help you. You know that."

"It's about Grandpa Clay's will."

"What about it?"

"Do you know what's in it?"

"Yes. He told me."

Free leaned forward with a frown. The noise from the other room seeped through the walls and the heavy glass on the closed door. "Why didn't you tell me about it?"

Tunis lifted his bushy brows. "But Roman said he told you."

"He didn't!"

"Well, well." Tunis rubbed his long fingers through his hair and then brushed the strands down with the palm of his hand. "That explains a lot of things."

"Not to me," said Free gruffly.

"Your pa has been acting very, very guilty lately when I've talked to him about you. I couldn't understand why. Now I do." Tunis brushed at his wide nose. "I always wondered why you didn't talk to me about the will. The way Clay left it and all."

"I can't understand why Grandpa said I had to be married to inherit his money and land."

"Didn't Lem explain?"

"Yes. But it sure didn't help. It doesn't seem right that I had to get married to get what Grandpa wanted me to have."

"He wanted you to have much more than what money could buy. He knew you wouldn't marry just to get the money. He knew you had too much integrity for that."

Free forced back a flush.

"Clay loved you more than you'll ever know, Free." Tunis moved pencil and paper out of his way and put his elbows on his desk. "He loved his family—all of you very much. But he didn't realize that until late in his life, too late to give all of you the things he wanted to give you."

Tears burned the backs of Free's eyes. He'd loved Grandpa with a fierceness that he'd never understood, and he'd felt the same love from Grandpa for him.

"Clay wanted you to value family, Free. He wanted you to know love was more important than great wealth, great success, or even great power."

An ache that felt as if it would take his life away started in the very pit of Free's stomach and spread through him. Since Grandpa had died, no one really seemed to love him. Now, he had a wife who didn't love him. Instead she was frightened of him and had married him only because he'd forced her into it. How could he ever expect love from her?

"What's wrong, Free?" asked Tunis softly.

Embarrassed, Free choked back tears. He was a man, and Pa had said more times than he could count that men didn't cry. "I miss Grandpa."

"I know." Tunis laced his fingers together and looked very serious. "Your grandpa learned of God's love late in life, and he wanted to share that love with his family. Clay had material wealth to leave behind, but he felt his spiritual wealth was of more value. He wanted each of you to personally accept Jesus."

In the back of his mind Free could hear Grandpa saying the very same words. When Free was about fourteen, he'd prayed with Grandpa, and he'd asked Jesus to be his Savior. But after Grandpa had died and after he'd left home in anger, he'd pushed that commitment aside.

Tunis brushed a hand across his face, then leaned forward again. "Free, you can have all the timber, all the grainfields, all the money you can spend, but if you lose your family, all of it means nothing."

Free stared down at his hat as he wondered if he believed Tunis. Free wanted timber and he wanted money.

Tunis cleared his throat. "I never told you this, Freeman, but today I'm going to tell you."

"What?"

"Your grandpa and I had a pact. A covenant we called it. He read in the Bible about the covenant that David and Jonathan cut together. It's as though two people become one—they look after each other's property and family." Tunis brushed moisture from his eye. "Clay and I were as David and Jonathan. Their covenant was never broken; each generation renewed it. I will not break my covenant with Clay. That's why I'm now looking after you and your holdings."

Free rolled the brim of his hat tight.

"Clay and I promised each other that we'd always watch out for each other. What was mine was his. What was his, mine. I promised him that I'd take care of all of you after he died. And, Free, I've tried to do it. That's why I butted in to get Roman to change. That's why I tried to make you understand your pa. And that's why I've been watching over you after you left home to live in the woods."

"I never knew," Free said solemnly.

"Remember the time the bear attacked you? I'd asked a woodsman who worked the same area to help you if ever you needed it. He chased away the bear."

Free rubbed his shoulder where he still had the scar.

"And I told Jig, that old woodsman who spends more time talking to God than he does anything else, to get you away from Willie Thorne."

Free sank back in his chair and stared at Tunis as if he'd never seen him before. "I never knew," he repeated.

"I'm glad you listened to Jig and quit working with Willie."

"Me too."

"And if I'd known you didn't know about Clay's will, I

would've told you. I love you, Freeman. I love you like Clay did."

Free quickly brushed a tear from his sunbrowned cheek. He'd known that Tune cared for him, but he had never understood how much.

"Now you're married, and Nina and I mean to watch out for Jennet like I've been watching out for you. I'm sure she's a wonderful girl."

Free looked down at his hat. He could never let Tune know the truth! "She needed me," he said hoarsely. "I guess we needed each other."

"So I understand from what she told Nina this morning."

Free realized from the look on Tunis's face that Jennet had not told the whole story. "I'd appreciate it if you kept your eye on her when I go to the lumbercamp in September."

"We'll be glad to."

"Tune, this covenant thing . . ." Free's voice trailed off.

"Yes?"

"I appreciate it."

"So do I, Freeman." Tunis nodded slowly. "There's even more to it."

Free lifted a brow questioningly.

"God cut a covenant with all of us through His Son. When we accept Jesus as Savior, we've entered into that covenant with God. All that is His is ours. All that is ours is His. It's an awesome truth. It's greater than the covenant that Clay and I have, even greater than the one between Jonathan and David. God Himself is a covenant partner with us!" Before Tunis could continue, a man knocked on his door, stuck his head in, and said, "I need a word with you, Tune."

"Be right with you, Wallis."

Free stood. "I have to see Lem before I go home. Thanks for taking time for me, Tune."

"My pleasure."

"Tune, I'd like you to keep my marriage to yourself. I want to personally tell my family."

"Sure thing." Tunis hugged Free tight and let him go. "See you at home."

"Yes. At home." Free clamped his hat in place and strode from the office.

Jennet slept away part of the afternoon, something she'd not done since she was a baby. She ate when she wanted, then she sat again in the rocker and waited. Without anything to do, the day seemed to last a lifetime.

When Free finally drove in about seven o'clock, shivers ran up and down her spine as she waited for him to take care of the horse. Through the kitchen window she watched him walk from the barn to the house. He carried his suit coat over his arm, and he looked tired.

Free walked in the back door and stopped short when he saw her waiting for him. He stared in surprise at her. He hadn't realized that she was beautiful. "Hello," he said, suddenly losing the other words he'd planned to say.

Jennet locked her hands behind her back. "Did you decide about tomorrow? Can I go visit my family?"

He draped his coat over a kitchen chair but couldn't look at her. "Maybe."

"I want to see them. I want to know if Ma is well. I want them to know I'm here where they can come see me."

"I'll think about it," Free said as he noticed how shiny her hair was and how pretty it looked hanging down her back. The dress he'd chosen for her fit just right and matched her eyes as he'd wanted it to.

Jennet gripped the back of a chair. Why was Free looking at her so intently? "And I want to find out if they've had word of Wex. When Marie last wrote, she said he might come home this summer. Have you heard?"

A muscle jumped in Free's jaw. "I spoke with my sister a

while ago, and she said that he wanted to come home for a short leave."

Jennet's eyes lit up and she smiled. "It will be so good to see him again!"

Free stabbed his fingers through his dark hair. "Just remember that you're married to me now."

The sparkle left her eyes and Jen nodded. "Do you want supper?" she asked stiffly.

"I ate with my sister."

"I'll go feed and water the horse."

"I already did."

Jennet rubbed the back of her hand and studied her blunt cut fingernails. "I'm not used to being idle. I don't know what is expected of me," she whispered.

Free walked to the stove and back to the table to stand beside her. "You have only yourself to tend. When I'm home, you can see to my meals and my clothes." His throat almost closed over at what he planned to say next. "When we have a family, you'll tend them."

A family! She flushed painfully.

Lem had told Free that they must have a true marriage so that Jennet's family couldn't have it annulled if they so desired. He didn't think they'd want that, but maybe Wex would if he came home this summer. And Wex was not going to have Jen! He wasn't man enough for her! Had he even tried to make her life better? Had he even tried to protect her?

Free cleared his throat and moved restlessly. He'd asked Lem not to tell his family about his marriage. "Anne said she'll come see you."

"It's been a long time since I've seen her."

"Pa still won't let her go to the farm. She hasn't seen the family since Wex left." Free turned away with a frown. He didn't want to talk about Wex. "What did you do while I was gone?"

"I met Nina Bowker from next door."

"She's a fine woman. Grandpa thought a lot of her and Tunis." Free led Jennet to the front room where they sat facing each other in the overstuffed chairs. Free told her about Grandpa Clay, the covenant that he'd cut with Tunis, and how Tunis had watched out for him. He told about the bear and about Jig. In the past Jennet had heard many stories about Clay from Wex as well as from Free, but Clay had died the year before her family moved to the farm, so she'd never met him.

Jennet listened without speaking, but a part of her mind was on the frightening time that was coming in bed with Free.

Later in her bedroom Jennet held Wex's hankie to her cheek and whispered, "I have a nice house to live in, and I don't have to work hard, but I am still a slave. This time to Free. He bought me, and I have to do what he says. I'm sorry, Wex. But I have to do what he says."

Just then the door opened and Free came in. Jennet jumped and dropped the hankie. Before she could pick it up, Free did. He held it out to her, then his eyes fell on the fancy "W" and he jerked it back. Jealousy shot through him, and fire flashed from his dark eyes.

"Whose hankie?" asked Free sharply.

"Wexal's," Jennet whispered.

"What are *you* doing with it?" Free's voice was thick with anger.

"I made it for him for his birthday," she said weakly. She sank to the edge of the bed. "He gave it to me when he went away."

"And what did you give him?" asked Free coldly.

She thought of the kiss that she'd wanted to give him, and she blushed to the roots of her hair.

Free scowled at the sight of her blush. Had she given herself to him? Had Pa been right about her after all? Free pushed the hankie in his pocket. "Forget about this hankie and forget about Wex. You're my wife!"

Jennet wanted to grab the hankie back and put it near her heart, but she didn't move and didn't say the angry words burning inside her.

"Get ready for bed," said Free in a low, tight voice. "I'll give you a few minutes alone, then I'll be back."

Her eyes wide in fear, Jennet watched him stalk out of the room.

CHAPTER

9

♦ In September, Jennet stood beside the open front door, held the satchel of clothes out to Free, and said dutifully, "Take care of yourself." She wanted to say, "I hate you for forcing me to marry you! I hate you for forcing me to share a bed with you!" Her body was used to him now, and at times when he was especially gentle and loving, she responded to him even though she tried not to. She'd actually enjoyed listening to his plans and dreams just as she had in the past before he'd left home. And that she couldn't allow! She wanted to stay angry with him. She wanted him to know she was angry and would never forgive him. How glad she was to see him leave a day earlier than he'd planned! A band tightened around her heart.

Free's mind was full of the wonderful adventure ahead in his lumbercamp, but he saw the relief in Jennet's eyes. Wouldn't she miss him at all? He had seen to her every need. He'd kept her safe and protected. What more did she want? Abruptly he pushed the thoughts away. He couldn't think about her feelings now. Finally he was a lumberman by name, and soon he'd prove he was a lumberman by reputation. He managed a smile. "I'll see you in the spring. Be sure to get someone to help you so you don't have to do heavy work in your condition."

Jennet barely nodded. She hated having him say anything that reminded her that she was going to have his baby in the spring. It was one more mark to show her that she was Free's slave. She had not wanted to share a bed with him, had not wanted to have a part of him growing inside her body. But she'd had no choice because she belonged to Free and he had a paper to prove it.

Free looked possessively down her slender body to the toes of her black shoes, then up to the pulse that throbbed in her neck. He liked the way she looked in her pale pink dress. A pink ribbon held back her long dark hair. He wanted to see her smile. "Nina and Tune will watch out for you," he said."

"They told me." She loved both of them, but she wasn't a child who needed to be "watched out for."

Glancing at the hired wagon stopped on the street, Free turned back to Jennet. She suddenly looked too young to become a mother. He should've sent her home in June, but he couldn't stand to think of her pa whipping her or his pa working her too hard. Her family didn't deserve to see her! Free watched the breeze blow a strand of hair across her smooth cheek that was once again rosy and healthy. He'd hated the thought of her seeing Wex again. Free hadn't wanted Wex around her. "Are you sure you'll be all right?" he asked softly.

Jennet nodded. Why didn't he leave?

Free wanted to pull her close and beg her to be happy. He wanted to take away the agony he saw in her eyes. He had so much to say to her, but all he said was, "I don't want you riding out alone to see your family." Free didn't want them to convince her to move back home.

Jennet pressed her lips tightly together to hold back a rush of angry words. She'd wanted to see her family since she'd been there, but Free would never take her and wouldn't allow her to go alone.

Free moved restlessly. A gust of wind blew in the door bringing in a faint smell of the Grand River several blocks away. The man in the wagon whistled as he waited. Although Free wanted to be on his way, he realized that he'd miss Jennet.

Jennet wanted him to leave, not say another word to her, but he just stood there as if he didn't want to leave. His white shirt buttoned to his throat made his brown hair seem even darker.

Free wanted to kiss her good-bye, but he'd never kissed her except in bed. Why shouldn't he kiss her when he wanted? He was her husband! He pulled her to him. She fit in his arms as if she'd been made for him.

Jennet felt Free's heart beat against her as he held her tightly to him. Her heart fluttered strangely.

Free pressed his lips to hers in a long, hungry kiss.

The kiss sent a tingle through Jennet, and she stiffened.

Free let her go with a slight frown. He saw the rigid set of her shoulders and the bleak look in her eyes. "Good-bye," he whispered.

"Good-bye," she said hoarsely.

Free strode from the house to the wagon. He felt frustrated and angry and didn't know why. He forced his mind off Jennet and onto the tracts of land that he'd be lumbering. This time the camp was his, the men were his, and the logs were his. He'd filed his logmark at the courthouse and each of his logs from now on would carry that mark—F and H hooked together inside a circle.

"Morning, Havlick," said the driver. "Great day, eh?"

"Sure is," said Free as he climbed on the wooden seat beside the driver. Free wanted to look back at Jennet, but he kept his eyes on the draft horses.

Clenching her fists angrily, Jennet watched Free ride

away with the man he'd hired to take him on the hard two-day trip to his lumbercamp. She closed the front door with a bang. How she wanted to tell him that she hated him, that she wanted to be married to Wex, but she'd kept her feelings and her words to herself.

Jennet brushed at her mouth, trying to rub away the feel of his lips on hers, then groaned because she suddenly realized she would miss having him with her. She trailed her finger over her mouth. How would it feel if she did try to love him, did try to talk to him and tell him her thoughts and feelings? Oh, that was impossible! She'd never care for Free!

With a long sigh she walked outdoors to feed and water Acorn. Since June, she'd learned to love the sorrel mare, and when Free didn't have her, Jen had taken her for rides, astride her or hitched to the buggy. A few times Free had taken Jennet for a buggy ride and talked to her about his dream of being a prosperous lumberman.

The pleasantly warm breeze pressed Jennet's long pink skirt against her legs. Just outside the back door near the bench the calico cat rubbed against Jennet's ankle, and she picked him up and brushed her cheek against him. He smelled of milk and dust. She'd learned that he was the mouser for the house and barn and no one had named him, so she had called him Cal, short for Calico.

"Cal, did you catch that mouse I spotted in the barn yesterday?" Jennet asked. Her voice sounded strained. She cleared her throat and forced herself to relax.

Cal mewed and Jennet laughed softly.

"Good morning, Jen," called Nina from next door as she walked across the wide yard, carrying her hat. "I haven't seen much of you lately."

"I'm sorry," said Jennet. When she'd learned from the doctor that she was going to have a baby, she'd kept away from Nina and Tunis as much as possible. Jennet didn't want to tell anyone, not even the kind woman and her husband who had become her good friends.

Nina hugged Jennet briefly. "I saw Free leave. The next seven months he's away will be lonely for you both. Maybe you could visit him."

Jennet shook her head. She'd never do that!

"What will you do with your time now?" asked Nina.

"I don't know." Jennet looked across the yard to the trees behind the barn. What was she going to do with her time?

Nina patted Jennet's shoulder and smiled. "It's up to you. You only have yourself to answer to."

The realization hit Jennet so hard it took her breath away. She didn't have to answer to anyone but herself for seven long months! Not Pa. Not Roman. Not Tait. And not Free! Was that possible?

What *would* she do? Suddenly she knew. She'd visit her family! She'd see Ma and the girls and maybe meet Tim. But she would not speak to Pa! All summer she'd wanted to go, but Free hadn't let her. Now he was gone, and she could do as she pleased. And if she wanted to go alone, she would! He wasn't around to tell her what she could do or what she couldn't do!

Her blue eyes sparkling, Jennet smiled at Nina. "I will visit my family," she said with more assurance than she felt.

"That'll be nice for you," said Nina as she set her hat in place on the carefully arranged gray hair. The fluttering wide blue feathers matched the blue of Nina's eyes.

Jennet nodded. "Yes. Yes, it will."

"It'll be strange for you to see them again since you're a married woman and not their little girl any longer."

Jennet frowned slightly. She had never been their "little girl," but it would be strange to know that she didn't have to put up with Pa's anger.

"And will you visit with Free's parents?" asked Nina as she brushed at the wide sleeves of her dress.

"No."

Nina caught Jennet's hand and held it as she looked in concern at her. Jennet had told her about her life on the farm. "Jen, don't let anger and unforgiveness keep you from learning to love your new family."

Jennet bit her bottom lip. "I don't think of them as family."

"But they are." Nina squeezed Jennet's hand. "With God's help you can learn to care for them."

She didn't want to argue with Nina. "I'll see you when I return, Nina."

Nina smiled and laugh lines fanned from the corners of her blue eyes to her gray hair. "Enjoy yourself, Jen. I'm on my way to meet Tunis for breakfast. He's taking me to the new restaurant that opened last week." Nina smiled and touched her hat to make sure it was on straight. "You're welcome to come along."

"Thank you, Nina. Maybe another time."

"I'll see you when you return." Nina hugged Jennet, walked to her waiting buggy, and drove away. At the corner she waved and Jennet waved back.

Feeling as light as dandelion fluff, Jennet went inside to the bedroom and changed into the blue dress that Free had bought for her. She wore only one petticoat to make driving easier, then forced herself to put on the hat that Nina had helped her buy. She glanced in the mirror with a frown. Her family would think she was putting on airs if she wore such a fancy hat. She agreed. Wrinkling her nose, she dropped the hat back in its box. Jennet quickly braided her hair in one long, thick chestnut-brown braid, coiled it loosely at the nape of her neck, and pinned it in place. She packed to spend the night and walked to the barn with her case. Cal ran along at her feet and almost tripped her. A blue jay scolded from the top of a tall maple. The smell of wood smoke drifted through the air and on up to meet the fluffy white clouds dotting the blue sky.

Just as Jennet finished harnessing Acorn she thought she heard a strange noise, almost like a baby crying. She cocked her head. Was she hearing things? She listened, but Acorn rattled the harness and covered any other sounds.

With a shrug Jennet led Acorn from the barn. Walking back to close the door, she caught a flash of movement from the corner of her eye.

"Is someone in there?" Jennet asked in a shaky voice. There was no answer. With all the courage she could muster she stepped into the barn and looked around. Trying to sound firm, she said, "I know you're in here. Come out right now!"

Finally a ragged colored girl carrying a bundle emerged from the shadows. She was about the same size as Jennet but younger. Her eyes were full of fear. Pieces of hay stuck in her tight black curls and on the sleeve of her faded brown dress. "I's come for help," she said weakly.

Jennet frowned. "Who are you?"

"Dacia, ma'am. The white lady tole me to come." Dacia thrust out a paper. "I's to give this to the man called Free dat lives here."

Jennet gasped as she quickly read the note: "I know you must leave tomorrow, but Dacia needs help. I'm being watched and can't get her to the next station. Please take care of her." It wasn't signed, but she knew it was from Free's sister Anne.

Jennet stared in shock from the paper in her hand to the runaway slave girl. Free had never breathed a word about helping his sister get runaway slaves to Canada. But Free was gone! "You'll have to go back to Anne. To the white lady who gave you the note."

Dacia shook her head as giant tears welled up in her eyes. "I's can't go back. I's never can't go back!"

Just then the low cry of a baby came from the bundle

Dacia held. Tears sparkled in her black eyes. "My Colin is hungry, ma'am."

Jennet pressed her hand to her throat. Finally she said, "You'd better come in the house."

"I's scared, ma'am."

The baby cried harder, and Dacia shook the bundle gently and crooned soothingly as Jennet peeked out the barn door. She knew Nina and Tunis were gone. The other neighboring houses were hidden among trees. No one was in sight.

"Come with me," said Jennet, taking Dacia's stick-thin arm. Jennet kept Dacia close to her side as she walked to the back door and stepped inside. Smells of breakfast coffee still hung in the air. It was not yet eight o'clock, but it seemed like an entire day had passed since Free had left.

Dacia set the bundle on the table, pushed aside the rags inside, and lifted out a tiny crying baby that Jennet could see was only a few days old.

"Sit down here," said Jennet, pulling a chair out from the table. "Feed the baby while I get you something to eat."

Sighing, Dacia sank to the chair and nursed the baby.

From the pantry Jennet brought bread, cheese, and ham. She poured a tall glass of milk and set the food on the table.

While the baby nursed, Dacia ate as if she hadn't seen food in a long time.

"What am I going to do with you?" asked Jennet, more to herself than to Dacia.

Dacia lifted startled eyes. "You won'ts send me back, will you, ma'am?"

"No."

Dacia gently burped the baby before she set him back to nurse again. "Dey knew I was gonna have a baby. Dey planned to take him right out of my arms after I had him and make me go wait on old Mas'r Jacob again. I begged 'em to let me keep him. And I didn't want to be sent back to Mas'r Jacob. But dey was gonna take my baby, no matter how much I begged. And dey was gonna send me back to Mas'r Jacob, no matter what he did to me." Dacia shuddered as she bent her head over her baby. "I run. I run fast as I could. When I gots North, but not to Canada, I had Colin right out in a field."

"When was that?"

"Prob'ly six days now."

"And you've been traveling ever since?"

Dacia nodded. "He's my baby. My Colin. I won'ts let nobody sell him. I run. I run and folks helped me. We gots to get to freedom land. We gots to be free!"

Jennet knew Dacia's anguish firsthand, and she determined to think of some way to help. Suddenly she thought of Pa and his help with runaway slaves. She'd take Dacia and the baby to Pa and let him see that they got to the next station. She knotted her fists in her lap. She'd ask Pa to help Dacia, but she wouldn't have anything more to do with him.

She glanced at Dacia and the baby. There were bounty hunters looking for runaway slaves. If she was caught with one, she'd be sent to prison. She'd just have to make sure that she didn't get caught!

Jennet jumped up and told Dacia, "You finish with Colin, and then you're going to wash that travel dirt off and dress in my clothes. We're going out in the country where someone else will help you to freedom."

Dacia caught Jennet's hand and pressed it to her cheek while tears filled her eyes. "Praise be to God! You be an angel, ma'am."

"I'm not," said Jennet dryly. "I'm Jennet Havlick."

Later in the bedroom Jennet helped Dacia change into the green calico dress. "You're a very pretty girl, Dacia."

Dacia ducked her head. "I be ugly on the outside. But inside I be beautiful like Jesus."

Dacia stepped close to the looking glass and stared and stared. "I feels like a old lady, but I looks like a little girl."

"How old are you?"

'Fourteen."

"You are a little girl! Do you have a husband?"

"No. Mas'r Jacob put that baby inside me." Dacia motioned to the baby asleep on Jennet's bed. "I wanted to rid myself of him, but I knowed I couldn't kill him just 'cause I hated Mas'r Jacob." Dacia ran a finger gently down Colin's light brown cheek. "I loves this baby. I won't let him be no slave to nobody!"

Jennet pressed her hand to her still-flat stomach, suddenly feeling the same way about her baby. She'd been forced to do what others had said all of her life. She would not let that happen to her baby!

Jennet found a basket, placed a blanket in it, and carefully laid Colin inside. She covered him lightly with a cloth to make it look like a picnic basket. Anyone pursuing Dacia might look for her *and* a baby since she was so close to delivering when she ran away.

"Let's go, Dacia," Jennet said softly.

Just then a new idea occurred to her. "Dacia, I'm going to dress you in Free's clothes and cut your hair. Folks will think you're a boy."

"I's do anything to reach freedom land, Miss Jen!"

Later, Dacia did indeed look like a boy. She stared at herself in the looking glass. "Ain't nobody can tell it's Dacia," she said, giggling slightly.

Their eyes met in the looking glass, and they both smiled. Jennet announced, "We'll call you Abe." That was the name of her butcher and the first name that popped into her mind.

"Abe." Dacia giggled harder.

A few minutes later Jennet sat beside Dacia in the buggy with Colin in the basket at Dacia's feet and drove down the sawdust-covered street. She passed several large homes, a furniture factory, a blacksmith, and a livery. As men in buggies and wagons lifted their hats to her, Jennet felt apprehensive: *Would they wonder about Dacia?* Dacia stiffened, then relaxed when nobody barked out a command to halt.

The sun sent warmth through the buggy's black canvas top. Several children played in one yard they passed, and Jennet heard their laughter and their shouts. Finally they reached the road leading to the Havlick farm. At the pace they were going, they would reach the farm just after noon. Birds sang in the giant trees that shaded the rutted road. She hesitated, then flicked the reins for Acorn to walk faster.

Jennet's heart skipped a beat at her daring plan.

"That man Free, he your husband, Miss Jen?" asked Dacia.

Jennet said very quietly, "Yes."

"You don't much like him?"

Jennet shot Dacia a startled look. "I didn't say that!"

"I's feels things, Miss Jen."

"He's all right, Dacia, but I planned to marry someone else."

"Why didn't you."

"He's off fighting in the war."

"Is your husband too old to fight in the war?"

"No. He wanted to stay here and be a lumberman." Jennet knew there was another reason that Free wouldn't talk about. She knew he wasn't afraid to go, but she had no idea what secret reason was locked inside him.

"Does he beats you?"

"No."

"You best forget about the man you ain't married to and love this man called Free."

Jennet's heart jerked strangely. "Why do you say that?"

"He be your husband, Miss Jen."

Jennet pressed her lips tightly together.

"I's didn't mean to make you feel bad, Miss Jen."

"I know." Her eyes full of pain, Jennet said, "Do you mind if we talk about something else?"

"We's can talk about anything you wants." Dacia smiled broadly.

Just then a man on horseback rode around them, dust puffing around the bay's hooves. The man glanced back at them, then looked again when he spotted Dacia.

Jennet saw his look and shivers ran down her spine. She heard Dacia's sharp intake of breath.

The man pulled in the bay and turned around, right in the way of the buggy. Jennet wanted to slap the reins down hard on Acorn and make a run for it, but she knew she couldn't. She had to act as if everything was normal.

"Please, move," she called to the man.

"A word with you, miss," he said as his bay sidestepped nervously.

Jennet pulled back on the reins and said, "Whoa, Acorn." She didn't dare look at Dacia, but she felt her fear.

The man brought the bay up next to Jennet, all the time watching Dacia. "I'm looking for a runaway slave girl. I thought maybe you and your darky might have seen her."

Jennet lifted her chin and tried to look years older than she was. "Sir, Abe and I are going to visit my family. We aren't out looking for runaway slave girls."

"Abe, you say?"

Jennet scowled at the man. Oh, what would she do if Colin started crying? "Abe. He's riding with me to see my family. My husband, Freeman Havlick, doesn't want me riding alone."

"Havlick." The man nodded. "I was at Roman Havlick's farm a few days ago."

"He is my husband's father."

"And is your husband off fighting to free the slaves?" asked the man with a sneer.

"He's a lumberman," said Jennet steadily. "Now, let me be on my way."

"I'll ride along with you since I'm going that way."

Jennet's heart beat so loudly she thought the man could

hear it. It took all her courage to say, "I would like to be by myself. I have much to think about."

"But you're not by yourself. Abe here is with you."

"I consider that being by myself, sir!"

The man laughed and slapped his thigh. "I'm sure glad to hear you don't call them colored folks equals like a lot of these Michigan abolitionists do."

Jennet fought against the panic rising in her. "I must be on my way!"

"Not so almighty fast there!" The man leaned over and looked right into Dacia's face. "You got them papers to show me who you are?"

Dacia shrugged, but Jennet knew she was too frightened to speak.

Forcing her hands to stop trembling, Jennet lifted her handbag. "I have his papers." Could the man even read? She'd show him the letter she'd started to Marie. If he could read, she'd think of something else. If he couldn't, they'd be safe. She fumbled with the drawstring on her bag. She pulled out the partial letter and thrust it at the man. "Here! See for yourself!"

He took the paper, scowled at it, and muttered, "Free." Finally he gave it back to her. His hand was dirty, his thick fingernails chipped. "I plan on finding that runaway girl."

Jennet glanced down at the letter, saw that she'd mentioned Free's name, and realized the man could read only the one word. She turned an icy stare on him. "You saw what you wanted, now get out of my way."

The man tipped his hat, turned the bay, and rode away in a cloud of dust.

"I's gonna faint dead away," whispered Dacia.

"Me too," said Jennet, closing her eyes to make the world stop spinning like the top her sisters had.

Colin cried a short, sharp cry, then was quiet.

Jennet laughed breathlessly. "I'm glad he didn't do that while that man was here."

"I's prayed he wouldn't," said Dacia, smiling. "Thank you, Jesus. You is one big miracle worker!

Jennet smiled as she slapped the reins against Acorn. "I hope nobody else stops us. I don't have enough strength or courage for that."

"We's got all the courage we's need, Miss Jen! Colin and me, we's gonna make it to freedom land! I jest knows it!'"

"I'm sure my pa will help you," Jennet said with more confidence than she felt. She frowned at the thought of seeing Pa and talking to him about Dacia as if nothing had happened between them. What if Pa wouldn't help Dacia?

Jennet pulled back on the reins and slowed Acorn. Fields of tall corn stretched for miles where once giant hardwood trees had stood.

"What's you scared of, Miss Jen?" asked Dacia.

"It's been months since I've heard from home." Jennet told Dacia a little about herself and her family. "What if Ma is sick again or maybe dead?" Jennet groaned. "Maybe I should turn around and go home." She saw panic reappear in Dacia's eyes. "I'm sorry, Dacia. I won't turn back!" she said with such force that Acorn pricked her ears.

About noon Jennet watched a wagon driven by a stout, bearded farmer approach them. The man lifted his hand in a wave, and Jennet did the same. She felt his stare but kept her eyes straight ahead.

"They's all stare at me," said Dacia with a loud sigh.

"We're almost there," said Jennet.

Several minutes later Jennet drove along the stretch of road between the pigpen and the farmyard and turned into the drive. Everything looked the same. Pigs still rooted and squealed in their pen. Cattle grazed in the fields next to the cornfields. It was too early to harvest the corn, and the wheat and oats and hay were already done, so there were no workers around. Pa and Roman would be in the woodlot cutting firewood for the winter. Next to the main house wash flapped on the clothesline stretched between two trees. Bright zinnias and marigolds swayed in the breeze along the front of the large white frame house. The house looked deserted even with several windows open, but Jennet knew Lillian Havlick would be inside, probably knitting wool socks for Roman for the coming winter. Kit, the hired girl, would already be starting supper, even though she'd probably just finished cleaning up after dinner. A chicken squawked and ran out of Acorn's way.

Jennet glanced back toward the road, longing to turn and drive away as fast as she could, but she continued past the big barn and the granary, and back along the narrow lane to the two-story log cabin. Butterflies fluttered in her stomach as she stopped Acorn. "We're here," she said weakly.

"Don't be scared, Miss Jen," said Dacia, patting Jennet's hand.

Jennet tried to smile but couldn't.

Jennet climbed carefully from the buggy, stiff from sitting so long, and tied the reins over the rail that she'd helped Pa split about three years ago. Where were the girls? Why didn't anyone step outside to see who had driven up? Maybe all of them were in the woodlot helping with the wood. It took a lot of wood for the cabin and the main house. She'd helped split and stack wood as long as she could remember.

With a quick look around, Dacia jumped to the ground, then reached for the basket. Colin didn't make a sound. "What you want me to do, Miss Jen?"

Jennet hesitated before answering, "You wait in the barn until I find Pa." Jennet walked Dacia to the barn, found a hiding place behind a pile of hay, and gave her a drink of water from the well. "Make yourself comfortable and I'll be back for you later."

"I's be just fine here, Miss Jen. Me and Colin will be."

Jennet made her way toward the cabin. Would the family be glad to see her? Would they guess that she was going to have a baby? How she longed to slip out of sight with Dacia!

Jennet glanced at the angel that stood over Baby Vernon's grave, sighed heavily, and walked to the cabin door. Blood pounded in her ears. What would Ma say when she learned that she was married to Freeman Havlick? Was Ma even alive?

Just then the door opened and Ma stepped out. She wore a faded gray dress with tiny faded red-and-yellow flowers all over it. She stopped short when she saw Jennet.

"Ma?" Tears filled Jennet's eyes. Ma looked young, healthy, and pretty!

"Jen! It's me. Marie! Not Ma!"

"Marie? Is it really you?" Jennet laughed and hugged Marie hard. Marie smelled like yeast and soap. Jennet stepped back from her. "You look just like Ma!"

"I know. It's funny, isn't it?" Marie fiercely hugged Jennet again, then let her go. "I heard someone drive up, but I thought it was the others coming in with a load of wood." Marie brushed tears from her eyes and laughed shakily. "Oh, Jen! It's really you!"

Jennet hugged Marie again as she struggled with the scalding tears that threatened to overflow. Marie had grown up while she was gone and she'd missed seeing it happen! It just wasn't fair! Jennet caught Marie's hands and held them tightly. "Where are the girls?"

"Still in the woodlot, but they should be back soon."

Jennet could barely get the next question past the hard lump in her throat. "And Ma?"

"With the girls and Tim."

Jennet's heart leaped with gladness. "Then she's all right?"

"Oh, yes! She's back to singing and telling stories!"

Jennet brushed a tear away. "I'm glad she's well again."

Marie looked Jennet up and down. "You look so different! So grown up!"

"So do you." Jennet flushed. What would Marie say if she knew about Free and the baby?

Marie squeezed Jennet's hand. "Jen, you're so pretty!"

"So are you."

Marie blushed, making her rosy cheeks even rosier. "Thank you. Come inside and I'll get you a cup of water and something to eat."

"Wait" Jennet's eyes darted toward the barn, then across the field to the woodlot.

"What?"

"Pa. Where's . . . he?"

"In the woodlot." Marie brushed back a strand of dark hair. "He's . . . he's changed, Jen."

"Oh?"

"He looks so old! He lost the spark he had. He took it real hard when you left."

Jennet clenched her fists at her sides. "He sold me!"

Marie nodded. "Try to forgive him."

Fire flashed from Jennet's blue eyes. "I can't! Please, let's not talk about it." She watched a grasshopper jump from one tall blade of green to another. "I would like the drink you offered."

"Oh, Jen." Marie wrapped her arms around Jennet and held her close. "He hurt you so much!"

"Yes. He did. But let's not talk about it. Please!" Hand in hand they walked inside. Jennet looked around the room and shook her head. "It still looks the same. I thought it would be different, but it's not."

Marie filled a glass with water and handed it to Jennet. She watched her finish it before asking, "Why didn't you write? Why are you here now? Where's Uncle Tait?"

"First, I have to see Pa."

Marie lifted her dark brow questioningly. "He'll be here soon. Just tell me how you came to be here."

"It's a long story." Jennet laughed as she sank to the bench at the table, the spot where she'd always sat. Who had taken her spot when she left over a year ago? "Marie, I did write. I wrote lots of letters."

"But we never heard from you!" Marie sat in Ma's chair and leaned toward Jennet.

Jennet told Marie about her life with Tait. Marie bristled with anger that intensified with each detail Jennet shared. After she described finding Marie's letters, Jennet added, "I still have the copies." Finally she took a long, steadying breath and said, "I'm married."

"Married!"

"To Freeman Havlick, and we live in Grand Rapids."

"Married to Free?" cried Marie.

"Yes. He stopped at Uncle's and saw me there." Jennet kept her eyes lowered. She couldn't tell Marie the whole truth! "He paid Uncle what was owing, took me to Grand Rapids, and married me."

Marie pressed her hand to her mouth, unable to take the whole story in. "Does Roman know?"

"No."

"I know Lillian doesn't or she would've told me. We're very close." Marie blushed and giggled nervously. "She likes me. I'm going to be . . . to be her . . . daughter."

Jennet's eyes widened in shock and her stomach knotted painfully. "Daughter?"

Marie nervously brushed a strand of hair off her flushed cheek. "Now that you're married to Free, I don't feel so guilty about this."

"About what?" whispered Jennet hoarsely.

Marie swallowed hard. "Wex and I are going to be married when his time is up."

"Married?" whispered Jennet. Pain ripped through her, then anger at Marie forced back the pain. "Just how did this happen?" Jennet asked coldly.

"We've been writing to each other, and we fell in love." Marie lifted her chin. "It's very romantic."

The wood in the cookstove snapped, sounding like a shot inside the cabin.

Jennet laced her fingers together and forced back the blackness that she felt washing over her. "What does Roman say about that?"

"Nothing. He likes me too. He's not as hard as he was, Jen. Both he and Pa have changed. Pa is easier to live with, and Roman doesn't get angry over everything. He feels like he lost both his sons. And Anne won't even visit him."

"He won't let her," said Jennet sharply.

"He won't? That isn't what Lillian says. She says Anne is too angry with Roman to step foot on the farm, and she won't let them go to her house."

Jennet shook her head. "Free said different. Maybe Roman told Lillian that just to keep her from taking it out on him."

"Do you suppose?"

"It wouldn't surprise me." Jennet glanced out the back window at the barn. She'd forgotten about Dacia! She'd be wondering what had happened. Jennet pushed aside her anger and jumped up. "Marie, I have to see Pa right now!"

"Is something wrong, Jen?"

"I just have some business with Pa."

"You could drive out to the woodlot if you wanted."

"I'd better," Jennet replied, dreading the thought of facing Pa again even though Marie had said he'd changed.

Her legs trembling, Jennet walked to the door.

CHAPTER

10

♦ Nearing the woodlot, Jennet spotted Pa trimming branches off a felled oak with quick swings of his ax. His shirt tightened across his back muscles as he worked. Sunlight flashed on the shiny ax blade.

Jennet's hands tightened on the reins. It wasn't too late to turn back. She forced herself to concentrate on her all-important errand, though, and urged Acorn on. She stopped near Pa's wagon. She hadn't seen Ma and the girls because of the thick growth of trees, but she had heard their shouts and laughter. She knew they'd be loading wood. She didn't want to see Ma until she finished her business with Pa.

He looked up and saw her and slowly lowered the ax. Gray that hadn't been there before streaked his beard and hair. His shirt was stained with sweat under the armpits and down his chest. Wide green suspenders held up his dark blue pants. His pant legs were stuffed in his heavy high boots laced tightly with leather thongs. Even though Pa stood at six feet, he looked small next to the giant tree beside him. Light leaped into his blue eyes, and she frowned. How dare he act like he was glad to see her?

Jennet heard the ring of another ax as she climbed from the buggy. Suddenly a picture of Pa swinging her high in his arms and laughing flashed across her mind. She'd forgotten that he once had laughed and played with her. Impatiently she pushed the memory aside.

"Jen," he whispered as he took a hesitant step toward her.

"Hello, Pa," she said coldly.

He seemed to devour her with his eyes. "Where's Tait?"

"Not with me," she said harshly.

Pa stabbed his thick fingers through his gray-streaked hair. The wind's rustling of the leaves and a crow's cawing filled the awkward silence. Pa leaned the ax against a branch and took another step toward Jennet. "Did you run away?"

Jennet shot an answer at him. "No, but I should have!"

His beard worked and finally he spoke. "How is it you're here?"

Jennet wanted to lean against the buggy before she collapsed, but she stiffened her legs and her spine. "I wanted to see Ma and the girls." But not you, never you, the expression on her face said.

Pain flashed across Pa's face, then was gone, but not before she'd seen it and been glad for it.

"But not me?" he asked gruffly.

"No!" Her abrupt response was louder than she meant for it to be.

He grabbed his hat from the ground where he'd tossed it earlier and rammed it back on. "Then why are you here talking to me?"

Jennet looked intently at him. It was hard to read his eyes now that his hat shaded them. "I have business with you."

Pa cocked a dark brow and fingered his beard. His trousers hung on his lean frame and would've fallen except for his suspenders. He had lost weight!

Jennet plucked at her skirt. "I brought a runaway slave for you to take to the next station."

"Quiet!" Pa barked as he looked around fearfully. He strode to stand before her, close enough that she could feel the heat of his body and smell his sweat. "What do you know of runaway slaves?"

Jennet wanted to run from him, but she stood her ground. "I brought a girl and her baby for you to help," she said.

Pa glowered down at Jennet, and she trembled with the same fear that she'd always felt when he looked at her that way. What had happened to her resolve to be strong before him?

"You say you brought a girl and her baby? Where are they now?"

"In the barn, hidden behind the hay."

Pa gripped her arm and she winced. "You get yourself to the barn, and you hide them in a safer place until dark."

"But where?"

Pa looked around, then lowered his voice even more and lightened his grip. "I have a hidden room in the tack room in the barn."

Jennet's eyes widened in surprise.

Pa wiped a shaky hand across his face. "There's a ring up where the harness hangs. Pull on the ring and the peg that holds the harness, and the door will swing open. It's a tiny room, but I've made it comfortable." He groaned. "Jen, Jen, what've you got yourself into?"

Jennet's heart turned over at the look of concern for her on Pa's face. "Shall I tell Dacia you'll take them out tonight?" Jennet asked.

"Yes."

"I'll have to see that she has food."

"I'll see to it! Once you put her in that room I don't want you near it. You hear me, Jennet?"

She nodded. His urgent tones made her even more aware of the serious nature of their undertaking.

"Did you run across anybody who questioned you on the way here?"

She told him about the man on the bay, and the color drained from his face.

"Blue Newmeyer! He's trouble," said Pa, stepping back a pace from Jen. "But since he was here a few days ago, he probably won't be around for a while."

"Does he suspect you, Pa?" Jennet asked, suddenly frightened for him.

"No. He was just looking for runaways. Somebody told him Roman hires coloreds at times."

Jennet turned back to her buggy, but Pa stopped her with a hand on her arm.

"Be careful, Jen."

"I will," she said stiffly, her heart thundering. Was he actually concerned about her?

"Take care of the girl and then we'll talk about Tait."

She pulled away from Pa. "No! We won't talk! I came to see Ma and the girls. Not you!"

"What about Tait?"

"What do you care? You sold me to him!"

His eyes darkened with grief. "I'm sorry, Jen. I'm so sorry!"

"It's too late for that!" Shaking with emotion, she stepped away from him and added, "I plan to stay the night."

"Fine."

"I'm surprised you'll let me."

"Aw, Jen . . . don't break my heart!"

"What heart?" Jennet climbed in the buggy and drove away from him before she did something she didn't want to do—talk to him, understand him, even forgive him.

At the barn Jennet found Dacia curled up and burrowed

partway into a pile of hay with Colin tight against her breast. They were both fast asleep. Jennet knelt down and gently shook Dacia's stick-thin arm. Dacia awoke with a start, then relaxed when she saw it was Jennet.

"Miss Jen, I's havin' a dream that we was free!"

"You will be, Dacia! Come with me. Hurry," said Jennet in a low voice. She knew Ma and the girls would be coming with a wagonload of wood any minute. "Pa said to hide you. He'll take you after dark."

"You be mad at your daddy, Miss Jen? You be glad you gots a daddy. Mine be sold away from me when I was nine. Colin won't never gets to see my daddy. Not now and maybe not never till we gets to heaven."

"Oh, Dacia, I'm so sorry!"

"Nobody's never gonna sell me away from Colin!"

"We'll make sure of that." In the empty stall Jennet found the ring that Pa had told her about and opened the hidden door, amazed that she'd never noticed it before. The small dusty-smelling compartment was big enough to hold three men if they stood side by side with their backs pressed to the back wall. Dacia could easily sit or lie down. A horsehair blanket was folded in the far corner. With the door closed Jennet knew no light would shine in it. "Pa will be in later to bring food and water for you. Will you be all right?"

"I's been in hell, Miss Jen," whispered Dacia, her dark eyes wide. "I's can stay in that nice room as long as I needs to."

Jennet wrapped her arms around Dacia and Colin. "I'll never forget you, Dacia."

"I's won't forget you, Miss Jen. You think on what I's said about your man named Free. You learn to love him."

"I'll think about it."

"And you love your daddy!"

Jennet kissed Colin's warm cheek. She would never love Pa again!

Jennet set the basket beside Dacia in the small room. "For Colin," she said hoarsely. "Good-bye, Dacia. Enjoy your freedom."

"I's will, Miss Jen. Colin will always be free. Thanks to you, Miss Jen."

Jennet closed the secret door. She stood for a long time, her eyes full of stinging tears and worry wrinkles creasing her forehead. She hoped they would be all right.

Finally she unhitched Acorn, rubbed her down, watered her, and let her out to pasture. Acorn kicked up her heels and ran from one side of the fence to the other, then settled down to graze on the lush grass.

Back in the house Jennet found Marie working over the hot cookstove. Smells of porkchops and sweet potatoes made her mouth water. Jennet remembered that she hadn't eaten anything since breakfast on this remarkable day. "What can I do to help?" she asked.

Marie laughed, looking even more like Ma. "I bet you don't know how to sit and be company, do you?"

"No." Jennet washed her hands at the washbasin and dried them with the rough towel.

Marie lifted the heavy lid off the porkchops and carefully laid it on the work table. She faced Jennet, the long meat fork in her hand. "Did you find Pa?"

"Yes."

"And?"

Jennet frowned. "I talked business with him and that's all! I told him I'm staying the night, and he said I could."

"I'm glad." Marie turned the porkchops. Grease spattered and sizzled. She turned back to Jennet. "Jen, Pa has changed. Honest. I know how hard he was on you, but he's sorry. I know he is. Can't you forgive and forget?"

"No!"

"Don't let your anger stay all bottled up inside you like Pa did or it might come out like his did."

Jennet thought of her baby, and she knew she'd never

beat him. She'd spank him when he needed it, but she'd do it out of love, not anger or hatred or frustration. "Can't I do something to help?"

"I guess you don't want to talk about Pa."

"You're right."

"It's still early, but you can set the table if you want."

While Jennet set the plates around, she tried to think of a way to bring up Wexal without showing her feelings for him, but she couldn't find the words.

Marie laid down the long meat fork and turned to Jennet. "Would you like to read my letters from Wex?"

Jennet's heart leaped, then dropped to her feet. "I don't know. They're probably too personal."

Marie grinned and shrugged. "I don't mind."

Jennet couldn't stand the thought of seeing Wex's words of love to Marie. "Just tell me how he is."

"He was wounded three months ago."

"No!" Jennet sank to the bench, her hand at her throat. "How bad?"

Marie dashed away a tear. "A bullet in the shoulder. It healed all right but left a scar. He said in the army hospital he saw boys with their arms and legs sawed off. He smelled their rotting skin. And he saw lots of them die."

"Oh, why didn't he stay here like Free did?" cried Jennet.

"He couldn't," whispered Marie, brushing away more tears. "He said he had to *do* something. He couldn't stay here while others were dying to keep the North and South together. And he had to help set the slaves free! That's just how Wex is."

Jennet tried to imagine Wex being strong enough to face danger without running, but she couldn't. He couldn't even face his own father without cowering like a scared pup. Free had stood up to his pa. Yet, Free hadn't joined the fight. She couldn't sort it out, and right now she didn't have the energy to think about Free or Wex. She heard the wagon drive up. Ma and the girls!

Jennet ran outdoors with Marie right behind her and watched as Ma stopped the wagon at the side of the barn where they'd unload the wood into the lean-to.

Ma caught sight of Jennet, and joy flashed across her face. She leaped from the wagon and ran to Jennet while Marie held the girls back to give Ma and Jennet time alone.

"Jen! Oh, Jen!"

Ma looked years younger than she had when Jennet last saw her. Her chestnut-brown hair was neatly pulled back in a bun, and her cheeks were rosy with health. Her blue serge work dress fit her well instead of hanging on a too-thin body. She hugged Jennet tight. Just the touch of Ma's skin, which smelled like a warm rose, raised Jennet's spirits, and she once again felt love flowing from her. Tears ran down Jennet's cheeks, and she clung to Ma as if she'd never let her go.

Finally Ma held Jennet from her but kept her hands curled around Jennet's arms. "Oh, Jen! You've grown so! You are beautiful! I've longed to see you. How I've missed you! Your pa said he'd go get you from Tait's before winter. But here you are!" Ma pulled Jennet close again and held her fiercely. "I've missed you so!"

"I've missed you, Ma," whispered Jennet through her tears.

"Are you here to stay?"

Jennet forced out words around the lump in her throat. "Only for the night."

Ma's face clouded over. "Must you go back to Tait?"

Jennet struggled with the desire to tell Ma just what Pa had done to her but couldn't bring herself to say anything that would bring sorrow back to Ma. "I don't work for Uncle any longer."

"You don't?"

Jennet shook her head. Her stomach fluttered nervously. "I am married, Ma."

"Married?" whispered Ma. "Married?"

Jennet nodded. "To Freeman Havlick." She couldn't find the courage to tell Ma about the baby.

"Does Roman know? Or Lillian?"

"No."

Ma smoothed back Jennet's hair that had come loose from her braid. "You've left me speechless. Married! Without a word to us!" She glanced at the girls who were bursting in their excitement to greet Jennet. "I'll try to come to grips with it while you talk to the girls."

Jennet touched Ma's soft cheek with her fingertips. "Ma, I don't want you to feel bad. It was all so sudden, and there wasn't time to talk to you about it."

"Is Free here with you?"

"No. He's away at his lumbercamp."

"I want to know everything!" Ma kissed Jennet's cheek and let her go. "You go see the girls before they explode."

Jennet ran to the girls, and they laughed and talked and hugged her in turns. They'd all grown so much that she couldn't believe they were the same girls she'd left behind.

After the noisy greetings Jennet helped them unload the wood from the wagon. Suddenly she felt as if she'd never left. All her life she'd helped bring in wood for the winter.

"We have to haul another load yet," said Ma. "Girls, go to the well for a drink, then jump in the wagon."

With shouts and laughter the girls gathered around the well.

Before Jennet could say that she'd help with the load, she saw Blue Newmeyer riding toward them. She felt his eyes on her, and she knew he recognized her. She fought the urge to run and hide. Since Pa was still at the woodlot, she'd have to find out what Newmeyer wanted—and she'd have to do it alone.

"Who is that man?" asked Ma with a frown.

"Pa knows him," said Marie. "I saw them talking together."

"I'll deal with him," said Jennet as she looked at Ma and the suddenly quiet girls. Newmeyer was still far enough away that he couldn't hear her. "You go get the next load while I take care of this."

"Are you sure, Jen?"

"I'm sure, Ma." Jennet made her voice sound strong and sure.

Ma nodded and climbed in the wagon while the girls scrambled in behind. "See you in about a half an hour," said Ma.

"See you then," Jennet answered.

"I'd better check on supper," said Marie. She hurried to the house and slipped inside.

Blue Newmeyer reined in the bay and tipped his hat to Jennet. "We meet again," he said.

Jennet barely nodded.

"Where's the negra boy?"

"Out and about."

"I want a word with him."

"My pa's out in the woodlot chopping firewood. He could be out there helping him."

"Your husband's daddy is Roman Havlick. Who is yours?"

"Vernon Cordell."

"Ah."

Jennet felt panic rising in her, but she forced it down. She kept her hands loosely at her sides. The warm breeze pushed her skirts against her legs and feathered loose strands of her hair over her cheek. She waited for Blue Newmeyer to speak.

His bay moved restlessly and Blue pulled him up short. "You say that colored boy is with your pa?"

"He's around here somewhere. Pa might know where he is. Abe's a hard worker."

"You read his papers?" asked Blue Newmeyer.

Jennet frowned. "You read them! He was born of free parents in a free state."

"Then he shouldn't be afraid to answer some questions. Should he?"

Blue Newmeyer pulled off his hat, scratched his head, and dropped his hat back in place. Without another word he nudged the bay toward the woodlot.

Jennet knew Pa would send Blue packing, but she shivered as she thought about what would happen to her and to Pa if they were caught helping Dacia.

Suddenly a terribly wonderful idea occurred to Jennet. What if she told Blue Newmeyer about Pa's work with the Underground Railroad? Pa would be punished just as he deserved to be for selling her to Tait.

Her head whirled as she thought about Pa getting punished worse than he'd ever punished her. Then she frowned. Pa would probably be hung. She certainly didn't want that to happen. Ma and the girls would have to fend for themselves. Besides, she really didn't want Pa to stop helping runaways.

Jennet gazed across the acres of corn as Pa's look of delight at seeing her burned into her heart. How could he be glad to see her when he hated her as much as he did?

Impatiently Jennet pushed thoughts of Pa out of her mind. She'd spend time with Ma and the girls, then go home. Maybe she could take one of the girls home with her to help her and keep her company while Free was gone. Would Ma part with one of them for that length of time? Probably not, but she'd make the suggestion anyway.

Several minutes later they all sat down to supper, with Jennet in her old place. She took in the whole scene and realized once again how much she had missed her family. The girls still giggled at the least little thing. They were clean with neatly brushed hair even though their clothes were faded and patched. Ma looked as healthy as she had before Baby Vernon. Pa smiled down the length of the table at Ma with such love in his eyes that Jennet had to look away. She'd forgotten the love between Ma and Pa. A desire to experience that kind of love welled up inside Jennet, taking her by surprise.

Now that Ma was back at the table, they prayed before they ate. To Jennet's amazement, Pa asked the blessing on the food. She'd never in her life heard him pray. A warm feeling wrapped around her heart, and she wanted to reach out and touch Pa the way she had as a little girl. But a picture of him whipping her when she'd innocently given Wex the birthday handkerchief flashed across her mind and stopped her. The anger she felt toward him replaced the warm feeling.

Pa ended his prayer with, "Thank You, Jesus, for bringing Jennet back to us today. Bless her and keep her. Amen."

Jennet wouldn't look at him as she lifted her head.

"We are thankful to have you home, Jen," said Ma from her end of the table.

"Ma, I'm glad you're well again," said Jennet, smiling around Nola and Lois at Ma.

"We all are," said Pa, smiling at Ma with such love that Jennet blushed with embarrassment.

As they ate, Jennet tried to answer all their questions. She told them about Eve and Joshua, but she didn't say anything about Tait overworking her or beating her. She'd leave that for Pa's ears alone so that he'd know just what he'd done to her. She saw the startled look on Pa's face when she said that she was married to Freeman Havlick. She didn't tell them that she was expecting a baby or that Free had married her so he could get his inheritance.

Darkness had fallen by the time they finished eating, and the lamp cast a soft glow over the room. Jennet couldn't remember when she had talked so much. Her mouth felt dry, and weariness was overtaking her. She tired quicker than she had before expecting a baby. She listened to her sisters tell her what they had been doing.

Pa pushed himself away from the table and stood up. "Me and Jen are going outside for a talk," he said, walking to the door and holding it open.

Jennet started to object but thought maybe he wanted to say something about Dacia and Blue Newmeyer, so she followed him.

Granger ran to Jennet and sniffed her, then wriggled all over the way he had as a puppy.

"Aw, Granger, how've you been?" Jennet rubbed his neck and between his ears and kissed the top of his head. To her surprise, Pa waited patiently without snapping at her for being slow.

They crossed the yard to a tall maple. Standing with her back pressed against the tree, Jennet glanced toward the dark shape of the barn where Dacia and Colin were still hiding. Then she turned her attention to Pa, who had bent over to pat Granger.

Pa cleared his throat. "Blue Newmeyer was mad as a hornet that he couldn't talk to that colored boy Abe." He continued to pat Granger, keeping his eyes on the dog.

"What'd you tell him?" she asked.

"To get out of here and leave us alone. I said Abe didn't have to see him or talk to him." He didn't even try to disguise his contempt for Newmeyer.

"When will you take Dacia and the baby away?"

"Later tonight."

She could tell that Pa had something else on his mind, but she didn't want to know what it was. She wanted only to tell him just how much she hated him. Nevertheless, the thought of the love she'd seen in his eyes kept the words from pouring out.

"Jen, you be careful of Blue Newmeyer! He's dangerous. Don't do anything else to help runaways."

His well-intentioned warning sounded like an order to Jennet. She told him, "I will help if *I* want, Pa."

Pa sighed heavily. "Don't do it just to get back at me."

"You can't tell me what to do any longer, Pa. I will do as I please, and it pleases me to help runaways." Jennet glared at Pa, daring him to say more. Maybe she'd be able to tell him just how she felt about him after all!

Pa persisted. "I'll get word to Free to stop you from such dangerous work."

"It's dangerous for you and you still do it," she challenged.

"But I can protect myself."

"I am not a child, Pa. You saw to that!"

He growled deep in his throat. "Forgive me, Jen! I can't sleep or eat with the guilt resting on my shoulders."

So, he had suffered! Good! He deserved to! A cloud uncovered the moon, and Jennet saw the anguish on Pa's face. She smiled grimly. She wanted to relish every detail of his pain.

"I have only myself to blame," Pa said just above a hoarse whisper. "You brought out my anger because you were always so sure of yourself, so strong. No matter how hard you had to work, you were cheerful. I couldn't be that way, and seeing you made it bad for me. Then when your ma got bad sick, I took it out on you. I need you to forgive me."

"He beat me, Pa," Jennet hissed. How could he think she'd forgive him? "Uncle beat me if I made a mistake. A mistake! He worked me hard." She took a step toward Pa, her face pale in the moonlight. "And he didn't give me much to eat."

Pa held his hands helplessly out to Jennet. "Jen, Jen. It's too much to bear!"

"And it's because of you, Pa!" Jennet shook her finger at him.

"I know!" Pa looked down at his hands and groaned from deep inside.

Jennet leaned toward him, her voice rising. "How can I forgive you, Pa?"

"I don't know. Only with God's help."

Without another word Jennet turned on her heel. She would not forgive him, not even with God's help!

The next morning Ma walked Jennet to Baby Vernon's grave. Ma touched the angel, but Jennet couldn't bear to see her with it. She looked up at the bright blue sky.

Ma squeezed Jennet's hand. "Jen, I've come to grips with losing Baby Vernon. I had forgotten that I could find peace in God." Ma smiled as she slipped her arm around Jennet's shoulder.

Jennet leaned into Ma's warmth and looked into her dear face.

"Jen, Baby Vernon is in heaven with Jesus, and I'll see him again someday." Ma blinked tears from her eyes. "Baby Vernon's body is buried here, Jen, but he is in heaven. We didn't need this angel and I told your pa so, but he'd already paid for it and had Baby Vernon's name on it."

Jennet felt the familiar rage building inside her, and she quickly turned away from the angel to look toward the barn where she'd hidden Dacia and Colin. Pa had secretly told her before breakfast that they were safely on their way to Canada.

Jennet turned back to Ma. "I'm going home soon, Ma. I wanted to ask if I could take one of the girls to stay with me a while."

Ma frowned slightly, considering the request. "Marie?"

Jennet knew Marie would talk constantly about Wex and she couldn't abide that. "No. You need Marie here."

"I do. And so does Lillian Havlick. She's come to depend a lot on Marie."

Jennet didn't want to hear how the Havlicks' felt about Marie. "What about Nola?"

Ma shook her head. "It would break Nola's heart to leave Tim."

Jennet hadn't meet Tim yet, but Nola had said she'd take her to the barn to introduce them while Tim was doing chores. She'd told Nola they'd go after her talk with Ma.

Ma brushed a tear off her cheek. "You could take Opal. Or Lois. But she'd have to be home in October before winter set in."

Jennet lifted Ma's hand to her lips and kissed the back of it. "Could you come? Oh, Ma, I need you!"

Ma pulled Jennet close and kissed first one cheek, then the other. "My dear daughter, I long to be with you, but I can't leave the girls and your pa. You can understand that, can't you?"

Jennet nodded slightly.

"Why don't you stay here, Jen?" Ma laughed in delight. Her light brown eyes glowed. "Yes! Stay here until Free comes home!"

Oh, but it sounded wonderful! Jennet's heart leaped. She could be with Ma and the girls every day! Then she thought of Pa and Roman and she frowned. She would not live under the same roof with Pa or on the same farm with Roman!

Jennet shook her head. "I can't stay, Ma."

Ma's face fell, then she smiled. "I know you want your own home. But if you change your mind, you're welcome to stay."

"Thank you, Ma." Jennet forced back the hot tears stinging her eyes. If only she could tell Ma what Pa had done to her! "I'll go find Nola so I can meet this famous Tim I've heard so much about."

"He's a fine boy, Jen. We love him as our own."

Jealousy flashed through Jennet, but she forced it away as she walked back to the cabin with Ma.

Later in the barn, when Jennet shook hands with Tim, she liked him immediately. He was tall and thin with red hair and freckles. He had an excitement for life that reminded her of Free. Abruptly she pushed thoughts of Free away and listened to Tim talk about the farm.

Just as Jennet was leaving the barn, Roman Havlick strode up. He wore dark work pants held up by a wide black belt—the same belt he'd used on her. Remembering his harsh treatment of her, Jennet flushed with anger. Roman stopped short at the sight of her. His face darkened, but she didn't know if it was from hostility or guilt.

"Jen," he said sharply. "This is a surprise."

"I'm on my way home now," she said coldly.

"With your uncle?"

"No. Your son Free." She waited until she saw the shocked look on his face. "He and I are married." How she loved to see his anguish!

Roman swallowed hard a few times and finally said, "Then he has a good wife."

Jennet couldn't believe her ears. Where were the enraged outbursts that she'd expected?

Roman glanced around. "Is he with you?"

"No. He's at his lumbercamp."

Roman responded predictably then. "What does he know of the lumber business? He was raised a farmer!"

"He has been working at lumbercamps since he was seventeen. He is a lumberman!" Why had she said it with such pride? Was it for Roman's benefit or Free's? She didn't know the answer and didn't want to sort it out.

"Come to the house with me to tell Lillian. She'll be pleased to learn that Free is married to you."

Jennet scowled. What was happening here? She was so sure that the Havlicks would be furious. She shook her head. "I'm leaving now."

"Do you live in Grand Rapids?"

"Yes."

Roman brushed an unsteady hand over his face. "Could we visit you?"

Jennet doubled her fists at her side. She wanted to tell

Roman she never wanted to see him again as long as she lived, but instead she said, "You can visit in the spring when Free is home."

Roman pulled his hat low, said good-bye, and walked toward the main house with the steps of a tired old man.

Her heart hammering, Jennet left Nola with Tim and hurried to the cabin to tell Ma and the other girls good-bye.

Suddenly she wanted to be home alone in her own house where she had to think about only herself and her feelings. She didn't want to share her quiet house with anyone, not even one of her sisters.

At the cabin Jennet saw that Acorn was already hitched to the buggy with a saddled horse tied to the back. She frowned.

Just then Pa came around the corner of the cabin. He smiled when he saw Jennet. "You can't go home alone," he said. "It's not safe. Especially with Blue Newmeyer nosing around. I'll drive you and ride back."

Pa's kindness left her speechless. She just nodded before entering the cabin.

CHAPTER

11

♦ Jennet peeked from the corner of her eye at Pa beside her in the buggy. His hat was pushed to the back of his head, and Acorn's reins dangled between his fingers. He looked deep in thought. Was he going to make the entire trip to Grand Rapids without speaking? Jennet moved restlessly, taking her eyes off Pa and watching Acorn pick her way around the deep ruts in the road. She had to admit Pa kept a nice rein on Acorn, not too tight and not too loose.

The buggy swayed and bumped as the large wheels rolled in and out of the ruts. With each bump the wooden seat bounced on its heavy steel springs, causing Jennet to grab the seat and brace her feet on the wooden floor. The black canvas top of the buggy shielded them against the hot morning sun. Pa's horse tied to the back of the buggy easily kept pace.

After driving almost an hour, Pa suddenly chuckled, and Jennet shot him an astonished look. Pa had chuckled right out loud!

Pa glanced at her, and she saw his blue eyes twinkle, actually twinkle! It almost sent her reeling. "Jen, I was just thinking about the time you were six and we went fishing together. I caught a few bass and you caught a perch no bigger than five inches, but you were proud of it."

"It was the first fish I ever caught," she said stiffly. She brushed dust off her skirt. "I'm surprised you remembered."

Pa pushed his hat further back on his head and smiled. "I remember a lot of good times we had."

"I remember the bad ones." She did remember some of the good times when she was least expecting to, but she wouldn't admit it to him.

Pa looked down the long stretch of road, then over at Jennet. With high-pitched cries flocks of grackles flew from the tops of the trees. For a minute the whir of wings covered the clip-clop of the horses' hooves. Pa smiled wider, showing a flash of white teeth. "I remember another time. An important time in your life."

"When?" Jennet asked, then could've bitten her tongue for doing so.

"When you were nine years old. Your ma read in her Bible that God loved you so much that He sent Jesus to die on the cross for you and you started to cry. She told you all about Jesus. You said you wanted Him to be your Friend and Savior. Ma prayed with you, and you accepted Jesus into your heart."

Jennet frowned. "I remember that you were angry."

Pa shook his head and clicked his tongue. "I was too dumb to know any better. But now I do. Because August last I asked Jesus to be my Savior."

Jennet stared in shock at him. She never thought she'd hear him talk that way. He'd always made Ma keep what he called her religion talk between her and the girls.

"When your ma got sick and Baby Vernon died, I almost hit bottom. But when I let you go with Tait, I hit below bottom. I wanted to go hang myself."

Jennet stared at him as if she'd never seen him before. Was this really Pa?

Pa groaned and his beard twitched. "I was a hopeless case. Hopeless! And then one night in a dream Jesus came to me and told me He loved me. He said He wanted to put my life back together again." Pa rubbed an unsteady hand over his moisture-filled eyes. "I woke up, and I felt as if Jesus was standing beside the bed. Right then I asked Him to forgive me and take my life and make it into something good." Pa cleared his throat and couldn't speak for a while.

Jennet's heart beat fast. It was hard to keep from reaching out to Pa or snuggling close to him the way she had when she was a little girl.

"I looked at your ma sleeping restlessly beside me. She had always said Jesus was a miracle worker. Right then I put my hands on Hannah, and I prayed for her. I didn't know how to pray, but I stumbled over some words. Jesus knew my heart. From that day on she started getting better." Pa slowed Acorn until the buggy was barely rolling. "Jen, I prayed that God would give me a chance to help you. Now He has. Let Jesus work a miracle in your life. Let Him take away the bitterness and anger you feel."

She felt herself softening and she almost nodded.

"Let Jesus help you forgive me and Tait."

"That's asking too much, Pa!" A black cloud settled over her, and she felt as if her heart had turned to stone.

"Jennet, Jennet. You've always been strong willed. Don't let what I did to you keep you from God." Pa waited until he passed a creaking wagon full of hay. Dust floated behind it, blocking out the bright sunlight for a while. Pa cleared his throat. "I learned that I have an enemy. It's Satan. He does all he can to wreck lives. I was letting him wreck mine! That made me mad, but it helped set me free. I was not going to let the enemy steal my wife, my family, or our happiness."

Suddenly Jennet remembered the Scripture she'd helped Eve memorize that said Satan had come to steal, kill, and destroy. And Jesus had come to bring life more abundantly. Eve had told her that when she stepped into the enemy's territory, he had the freedom to harm her, but when she stayed close to God and obeyed His Word, Satan couldn't hurt her. "Satan will tempt you to do wrong," Eve had said. "It's up to you if you give in to that temptation. When you give in, that puts you right in his territory and he tries to make you as much a slave to him as the colored folks in the South are to the white folks."

Eve's words seemed to echo inside Jennet. She knew she was in Satan's territory when she remained angry and unforgiving.

"You're awful quiet, Jen," said Pa softly.

"I have nothing to say!"

"I've been praying for you."

Pa had prayed for her! She quickly brushed away a tear that slipped down her cheek.

The buggy swayed harder and Pa's leg bumped Jennet's. What Pa had said played over and over in her mind. She *was* tired of being a slave—first to Pa, then Tait, now Free. Was she a slave to Satan?

Jennet thought of the book of Romans that she and Eve had memorized together. She remembered that as a child of God, no matter what came against her, she couldn't be separated from the love of God. Only she could bring that separation by sinning. She knew very well that unforgiveness was a sin.

But could she forgive Pa? She saw tears running down his sun-darkened cheeks into his beard, and her heart almost broke in two.

Pa stopped Acorn at the side of the road. He turned to Jennet and took her trembling hands in his. "Jennet, I love you. I want you to be free to be happy again."

Jennet gripped his hard, work-roughened hands. "Pa, you don't love me or you wouldn't have sold me!"

"I do love you!"

"You sold me!"

He bent his head, and his broad shoulders shook with sobs. "I am so sorry for the wrong I did to you. Please believe me! Please forgive me! Your ma has."

Jennet dropped Pa's hands and looked at him in disbelief. "But I never told Ma anything about . . ." Jennet couldn't go on.

"Last night your ma asked me why you were so mad at me, and I told her the whole truth."

"Oh, Pa!"

"But she forgave me, Jen." Pa swallowed hard and sniffed. "She forgave me! And she said she'd pray that you'd forgive me too."

"Oh, Pa," whispered Jennet. Dare she believe him? Had he told Ma, and had she really forgiven him?

"I did wrong, Jen. I'd take it all back if I could. But I can't!"

Almost against her will, Jennet flung her arms around Pa. Tears flowed up and out and down her cheeks to wet the front of Pa's jacket. Her voice muffled against him, she said, "I forgive you, Pa. I do!"

Fiercely Pa held her to him as he sobbed out his anguish for what he'd done to her, then he lifted her face and kissed her damp cheeks. His beard felt strange against her but brought back the memories that she'd hidden deep inside her of the times he'd rubbed his beard against her cheeks and neck just to make her laugh.

"Your ma will be glad to hear of this," he said in a husky voice.

"God answers prayer," whispered Jennet, brushing fresh tears off her cheeks. A warmth spread through her, and she realized all her anger and hatred toward Pa had melted away.

Just then Jennet saw a rider coming fast down the road toward them. "Pa, it's Blue Newmeyer! What'll we do?"

"Act normal," said Pa, but his voice shook a little. "We'll tell him Abe left during the night and I wasn't going to wait around for him to come back."

"Good," said Pa, patting her arm.

Blue Newmeyer reined so quickly to a stop beside them that his bay reared and snorted. Acorn bobbed her head, and Pa quieted her with a firm, but gentle word.

"Where's the colored boy?" snapped Newmeyer without wasting any time on pleasantries. He didn't bother to tip his hat.

"I refused to wait on him! If he wants to get back to Grand Rapids, he'll have to do it on his own," Jennet said matter-of-factly.

Newmeyer barked out an ugly laugh and slapped his leg. Dust rose from his gray trousers. "You got the right idea, missy. Too bad more people don't see it that way. Let the niggers do it on their own. Then we'd get 'em for sure. All abolitionists should be hung!"

Blue Newmeyer's wild look frightened Jennet. She was glad that Pa had insisted on driving her home.

"We're a free state, Newmeyer," said Pa coldly. "We have the freedom to be against slavery."

Newmeyer's eyes thinned to slits of blue steel. "But you don't have the freedom to help runaways!"

Jennet sat very still while Pa and Newmeyer stared each other down. Finally Newmeyer kicked his bay and rode away.

Much later Jennet showed Pa through her house and gave him some food and a tall glass of cold well water. It would be suppertime before he got back home. She walked to the barn with him to get his horse. Suddenly she didn't want him to go. The feeling surprised her after being angry with him for so long.

"Pa, come see me when you're in town," she said, trying to keep her voice normal.

"We will. Your ma and me. But it'll be a while before we can get back."

"I know."

"Come see us again," he said. "But, Jen, don't come

alone. Who knows just how long Newmeyer will stay in the area." Pa caught Jen's hands and held them tightly. "We'll be praying for you and you pray for us, Jen."

"I will, Pa." Tears glistened in her eyes.

Pa hugged her close, then swung into the saddle.

Calico rubbed against her and purred. Jen picked him up and held him as she watched Pa ride down the street past the neighbors' houses and out of sight.

"Jennet!"

Nina was crossing the yard at top speed, her rose-colored dress bouncing around her ankles. "I'm so glad you're back!" Nina reached out and hugged her. Looking closely at her, she announced, "Something's different. I can feel it."

Jennet smiled. "Come inside and we can talk."

Jennet opened the windows to let in the pleasant breeze, then sat in the front room in a soft chair across from Nina. She told Nina about her visit, all except the part about Dacia and Blue Newmeyer. It wasn't safe to let even a good friend know that she'd helped a runaway.

"Tunis will be delighted to hear your news," said Nina. "He spends a lot of time praying for you and Free."

Just then someone knocked on the door. Jennet lifted her brow in surprise. Who would visit her aside from Nina?

Jennet peeked out the window and saw Free's sister, Anne, standing there, her face pale. She was short and slight with Free's dark hair and eyes. Jennet glanced at Nina. "It's Anne."

"She was here yesterday to see you," said Nina. "She came to ask me if I knew where you were. I told her and I mentioned that you'd probably be back today."

Jennet opened the door and Anne walked right in. "Jen, I just learned Free left Monday instead of Tuesday. . . ." She stopped short when she noticed Nina. "Hello, Nina."

"Anne, I hope everything is all right," said Nina.

Nervously Anne pulled off her hat. "Nina, I must speak in private to Jennet," said Anne. "Please excuse us."

Nina nodded. "Of course. I'll go home and leave you girls alone. But if there's anything I can do to help, let me know."

Jennet frowned slightly at Anne as she held the door open for Nina. What was wrong with Anne? It wasn't her place to send a guest home.

Anne waited until Jennet closed the door again, then she said, "Jen, I sent someone here for Free to help."

"I know, Anne. I took care of Dacia and the baby."

Anne sank to a chair, her hand over her heart. "You did? Oh, I've been beside myself!"

Jennet sat in the rocker and quickly told Anne about finding Dacia and taking her to someone she knew would help. She didn't say that it was Pa. "Dacia and her baby are well on their way to Canada."

"Free will be so angry with me!" cried Anne. "He made me promise never to involve you in helping the runaways."

Jennet frowned. "Why should he make you promise that?"

Anne spread her hands wide. "He said it wasn't safe for you. He didn't want anything to harm you."

Jennet's heart jumped a strange little jump. Was that really Free's reason?

Anne sprang up and paced from the doorway to the fireplace and back again, her face flushed.

Jennet watched her with growing agitation. Something was wrong. Had something happened to Free that Anne was afraid to say? Jennet gripped the arms of the rocker. "Anne, what's wrong?"

Finally Anne sank to her chair again, her eyes boring into Jennet's. "Jennet, I need your help, no matter what Free said."

"What do you need?"

"My place is being watched too closely to be the drop-off spot. Can we use your barn?"

Relief washed over Jennet. It wasn't bad news of Free! "Of course you can use the barn!"

"Free will be very upset." Anne took a deep, steadying breath. "But right now getting runaways to freedom is more important. Jen, I cannot live with myself if I sit back and do nothing to help those people! I cannot!"

Jennet locked her suddenly icy hands in her lap. "I want to help. I'll do anything you say."

"I'll send word to my contact to use you until I let them know differently." Anne ran her fingers through her masses of dark hair, then flipped the curly tresses over her slender shoulders to let them cascade down her back. "When will this war end? I had a very disturbing letter from Wex last week."

Jennet waited for her heart to jump at the very mention of Wex's name, but nothing happened. "What did he say?"

"He was wounded again."

"Oh, no!" Marie would be beside herself. "How badly?"

"He might lose his left leg."

Jennet gasped, her hand over her mouth.

"It makes me feel terrible for helping him join." Anne nervously plucked at the sleeves of her gray dress, and tears welled up in her dark eyes. "I don't want anything to happen to him! But somebody had to stop the South!"

"Wex wanted to go," said Jennet.

"I know." Anne sighed heavily. "I tried to convince Free to go, too, but he wouldn't.

"Why wouldn't he go?" Jennet leaned forward slightly.

"He says killing people is not the answer. He has been helping with the Underground Railroad since he was about fifteen years old."

"I never knew that!"

"No one did but me. Most people think he stayed here when Wex joined just to get rich being a lumberman. He wanted them to think that so he could do more without getting caught." Anne studied Jennet thoughtfully. "Are you sure you're capable of keeping our secret?"

Jennet nodded.

"My contact Rafe, will bring the runaways about dawn. You're to leave a bundle of clothes, blankets, and some food in the hidden room. But don't let anyone see you do it."

"What hidden room?"

"It's under the floor in the tack room. You have to move aside the bench and lift up a hidden door." Anne told Jennet exactly how to find it and to take the things out there just after dark. "Rafe knows about the hidden room. Grandpa Clay had it built before he died, and he told Rafe about it. Grandpa never did know that I helped Rafe." Anne smiled, then sobered. "Rafe will leave the slaves about dawn, they'll stay hidden all day, and tomorrow night you'll drive them outside of town to Meek Arlan's farm." She told Jennet the route to take. "It'll take you about an hour there and an hour back. Can you manage that?"

"Yes."

"You won't be too frightened?"

"I'll be scared, but I can do it anyway."

"Good for you. You might want to take a ride past the Arlan farm during daylight just to get your bearings." Anne grabbed up her hat and set it at a jaunty angle on her head, then tied the wide bow to the side of her chin. "I feel much better. I'm glad you're willing to help."

"How will I know what clothes to leave in the room?"

"I brought a bundle in my buggy. Come visit me in a few days and I'll give you another bundle." Anne walked to the door, smiled, then hugged Jennet. "I'm glad you're going to help."

"I am too."

"I want to get to know you better, Jen. I was very surprised that Free married you when Wex wanted to." Anne's voice faded away and she flushed. "I'm sorry. I shouldn't have said that."

"It's quite all right. I am married to Free. And from what my sister Marie says, she is going to marry Wex."

"He told me in a letter, but I didn't know if I should say anything."

"It's all right. We can't set back time, can we?"

"No. No, we can't."

When Anne drove away, Jennet carried the bundle Anne had given her inside the barn and set it on the floor of her buggy. Calico rubbed against her ankle and purred. Dust particles danced in the sunlight. In the tack room Jennet glanced at the harness hanging on the back wall, the shelf that held saddle soap, brushes, and other things, then down at the wooden bench. She'd sat on the bench many times but never once knew a door was hidden under it. Even though she peered closely at the floor under the bench, she couldn't spot the hidden door.

"Jennet?"

She jumped, then turned to find Tunis Bowker standing in the open doorway, his hat in his hand. Wind ruffled his gray hair. She smiled and walked toward him.

"How're you making out with Freeman gone?" Tunis asked as he slipped an arm around her shoulders.

She shrugged. "He's only been gone a couple of days." Jennet saw the newspaper under Tune's arm. "How many Michigan men on the list this week?"

"Fifty."

"But not Wexal Havlick?"

"No. Thank God!"

"Anyone you know?"

Tunis nodded sadly. "A boy who once delivered papers for me."

"I am so sorry! When will this war end, Tune?"

Tunis sighed heavily. "I pray it'll be soon, but this war

will not be over when the end does come, Jen. It'll touch all of us for years to come."

Jennet led Tunis across the yard to the bench near the back door, and they sat down. The smell of wood smoke drifted on the warm breeze. Calico jumped up on Jennet's lap, curled up, and purred happily.

"Nina told me about your visit with your family. I'm glad you're free of all that anger."

"Me too." She and Tunis had talked before about her family, but she'd closed her ears to any advice he'd offered concerning them.

"Now you're ready to learn what God has for you. God has a purpose and a plan for every person. He wants to reveal His plan to you for your life."

Jennet had never heard anything like that before. "What purpose could God have for me?"

"God is a personal God, Jen. He doesn't look at the masses, but at each individual. He looks right at you and He knows you. He has something special just for you to do that only you can do."

Jennet's eyes widened. "What could it be?"

Tunis smiled. "One plan that God has for me is to help watch out for you and Free."

"Oh?"

"I promised Clay Havlick before God that I'd do just that. And I meant it, Jen. What's mine is yours." Tunis rolled the brim of his hat as he studied Jennet. "I also promised Clay that I'd teach you and Free all I know about God."

"I'm glad, Tune! I really do want to know Him. I learned a lot of Scriptures already."

"You can know the words without understanding their meaning. I want you to know that you have a covenant with God. He promised great promises to you, and He stands behind every one of them. He will answer prayer for you. He will meet all of your needs according to His own riches in glory. He will help you with your little problems and your big ones. He's your heavenly Father, and He loves you very much."

Jennet watched a bird fly around the zinnias in the Bowkers' yard. "Tune, I haven't been able to plan my life by myself." She was thinking of Free. "How do I know that I am not already out of God's plan for me?"

"Honey, you have to take your life as it is today and go from there. You can't go back and change things. It's impossible. But God can take your life the way it is today and show you what to do with it."

She thought of helping the runaway slaves, and she knew that God did indeed want her to help them to freedom. He would help her do that. "You are a good friend, Tune. A true friend."

"That's what I aim to be, Jen. I know you and Free had a weak start in your marriage, but that doesn't mean it'll be a bad marriage. You have God to help you."

Her face red, Jennet looked down at an anthill. It embarrassed her that Free had forced her to marry him. She wondered if Tune had guessed.

Jennet talked with Tunis a while longer. Then he said he had to get home for supper. She watched him cross the yard before getting up and going inside. The house seemed empty and quiet. Tonight she'd sleep alone for the first time since she was married in June. She realized the anger that she'd usually felt for Free was gone. An empty space remained.

Just after dark Jennet crept to the barn with a basket of food. There was no moon, but she could see well enough to pick her way without stumbling. Acorn nickered softly as Jennet slid open the barn door.

In the tack room Jennet moved the bench, lifted the hidden door, and dropped the bundle of clothes and blankets down. She heard them land with a gentle plop. She picked up the basket of food and carefully felt her way down the few steps. She wanted to look around the room, but she couldn't see and didn't dare light a lantern. She set the basket and the bundle of clothes to the side of the steps, then crept back up and closed the door. Her heart thudded loud in her ears, and she felt as if a dozen eyes watched her movements. Calico mewed and Jennet jumped, then stifled a nervous giggle.

"Go catch a mouse, Cal," she whispered as she bent down and scratched Calico on the neck.

Several minutes later Jennet slipped into bed and pulled the light cover over her. Last night she'd shared a room with all of her sisters, and it had taken her a long time to fall asleep with the giggling and whispering, then the gentle snores of so many. Tonight the silence, interrupted only by a cricket chirping outside her windows, kept her awake.

She reached out to touch Free's pillow and whispered, "Heavenly Father, take care of Free tonight." She stopped short. Had she actually prayed for Free?

Jennet frowned slightly. He was her husband, and she really should pray for him just the way Ma had always prayed for Pa. It was only right.

Hesitantly Jennet prayed, "Father, keep Free safe and help him to forgive Roman for how he treated him. Help him to love You and his family." She was on the brink of asking God to help Free love her, but she couldn't get the words past her suddenly dry throat.

With a sigh Jennet turned on her side and closed her eyes.

At camp Free awakened from a sound sleep. He lifted his head and listened for an unusual sound that could've awakened him. He heard a wolf howl and smelled the wood burning in his stove.

Wearily he dropped his head on his pillow and closed his eyes. He wished Jennet were beside him. Did she think about him at all? Or miss him as he did her?

Just then a peace he hadn't felt in a long time settled over him and he smiled.

CHAPTER

12

♦ With blood pounding in her ears, Jennet hitched Acorn to the buggy. The wind chilled her even through Free's jacket and pants. One of his hats covered her mass of hair she'd braided and pinned up out of sight. She'd decided it was safer to dress in Free's clothes and pass herself off as a boy.

All day long she'd tried to do her usual chores and not think about the runaways hidden in her barn. During the afternoon, she'd driven the route to the next station, making careful note of the road and the directions. Finally it was time to open the hidden door.

Jennet lifted the door and listened but heard only Calico purring at her feet and her own heart thudding. "You can come out now. It's time to go to the next station." She kept her voice low, but it seemed to boom out into the night. Slowly a man well over six feet with shoulders almost as wide as the opening climbed out. Right behind him were three children under the age of ten. None of them made a sound as they looked expectantly at Jennet.

She closed the door, and the man set the bench in place

as easily as if it were a feather duster. She led them to the buggy, and the children climbed in the back seat while the man sat up with Jennet.

Several miles out of town after she'd passed the road that led to the Havlick farm, Jennet heard a rider coming. She quickly pulled off the road and stopped behind a clump of trees. Nervously watching and waiting, she remembered that God was always with her and He sent angels to guard her. Silently she thanked God for His help and protection. "Father, please keep Acorn quiet," she mouthed.

The rider slowed his horse to a walk, and Jennet thought he was going to stop. Despite the chill in the air, perspiration pricked her skin. She heard the shallow breathing of the children and the man. Finally the rider passed them. She sat stiffly with her head up until she couldn't hear the hoofbeats. She jumped when a wolf howled and another answered. Acorn bobbed her head and moved restlessly.

Jennet flicked the reins, and Acorn circled the trees to the road and picked her way around the ruts. Moonlight silhouetted trees lining one side of the road.

"You are a brave boy," said the runaway. His voice was deep and cultured, and that surprised Jennet.

"Thank you." Jennet let him think she was a boy. She wanted to know who he was, but she rode in silence. Anne had stressed the importance of silence, especially since she didn't have a hidden compartment in her buggy to hide the runaways.

When Jennet reached the Arlan farm, she stopped in the woodlot and watched the house and barns for any activity. "It's safe," she muttered.

Before Jennet could lift her hands to slap the reins against Acorn, the man caught both her hands in one of his. He whispered, "Wait!"

She was suddenly frightened of the man. What if he wasn't a runaway slave? He didn't sound like one or act like one. No black man would put his hands on a white person. Maybe he was sent to spring a trap on the Underground Railroad.

The children were so quiet that she had to glance to the back seat to make sure they were even there. They were huddled together in fear.

"When that cloud passes over the moon, then drive ahead." The man's breath fanned her cheek, and she smelled the dustiness of his jacket.

Jennet looked up at the sky to see that a cloud was on the brink of passing over the moon. She felt weak with relief. Just as the cloud covered the moon she urged Acorn ahead. In a few minutes they reached the granary between two barns, and Jennet stopped Acorn near a half-open door just as Anne had said to do. "You're to hide inside," Jennet said in a low, tight voice. "Someone will get you tomorrow night and take you on."

"Thank you," whispered the man. "God bless you!" He eased out of the buggy, and it swayed under his weight. He lifted down the children, and they slipped like shadows inside the granary.

Jennet flicked the reins and Acorn stepped out, swung around, and walked back the way they'd come. Only when they were well away from the farm did Jennet breathe easily.

The night pressed in around her, and she started thinking about how she'd come to have enough courage to do such a bold thing. Free would be very angry if he knew.

Just why was he so concerned about her?

Abruptly Jennet pushed the disconcerting question aside and concentrated on the road ahead. The hour's ride seemed to take five.

She reached home without mishap, unhitched Acorn, then crept to the house. Soon dawn would break, and the birds would be twittering as they awoke.

Inside Jennet sank to a kitchen chair, her legs suddenly

too weak to carry her further. She rubbed her unsteady hands up and down the arms of Free's jacket. The faint smell of wood smoke and the distinct odor of vinegar from the pickles she'd canned helped calm her jangled nerves. Without warning tears filled her eyes and ran down her cheeks. She had accomplished a dangerous mission and returned unharmed! She had helped runaways on their way to Canada!

"Jesus, thank You for Your protection. Help the runaways reach freedom."

Just then she thought of Free. She wanted to tell him about tonight and explain why she'd helped. Maybe he'd understand.

A week later Jennet pulled off her bonnet and let the pleasantly cool September breeze blow against her hair. She looked at Tunis as he drove the buggy along the rutted road through the miles of stumps. What would he say if he knew that she had made two trips to the Arlan farm with runaways during the past week? Did he even know about the hidden room in the barn?

She smiled over at him. "Thank you for letting me tag along to Prickett with you, Tune."

"I'm glad for the company," he said.

A few days ago Tunis had mentioned that he was going to Prickett on business, and she'd asked to go along to see Eve and Joshua to beg Eve to leave Tait and move in with her. She'd thought of Eve often lately and had tried to think of ways to get her away from Tait. It wasn't right for Eve to live with such a hateful man.

Jennet patted the drawstring handbag on her lap. She'd asked Lem Azack for money so that she could pay Tait's debts if he still couldn't. She wanted him to be owing to her. She might even kick Tait out and turn the businesses over to Eve! The heady thought made her chuckle.

"What's making you laugh, girl?" asked Tunis.

Jennet pushed her coat off her shoulders and shrugged. "Do I have to have a reason to laugh?"

"I guess you're not going to tell me."

She patted his arm and smiled. "I guess I'm not." It felt good to have the freedom to say that to him. In the past she'd have answered just because she wouldn't have had the courage not to. She hadn't realized that she'd gained enough confidence to say what she wanted to say. She sat up straighter and looked off across the open field dotted with stumps.

Tunis waved his hand out wide. "I remember when all this land was covered with huge trees." His voice was sad. "Now look at it! Stumps as far as you can see!"

Jennet scanned the countryside, and for the first time she really noticed how ugly it looked. On the Havlick farm she'd seen stumps, but they'd been uprooted and burned to leave the land free to plant.

"Someday Michigan will be bare without a tree in sight."

She frowned at the stumps jutting up like giant pawns on a giant chessboard. Weeds grew here and there but couldn't cover all the bare torn-up earth. A few spindly pine trees remained.

"The lumbermen are turning the trees into lumber, and the farmers are turning the land into grainfields and orchards. To the farmers, the trees are a bother. To the lumbermen, they're money." Tunis shook his head sadly. "Your children and your grandchildren might never know what a forest is."

Jennet thought of her baby and frowned, barely able to comprehend that he might never see a forest. There would always be forests, wouldn't there? What if Tune was right? "How could we stop that from happening?" she asked as he drove off the road to keep the buggy wheels from falling into a rut over a foot deep, then around a few stumps.

Tunis drove back on the road before he answered. "Someone could buy this land, then let it set. The few trees that remain would grow and as time goes by reseed until once again the land would be covered with trees."

Jennet was silent for a long time as an idea popped into her head and grew into a plan. "I could buy this land," she said, sounding uncertain in her own ears.

Tunis lifted a shaggy brow. "Yes. You could if you wanted."

"Lem Azack told me how much money I have. He said it was enough to buy land, a big new house, and still have some left."

"Free might object to you spending the money."

"Lem Azack said it was my money. Not Free's."

"I see."

"But why should Free care? He'd want his children to see forests." Jennet flushed at the thought of children. It was hard to come to grips with the knowledge that she was expecting one child—let alone more. Each day she checked in the looking glass to see if she could tell that a baby was growing inside her, but she looked the same. She never experienced morning sickness like Ma had with Baby Vernon. Sometimes she tried to pretend she wasn't going to have a baby.

Tunis nodded thoughtfully. "You're probably right. Clay Havlick's grandson would want that. I'll help you check into buying this." Tunis waved a hand to indicate the vast area of stumps. "The owner is probably a lumberman, and now that the trees are gone he'll be willing to sell. Could be a farmer already bought it, though." Tunis shrugged. "I'll check tomorrow when we get back."

"It feels strange to have enough money to buy land." Jennet looked at the acres of stumps and imagined them to be giant pines and hardwoods again. She'd show her grandchildren the trees and tell them that she'd saved a forest for them to enjoy. "I never had enough money before to buy candy!"

"I guess we can all remember times like that." Tunis told

her about his lean years as a newspaperman, and she listened with interest. "Then I met Clay Havlick and we became best friends. He came to my office one day and said he wanted me to write about the beaver and how fast they were disappearing. I did, but it seemed nobody cared." Tunis sighed heavily. "Clay said he wanted to help me, so he lent me some money to invest in grain. I made enough to buy my house and have money for my old age." Tunis shook his head. "Yes, Clay and me were best friends."

That made Jennet think of Wex. He had been her best friend. She realized that she'd not fallen into the old habit of talking to Wex. She couldn't pinpoint the time she'd stopped. Come to think of it, she didn't touch the spot where once she'd worn his white hankie. Maybe it wouldn't hurt to see him with Marie when he returned.

Jennet and Tune rode in silence for a while as her thoughts returned to the disappearing forest. "Lem Azack said Clay Havlick left some tracts of white pine for me somewhere north of Big Pine."

"I've seen 'em. Beautiful. Tall and straight. Most of them are at least five foot through."

Jennet stared down at her handbag. "I could keep those trees. Not let anyone cut them down."

Tune studied her thoughtfully. "That you could."

Jennet looked at Tunis and nodded, suddenly determined to protect the white pines from the shanty boys' axes. "I don't want Michigan to be a land without trees. I want my children and my grandchildren to see a forest. Clay Havlick would have liked that, wouldn't he?"

"He would. He would at that."

As soon as Jennet could, she'd go see that land and those white pines that stood tall and straight and at least five foot through. She'd see for herself the forest that she was saving for future generations. She slipped her arm through Tune's and hugged it. "Maybe one plan God has for my life is to save the forest, Tune!"

"You could be right."

About five o'clock Tunis reached the river and followed the road along the bank until he reached Prickett. The smell of pine was mixed with the fishy odor of the river.

The terrible loneliness and fear that she'd felt when she'd come here with Tait swept over Jennet. How foolish she'd been to come with Tunis! Could she face Tait without turning into the cowering slave that she had been?

Tunis pulled around a team of workhorses hitched to a big wagon and stopped at the hitching rail outside the boarding house. Smells of fresh baked bread drifted from the dining room.

Jennet looked down the street past the shoe factory toward Tait's store. She *would* face Tait! She'd make him sorry for treating her the way he had!

Tunis stepped to the ground, rocking the buggy as he did, then turned to help Jennet down, even though she'd been jumping in and out of wagons and buggies all her life.

Tunis smiled at her. "We'll get rooms and carry in our luggage. What say we eat supper before we go about our business?"

Jennet's stomach flip-flopped at the thought of facing Tait. She couldn't eat a bite now if she tried. "You go ahead and eat without me. I'll check in, then walk over to see Eve." She'd visit Eve first, then Tait. Oh, what a shock he was in for!

Several minutes later Jennet walked along the wooden sidewalk to the far side of the shoe factory, then left it to follow the path that led behind Tait's store to his house in the woods. The clean smell of pine hung heavy in the air, and she sniffed deeply in appreciation. Jennet's skirts flapped about her ankles as she rounded a clump of blueberry bushes. Boys shouted from a raft on the river several yards away. Birds sang in the trees. Jennet shifted the paper-wrapped bundle in her arms; inside were a baby quilt for Joshua and a new cape for Eve.

Jennet walked through the gate of the white wooden fence, around the two tall pines, and stopped outside the house. For just a moment she thought of running back to the boarding house, but she squared her shoulders and walked to the door. The late afternoon air had a nip of fall to it, and she pulled her dark blue wool coat firmly about her. She'd left her hat in her room. She touched the silky strands of chestnut hair curling from her temple. She'd pulled her hair loosely back and pinned it in place on top of her head. Would Eve even recognize her without braids and the unhealthy, gaunt look she'd had when she'd lived here?

Jennet knocked gingerly. She waited for the sound of footsteps, but none came. Had Eve taken Joshua and run away from Tait?

A squirrel chattered noisily from a low branch of a pine.

Jennet knocked again, louder this time, then called out, "Eve. Are you home?"

What had Tait done with Eve? She had always been home this time of day. Tait wouldn't allow her out and about for fear someone would mock him for marrying a Pottawatomie, and worse yet having a child with her.

"She's not home," muttered a disappointed Jennet. She opened the door and called softly, "Eve?" Silence hung heavy inside the house. Jennet smelled the faint aroma of porkchops and saw a small wooden rocking horse beside the coat rack. Eve's old coat hung on the rack.

With a deep sigh Jennet laid the bundle on the chair just inside the door. She left the house where she'd had the only hint of happiness during her stay in Prickett.

Jennet's face hardened as she thought of Tait. If he'd hurt Eve or Joshua, he'd be sorry! She gripped her handbag that held her money. Tait would pay for every minute of agony he'd caused her and Eve!

Suddenly Jennet remembered that she'd forgiven even Tait, and she slowed her steps. She dare not be bitter toward him or do anything to get even! "Help me, Lord! Without You I can't stop hating Tait."

By then Jennet was in front of the store where she'd spent so many agonizing hours. She glanced in the wide windows, which were filled with merchandise just as they had been when she'd left. Smoke curled from the chimney. Who chopped the wood for Tait now that she didn't do it?

Pushing open the heavy door, Jennet noticed that the store smelled the same—leather, smoke, kerosene, and black licorice candy. A small woman stood behind the counter with her back to Jennet. At the sound of the door she turned and Jennet gasped.

It was Eve! Eve was dressed in a dark green wool dress, which showed off her slender figure. Her hair hung below her shoulders and was held back with a green band around her head.

"Eve," whispered Jennet as she stepped forward.

Eve's dark eyes widened, then with a cry of joy she ran to Jennet and flung her arms around her. "Jen! It is you! Oh, Jennet!"

Tears streamed down Jennet's flushed cheeks as she clung to Eve. Finally she pulled away and wiped at her tears with the back of her hand. "Eve, what are you doing in here? What will Tait say? Where is Joshua?"

Eve laughed softly and hugged Jennet again, then stepped back from her and looked her up and down. "You look so different! No sad face. No dark circles under your eyes. And your dress is grand!"

"You look different too! And you're here!"

Eve smiled and nodded.

Jennet looked around, expecting Tait to walk in with an angry roar. "Eve, should you be in here?"

Eve caught Jennet's hand and held it. "God has answered my prayer, Jen. Tait is no longer ashamed of me. I work here with him."

"No!" Jennet couldn't take it in.

"It is a miracle. I learned the business fast, he says."

"But where's the baby?"

"Asleep in the back room. Come. I will show him to you. I believe it was Joshua who softened Tait's heart enough to let love in."

Jennet followed Eve to the doorway of the tiny room that had once been hers. It looked and smelled clean. Fresh curtains hung at the window. No spider webs swung from the wooden ceiling. A baby lay on his stomach asleep on the same narrow cot where she'd slept. She wanted to run to him and hold him close to her heart, but she didn't want to wake him. "He's so big!"

"Nine months. Two teeth already. And he can say Da."

"He's beautiful, Eve! Such a lot of dark hair!" Jennet thought of her baby, and a gentle yearning to see him and hold him stirred inside her.

The two women went back to stand at the counter beside the cash register. "Where is Tait?" Jennet asked.

"At the mill. He'll be here soon."

Jennet's stomach knotted. Maybe she should leave without seeing him. "Eve, does he treat you well?"

Eve nodded. "He's not perfect, but he loves me."

"Does he beat you?"

"Not for a long time."

"If you had a chance to leave him, would you go?"

Eve shook her head hard. "He is my husband, Jen!"

"I was going to ask you and Joshua to come live with me."

Eve patted Jennet's flushed cheek. "I love you, Jen, but I won't leave Tait."

Jennet nodded. She told Eve about accepting God's love back in her life and about forgiving those who'd treated her badly.

"I prayed for you, Jen. That you'd let the Scriptures we learned work in your heart."

"Thank you, Eve.

"I got another Bible, and Tait has been helping me learn the Scriptures."

"Tait?"

Eve nodded and smiled. "One of these days he will let the Scriptures work in his heart. It is very hard for him to forget the pain of his childhood."

"What pain?"

"Did not your father talk about his growing-up years?"

"No."

"He and Tait grew up in Pennsylvania. Their father was a cruel, hard man, a farmer. He worked the boys long hours and whipped them even when they didn't deserve it. Their mother died when the boys were young so they had no soft woman's touch. Tait said I am the first one to ever love him. Joshua the second."

To her surprise, Jennet felt sorry for Tait and for Pa, but especially for Tait. Pa had seven daughters and a wife to love him. Jennet glanced down at her handbag. Maybe she shouldn't do anything to make more trouble for Tait.

Just then the heavy door opened and Tait walked in. He wore a white shirt and black tie and a dark suit. He stopped short when he saw Jennet. "What are you doing here, Jen?"

Jennet squared her shoulders and looked him in the eyes. "I came to see Eve and Joshua."

"You're not welcome!"

Eve touched Jennet's arm. "I will talk to him."

Jennet shook her head. "It doesn't matter." She smiled at Eve. "Good-bye. I'm glad all is well with you."

"Good-bye, Jen."

Jennet walked toward the door, but Tait caught her arm. The old fear returned as she looked up at him.

"I spoke too soon, Jen," Tait said gruffly. "If you came for a job, you can have your old one back. With pay," he added quickly.

"I don't need a job," she said evenly.

He dropped his hand. "Are you living with your pa?"

"No. I'm married to Freeman Havlick."

"Married, you say! So he bought himself a wife!"

Eve gasped but didn't speak.

Jennet's face flamed.

Tait rubbed a hand over his mustache and neatly trimmed beard. "I thought there was something funny about him taking you. I couldn't figure why a man like him would do that."

Jennet thought that Free had not considered marrying her when he'd taken her from Tait. But maybe in the back of his mind he had planned to wed her. An icy band squeezed her heart as Jennet started for the door, her steps as heavy as her heart.

"If you want to stay here instead of going back to your husband, you can keep my books."

"Jen belongs with her husband," said Eve softly.

"Even if he bought and paid for her?" Tait asked bluntly.

"Even then," said Eve, looking right at Jennet.

Jennet bit her bottom lip as she looked helplessly at Eve. Would God work the same miracle for her as He had for Eve?

"Miracles happen," said Eve as if answering Jennet's unspoken question.

"I couldn't pay you much since things are still tight, but you could have your old room back," Tait said.

"Did Swanson ever pay his account?" asked Jennet.

"No. Died before he could."

"What about Heppelink?"

Tait shook his head. "Joined the war."

"Betzer?"

"Got his leg tore off working as a river hog."

The money in Jennet's handbag suddenly felt too heavy to hold. She knew she didn't want Tait owing her, but she did want to help because of Eve and Joshua. She walked to

Eve, pulled open the drawstring bag, and handed the money to her. "This is for you. You pay those bills, and part of this business will belong to you if you want it to."

Eve's wide, dark eyes misted with tears. "How did you come by this money, Jen?"

"It is mine legally." Lem Azack had told her that when she'd hesitated about taking it.

"Hold on there!" cried Tait, his face red. "You can't do that."

Jennet's eyes flashed. "I can and I will. It's my money, and I am giving it to Eve as a gift. She can do as she pleases with it."

"Why would you give it to Eve?"

"She was my friend when I needed one badly. I love her. And Joshua."

Tait scowled until his dark brows almost met over his long nose. "She's Pottawatomie!"

"I know. She was good to me."

"When?" snapped Tait.

Eve told him, her voice steady and her head high.

Tait glowered at her and mumbled under his breath. Finally he turned to Jennet. "Since we're telling tales, I'll tell you about your letters from your family."

"I found them," said Jennet coldly.

"But you didn't take them."

"I read them, copied them off, and put them back so you wouldn't know." She gripped her handbag tightly. "How could you do that to me? Why did you?"

Tait ran unsteady fingers through his hair, leaving it on end. He looked old and haggard.

"He is sorry," said Eve softly.

"I can speak for myself, woman!" He rubbed his hair flat and tugged at his high collar. "It was wrong for me to do that. But it's done and I can't make it right." He cleared his throat. "I take back what I said before. You are welcome here. If you want to sleep at our place or here, you can."

"I already have a room at the boarding house." Jennet turned to Eve. "I left gifts in your house for you and Joshua. I thought you'd be there, so I went there first."

Eve hugged Jennet close. "For the gifts I thank you. And for this." Eve pulled away and held up the money. "I will give it to Tait to help pay his bills. But I do not need a part of his business. It's enough that Joshua will have it someday."

"When did I say that?" Tait shot the question at her.

"*I* say it," said Eve softly but firmly.

Tait glared at her, then shrugged. "Sure it'll be his. He is my son."

Eve smiled at Jennet as if to say, "I told you so."

With a soft good-bye Jennet left the store. The last of her hatred for Tait fell away, and she smiled.

At the lumbercamp Free stood outside his office and listened to the ring of axes. Smoke drifted up from the cookcamp where the cook and his helpers were making supper. Inside the office the bookkeeper whistled as he worked. The camp consisted of four principal buildings: cook and eating camp about sixty-five feet by thirty-five feet; the bunkcamp with sleeping room for about a hundred men; the barn and stable, which could hold eighteen teams and hay and oats to last the season; and a blacksmith and tinker shop where the massive sleighs were made and all the tools were repaired. Three smaller buildings were homes for himself, his foremen, and his cook. Near the office was the store where clothing and tobacco were kept for the men. Free looked around his camp and puffed up with pride. His dream was finally coming true! He would indeed make his mark in lumber!

This winter they would finish the trees in this area, then he'd move on to the huge trees that Grandpa had left him. Free frowned slightly. Grandpa had actually left them for Jennet, but he'd convince her to sign them over to him so that he could lumber them off. She didn't have enough spunk to hold out against him, even if she had a mind to. He hooked his thumbs around his suspenders and smiled. With those trees he'd be right up there with George Meeker and Abel Witherspoon.

Just then he caught sight of Jig walking into camp, his pack on his back and his muzzleloader in his right hand.

"Supper on?" called Jig when he spotted Free.

"Soon." Free strode to Jig and slapped him on the shoulder. "It's good to see you again, Jig!"

"I figured I could be the preacher man here of a Sunday. Unless you already got one."

"Not a one. You're welcome to stay."

"I knew Clay Havlick's grandson would say that."

"I'll rustle up a cup of coffee for you while we catch up on things and wait for supper." Free led Jig to his office as Jig talked.

C H A P T E R

13

♦ Humming softly, Jennet stepped into the barn
to look for Calico. He'd been missing all day. The bright
October moonlight shone into the barn for Jennet to see to
light the lantern. The match flared, sending out a smell of
sulfur. It was warm for an October night, warm enough that
she'd not grabbed a shawl to drape over her dark blue wool
dress, which to her alarm had been almost too tight at the
waist to button. She didn't want to be reminded that she
was expecting a baby.

"Cal," Jennet called as she lifted the lantern high. She
waited, expecting the cat to run to her, but he didn't come.
"Where is he?"

Acorn nickered from her stall. Suddenly the hairs on the
back of Jennet's neck stood on end. Was someone hiding in
the barn?

Frowning at her foolishness, Jennet went to the tack
room to look in Cal's special sleeping spot on an old rag rug.
Just inside she stopped short and stared at the bench that
usually sat over the hidden door. It was out of place! Her
hand shook, and the light from the lantern bobbed. Anne
hadn't sent a message to expect someone. Had someone

entered the barn and moved the bench for some other reason? Only Tunis or Nina would come here, and they were gone to Detroit for several days. Should she open the hidden door and see if someone was inside?

When she heard a movement outside the tack room door, goose bumps covered her arms. Silently she prayed for help, then she slowly, cautiously, turned. Maybe it had been only Calico. But in her heart she knew it wasn't. She knew someone was there, someone was watching her.

With all the courage she could muster, Jennet walked out of the tack room. The light from her lantern caught the toes of black boots and the cuffs of gray tweed trousers. She sucked in her breath. "Who is there?" she asked sharply.

The man stepped forward. Blue Newmeyer! Jennet's blood turned to ice, and for a moment her legs trembled so badly she thought she'd fall.

"Jennet Havlick," he said with a low chuckle. "I might've guessed our paths would cross again."

Jennet forced back her panic. She wanted to run to the house, but she stood her ground. "What are you doing trespassing in my barn? I want you out of here now!"

Blue Newmeyer took a menacing step toward her, but she didn't move. "I followed a runaway to this here barn, and I won't leave till I have my hands on him!" Newmeyer called the runaway names that burned Jennet's ears.

A runaway! So, someone was hidden here! Perspiration dotted Jennet's forehead. She dare not let the man see how frightened she was. "Mr. Newmeyer, you have no right to sneak into my barn in the middle of the night. Now, get out before I scream for help." Jennet knew no one could hear her since Tunis was away, but she hoped Newmeyer wouldn't know it.

"You scream all you want, girl, but I'm finding me that runaway and you ain't gonna stop me!" Newmeyer grabbed the lantern and wrested it from Jennet's grip. Then he pushed her aside and strode toward the back of the barn. She ran after him, demanding that he leave.

Acorn nickered and pawed the straw-covered floor in her stall. Outside Newmeyer's horse answered.

"Mr. Newmeyer, you can't do this!" cried Jennet as she tugged at his arm to pull him away from Acorn's stall.

Newmeyer gripped Jennet's arm in a vise of steel. He pushed his face down close to hers, and she could smell his tobacco breath. "Don't cause me no grief, girl, or I'll bust your head wide open. When I find that runaway, I'm gonna hang him on the spot and you beside him." Newmeyer looked up at the hand-hewn support beam as if he could already see a rope dangling from it. Abruptly he flung Jennet away.

Jennet fell against the opposite stall beside the buggy and caught herself before she crashed to the floor. Pain sliced through her. The baby! Just how much of a fall would it take to harm the baby? She bit back a cry of pain and fire shot from her eyes, but she stayed away from Newmeyer. Trembling, Jennet watched Newmeyer thump on the back wall and the walls of each stall, even Acorn's. With the lantern in one hand he climbed up the ladder to the loft. Particles of dust and hay trickled through the cracks as he walked across the floor. Jennet heard him stab a pitchfork in clumps of hay. With an oath he flung the pitchfork from him, and it bounced down the ladder and landed with a thud on the barn floor.

Jennet pressed against the buggy wheel and watched Newmeyer drop down the last several rungs of the ladder. The lantern swayed, making shadows dance on the wall. Hay clung to Newmeyer's trousers. The second button of his blue shirt was missing, revealing his dirty-gray long johns.

Jennet's heart almost stopped as Newmeyer walked into the tack room. Free had been right! This was too dangerous for her.

Jennet glanced at the pitchfork, then stood outside the tack room door, ready to grab the pitchfork if Newmeyer found the hidden door. She watched him tug at the harness on the back wall. He knocked down the can of oil that she used on the harness and saddle. It landed on the hidden door, but even then he didn't see it. Swearing under his breath, he grabbed a shovel from the corner where several tools stood. He thumped the floor with the shovel handle to check for hollow sounds. He thumped the hidden door, but the sound was the same.

Swearing more vigorously now, Newmeyer hung the lantern on a peg. He jerked off his hat, wiped his sweaty forehead, and stabbed his fingers through his oily dark brown hair, then clamped his hat back in place. "I know he's in here! I saw him sneak in here. And he didn't run out the back door or I'd have saw him. You slave lovers make my blood boil!"

Jennet kept her back stiff as she walked toward the lantern. "I'm going to shut up the barn and go inside."

Just as Jennet reached for the lantern, she heard him move. He grabbed her from behind and she cried out in alarm. Was he going to kill her and the baby? He lifted her off her feet and swung her around, sending her sprawling. Her head struck the floor, and the pain almost made her pass out. Pins slipped from her hair, setting the long braid free of the coil at the nape of her neck.

Newmeyer grabbed her arm with his rough, dirty hands and hauled her to her feet.

"Take your hands off me!" she screamed.

"Where is he?" Newmeyer asked in a savage voice. "I'll break every bone in your body if you don't tell me."

"Let . . . me . . . go!" Jennet gasped, struggling to break free. Her head ached and she saw black dots before her eyes. She kicked out at Newmeyer's leg but missed.

Newmeyer gripped her left fist with his right hand and

squeezed, and she thought he'd crush the bones into powder. She cried out in agony.

Suddenly Jennet saw a huge shadow loom above Blue Newmeyer, and the scream died in her throat. It was the runaway!

Before Newmeyer knew what happened, the black man had him in a bear hug, making him lose his grip on Jennet. The runaway was the huge black man who had been with the three children Jennet had helped last month. He wore rumpled and dirty dark trousers and a wide-sleeved once-white shirt that had lost its collar.

The runaway shook Newmeyer like a rag doll, then flung him across the barn. He crashed into a stall with bone-jarring force.

The big black man looked into Jennet's face, and his eyes widened. "You are the boy," he said in his deep, cultured voice.

Jennet nodded. "Why are you here?" she whispered hoarsely.

Just then Newmeyer grabbed the pitchfork and lunged at the runaway. The black man leaped easily aside, as light on his feet as if he'd been a slight, wiry boy. He cuffed Newmeyer on the side of his head, sending him reeling. The fork fell to the floor. In a flash Newmeyer leaped up, gripped the fork, and flung it tines first at the runaway. He turned, but the tines caught his right arm. Immediately blood soaked his sleeve.

Jennet sprang forward to grab the pitchfork, but Newmeyer caught her braid and jerked her off her feet. Pain stung her head and tears filled her eyes. She lay in a heap against the tack room wall.

The runaway balled his fist and jabbed at Newmeyer. He ducked and danced away, then threw a punch that connected with the runaway's chin. The snap seemed to echo throughout the barn. The runaway grabbed for Newmeyer, caught his arm, and spun him around. The huge man wrapped an arm around Newmeyer and pulled his back up against him, twisted his head, and snapped his neck. The toes of his scuffed boots an inch off the floor, Newmeyer hung limply in the man's arms. Finally he let Newmeyer slide to the floor. With a low, anguished moan, the runaway stood there with his broad shoulders bent and his head down.

Jennet ran to Newmeyer and knelt beside him. She shot a startled, frightened look up at the runaway. "He's dead," she whispered.

"I know." The black man helped Jennet to her feet and turned her away from Newmeyer's crumpled body. "Don't look at him."

"What'll we do now?"

"You go inside. I'll take care of the man, then be on my way."

Suddenly she saw the blood flowing from his arm. "But you're hurt! You're bleeding!"

"I will survive."

"You take care of Newmeyer, then you come inside and let me dress your wound and feed you," she insisted.

The man finally tipped his head in agreement. Gray streaked his mass of tight curls. He glanced around the stall. "Where will I find a shovel?"

"A shovel?"

"I must bury him."

"Here?" Jennet cried in alarm.

"If I drop him in the river, his body will be discovered and questions asked."

"You're right," Jennet said weakly. "I'll water his horse and put it in the stall beside Acorn. You ride it when you leave."

The man nodded, then peered closer at Jennet. "You look ready to faint. Go inside and let me tend to the dead man and his horse."

Jennet absently brushed dirt off her dress and whispered, "I'm fine. I can do it."

"You are brave and you are strong, but you let me take care of this." The huge man turned her and gently pushed her toward the door.

"You sit down inside and drink a glass of water. I'll be in as soon as possible."

Jennet walked to the house, filled a glass with water, and sat at the kitchen table, hardly aware of her movements. She ached all over and her head hurt. She gingerly touched her barely rounded stomach. Was the baby safe? Jennet frowned and downed the glass of water in two gulps, then leaned her elbows on the table and cupped her chin in her hands. Trembling started in her legs and moved up her body until she shook like the gold-and-red leaves on the giant maples and oaks in the pasture behind the barn.

Would the runaway bury Newmeyer in the pasture behind the barn? Jennet groaned and closed her eyes tightly.

Jennet pulled herself together, washed her face and hands, added wood to the range, and sliced ham and potatoes into a skillet. She brought a loaf of bread and crock of butter from the pantry. She felt as if she was in a dream, but as long as she concentrated on what she was doing, she couldn't think about the runaway and the grave he was digging.

Several minutes later the black man stumbled in and sagged against the back door. His shirt was wet with water, and water sparkled on his ebony face. Jennet knew that he had washed at the horse tank. He moaned, and she ran to him and helped him to a kitchen chair.

"I lost too much blood," he said as he looked down at his right arm.

She looked at the gaping wound, and her stomach turned at the sight of the torn flesh. "It stopped bleeding." She handed him a glass of water, and he drank it thirstily. "You eat and then I'll dress it."

"Thank you."

Jennet set the plate of food before him, sat across from

him, and watched as he bowed his head in prayer a minute, then ate quickly as if he hadn't eaten in a long time.

"You're not a slave, are you?" Jennet asked when he'd finished.

"No."

She sucked in her breath. "Who are you? What are you?"

"My name is George Washington Foringer, and I was a professor of English and journalism in a university in Pennsylvania."

"Then why are you here?"

"I had to do something!" George Washington Foringer said determinedly. "In the past year I've led several people to freedom. I'm on my way back again."

"But why did you stop here?"

"The man . . . ," Foringer motioned to indicate he meant Newmeyer, "the man got on my trail south of here. I showed him my free paper and he knew I was a free man, but he was out to kill any Negro he saw. I got away from him and hitched a ride in a lumber wagon that came to Grand Rapids. I thought I'd lost him, but I hadn't. He followed me here." Foringer held his large hand out to Jennet. "I truly am sorry for the trouble and pain I've brought to you."

"Don't give it another thought. I'll dress your wound and stitch up that tear in your shirt. You're too big to wear my husband's clothes or you'd be welcome to them."

"Don't trouble yourself with me."

"Please take off your shirt." Jennet sounded very firm, and it pleased her. She helped him off with his shirt, put it to soak in a dishpan of cold water, then carefully washed and dressed his wound. "How long has it been since you've slept in a bed, Mr. Foringer?"

He laughed a deep laugh. "A very long time."

"Tonight you sleep in one of the spare rooms. Sleep as long tomorrow as you can. When it's dark tomorrow night, you can be on your way again."

"I can't accept such a generous offer." He stood, swayed backward, and sat back down. "It appears that I shall accept your kind offer. I thank you, and I thank God for providing."

They talked a while longer, then Jennet led Foringer to the spare bedroom nearest to the kitchen. She returned to the kitchen to wash his shirt. Carefully she stitched the jagged tear and hung the shirt near the stove to dry. She banked the fire before finally going to bed.

The next morning Jennet peeked in to see Foringer sleeping soundly. She guessed him to be about Pa's age, but it was hard to judge because his face was full and un-lined. Quietly she went about her chores and finally forced herself to go to the barn to tend Acorn and Newmeyer's horse.

Where had Mr. Foringer buried Blue Newmeyer?

Jennet let the horses out to graze, thankful that Nina and Tunis were not home to question her about the strange horse. She stood at the gate, shielding the sun from her eyes with her hand as she looked around. She couldn't find the terrible spot. Mr. Foringer obviously knew how to take off the sod, dig a hole, bury the body, cover it, and lay the sod back in place. No one would be able to find the body. Sighing in relief, she walked back to the house.

Just then Calico ran to her and rubbed against her ankle. Jennet picked him up, sat down on the bench beside the back door, and cradled Cal to her. "I see you have a bit of fur torn off, Cal. You'd better stay home after this and stay out of trouble." She laughed shakily. "I stayed home last night, but I didn't stay out of trouble, Cal. Oh, I missed you!"

Calico purred contentedly.

Just after dark, George Washington Foringer said good-bye and rode away. Stars shone brightly and a chilly wind blew down from the north. "God, bless him," Jennet whispered.

Jennet thought about George Washington Foringer off and on for the next several weeks. She tried not to think about Blue Newmeyer. She was glad when snow finally covered the pasture where he was probably buried.

After having Thanksgiving dinner with Nina and Tunis, Jennet watched snow swirl in the air as she sat near the window to stitch a quilt for the baby. The past several weeks had dragged by. Just last week when even her loosest dress no longer hid her secret, she'd told Nina about the baby. Nina had been delighted. She'd convinced Jennet to start sewing baby clothes and the quilt. Jennet had to admit that it helped pass the time.

Jennet had had one short letter from Free, saying that he was well and work was progressing as it should. He didn't mention the baby, and she was glad. Ma had written twice and Marie once. Even Pa had written, asking if she'd spend Christmas with them. He said he'd pick her up and she should plan to stay with them a week or so. She agreed to go, even though she knew they'd see that she was expecting a baby. She blushed scarlet just thinking about their knowing.

Just then the baby moved and Jennet smiled. The first time it had happened she'd been so alarmed that she'd run to tell Nina about it. Nina had laughed and said it was a good sign of a healthy baby.

Jennet touched her stomach. "Baby, I promise I'll get over being embarrassed about you. Nina says I have nothing to be embarrassed about, but I still am." A movement out the front window caught her eye, then a short time later she heard a knock at the back door. She laid the quilt on the rocker and went to the door. A gust of wind blew giant flakes of snow in on her. She pulled her shawl more tightly around her.

A ragged boy, no older than twelve, stood at the door with a younger girl just behind him. The boy smiled, but the smile didn't erase the haunted look in his blue eyes. His face was pinched and blue. He held a red wool cap in his dirty hands. "Ma'am, you got any wood that needs split?"

"I'm sorry, but I don't."

The boy stepped aside and pushed the girl forward. From under her red wool cap her light brown hair hung in ragged tails to her thin shoulders. Her dark green wool coat was full of holes, and her toes showed through holes in her shoes. She looked ready to cry. "She wants to know if you got any mending needs done or floors need scrubbed."

Jennet stood aside. She couldn't abide sending the children away without feeding them and letting them warm themselves in her kitchen. "Come inside and we'll talk about it."

The girl walked in and the boy reluctantly followed.

"I'm Jennet Havlick." They didn't offer their names, so she asked them.

"I'm Will and she's Meg."

Jennet had them hang their coats on hooks beside the back door, then led them to the kitchen table and asked them to sit down. She set out a plate of cookies that she'd planned to take to Tunis since he loved her oatmeal cookies with raisins. She filled three glasses with milk and sat at her usual place.

She held the plate of cookies out to Meg. Meg looked at Will, and he nodded slightly. She took a cookie and wolfed it down as Jennet held the plate out to Will. He ate his more slowly, but Jennet could see it took a big effort on his part.

From the pantry Jennet got some of the leftover turkey Nina had sent home with her. She sliced thick pieces of bread and set out butter. She made turkey sandwiches and gave them to the children.

"Where do you two live?" Jennet asked when they'd eaten.

"In town," said Will.

"We live in a box," said Meg.

Jennet was as much surprised at the answer as she was by Meg's speaking.

"She don't got to know that," said Will sharply.

"Where are your parents?"

"Dead," said Meg.

"Why don't you live at the Home for Orphans?" asked Jennet.

"Me and my sister can make it on our own," said Will, squaring his thin shoulders. The answer sounded as if he'd given it many times before.

Jennet couldn't stand the thought of the children being on their own. She decided to put them to work even though she really didn't need the help. "I could use someone to clean the barn."

Will jumped up, his blue eyes sparkling. He wore a threadbare red plaid flannel shirt and ragged black pants held up with old suspenders. "I'll get right to it."

"And brush my mare Acorn," said Jennet.

"I can do that too," said Will, nodding so hard his dirty brown hair flopped.

"I could do it," said Meg, jumping up to stand beside her brother. Her faded brown-and-yellow calico dress hung loosely on her too-thin body.

Will looked expectantly at Jennet. She shrugged and said, "She could do it, but I thought she might do the dishes and help me a little in here."

"Yes," said Meg quickly with a nod. "I can do that."

"Will, you come back inside when you're finished," said Jennet. "The calico cat you'll see out there is Cal, short for Calico. He likes to be petted and talked to."

"I like cats too," said Meg as she set water on to heat in the heavy teakettle.

The afternoon passed quickly and pleasantly for Jennet. She liked having Meg to talk to while she stitched the baby quilt and Meg dusted furniture that didn't need dusting.

After supper Jennet paid them both ten cents, and they acted as if she'd given them a fortune.

Jennet reluctantly opened the back door for them. Wind blew large snowflakes against the children as they stepped outside. It was already dark. "I could use you again tomorrow," Jennet said.

"We'll be here at six," said Will.

"Fine." Jennet smiled at Meg and wanted to ask them to stay the night, but she was sure Will would refuse.

Jennet watched until they were out of sight. She picked up the baby quilt and sat back in the rocker. Free had told her to hire someone to do the heavy work, so why not hire Will and Meg? She would hire them and give them a place to stay for the winter, maybe even find a permanent home for them! She nodded in satisfaction.

To Jennet's delight, after a week of coming to work every day, Will agreed that they could stay. Jennet gave them each a bedroom, laughing with pleasure at the joy on their faces. She introduced them to Tunis and Nina who were immediately taken with them. Nina went shopping for them and outfitted them in clothes like they'd not seen since their parents had died two years earlier. Each afternoon Jennet did with them what Ma had done with her and the girls—sat them at the kitchen table and taught them to read and write. Will was embarrassed that he didn't know how, but he learned quickly. It was harder for Meg, but she gradually caught on. Jennet read them Scriptures and helped them memorize verses. They went to church with her each Sunday and sat beside her as if they were family. Meg had been very excited when Jennet had told them about the baby, but Will hadn't said-much at all.

The day before Christmas Pa arrived to pick up Jennet and take her home for a two-week visit. Nina begged Meg and Will to stay with her, but Will said they could take care of themselves, so Jennet left them at her house. Nina promised to keep an eye on them.

"We have a surprise for you, Jen," said Pa as he turned the sleigh into the drive on Roman Havlick's property. The sleigh bells jingled, making the snowy day seem even more like Christmas.

Jennet pulled her coat tighter about her under the heavy robe wrapped around her. "I have a surprise for you, too, Pa." She wanted to wait and tell all of them about the baby at the same time. How would her family take the news? Should she tell Free's family? She trembled nervously just thinking about speaking to them.

Pa drove past the huge main house. An evergreen bough tied with a wide red ribbon hung on the front door. Pa drove past the barn where Roman had whipped Jennet, past the granary. The large rock where Pa had sat to spank Jennet was covered with snow. Instead of stopping at the two-story cabin, Pa drove up to a big white frame house that Jennet had never seen before. "Here it is. The surprise," said Pa proudly.

Jennet stared at the house with the white clapboard siding and tall windows. Her breath hung in the cold air. "Whose house is this?"

Pa's beard moved as he grinned. "Ours. We built it. Three bedrooms upstairs and one downstairs. Even a bathroom. That was your ma's idea. She said we should all be able to take a bath in private."

Jennet remembered all the times when she'd said, "Turn your backs," just to have privacy when she needed it. They all knew the rule to keep turned until the person said it was all right to look.

"Do you like it?" asked Pa, sounding nervous.

"It's wonderful! It's left me speechless."

"Roman said he owed us a house for all the years of working all of us and not paying anybody but me."

"I'm shocked!"

"He's trying to set things right," said Pa.

"Has he written to Free and Wex?"

"Marie said he did, but he didn't have the courage to mail his letters. Lillian wrote, but he wouldn't send those either."

Just then the wide front door opened and Ma and the girls streamed out, crying a glad welcome. Granger ran from the barn, wagging his tail.

Jennet jumped to the ground and hugged Ma tight. Ma hugged her back, then held her away and looked into her eyes. Jennet flushed painfully. She knew Ma had felt the firm roundness of her stomach.

"Jen?" Ma whispered.

Jennet nodded slightly, and Ma hugged her hard again.

"I don't know if I'm ready for this," whispered Ma in her ear, and Jennet laughed. She knew *she* wasn't ready for it!

Jennet reluctantly pulled away from Ma and hugged each of the laughing girls, making sure she didn't hug them tight to her.

"We waited to put up our Christams tree till you got here, Jen," said Evie, jumping up and down. "I strung popcorn, and Nola made a silver angel for the top of the tree."

The girls all talked at once as Pa herded them indoors.

Jennet scanned the comfortable-looking room. The walls were covered with wallpaper of red roses and ivy. On the wall between two closed doors two sconces with red candles hung on either side of a large painting of red and yellow apples in a woven basket. Two rocking chairs were pulled up close to a potbellied stove on the wall to Jennet's left. To her right stood the kitchen trestle table with chairs instead of benches around it. The big cast-iron kitchen woodstove from their old house stood on bricks against the back wall covered with bricks. Nine people were not crowded in the big room. A doorway led to a bedroom, and another to the famous bathroom. The stairway was built in, but the door stood open for heat to rise to the upstairs rooms. "This is wonderful!" cried Jennet.

"Now tell us your surprise before I do my chores," said

Pa from where he stood near the front door, his hat in his hand.

Jennet reached out and gripped Ma's hand. She cleared her throat and kept her eyes glued to Ma. "I'm going to have a baby in the spring."

No one said a word for so long that Jennet wanted to dash from the house. Then they all exclaimed their delight. The girls tried out their new title of aunt, laughing as they did.

Finally Jennet found the courage to look at Pa. Tears glistened in his blue eyes.

"Your ma was about your age when she had you," Pa said. "I don't rightly know if I can see myself as a grandpa, though. Nor your ma as a grandma."

Jennet nervously plucked at her coat draped over her arm.

"You'll make a fine mama," said Pa, nodding. "A fine mama."

"You've had plenty of practice," said Ma, hugging Jennet again. She took Jennet's coat and handed it to Lois to hang on a hook near the door with the other coats. "Does Free know?"

"Yes."

"And is he happy?"

Jennet nodded. She knew his happiness came from inheriting more land at the birth of a child, but she didn't say so.

"Will you visit with Roman and Lillian while you're here?" asked Ma.

She looked helplessly at Ma. "I don't know."

"They'll be happy and proud about the baby," said Marie.

It was hard for Jennet to believe that, but she didn't say anything.

Ma turned to the girls. "Get supper started, girls. We don't want Jennet to starve, do we?"

"The sooner I get at them chores, the sooner they'll get

done," said Pa as he set his hat in place. "The temperature is dropping fast. Your tongue would sure stick to the pump handle today!"

They all laughed because they'd heard Pa's story many times: Tait had dared him to stick his tongue on the pump handle one winter day when he was six, and he'd done it. He had a sore tongue for a long time after. And he never took that kind of dare again.

As Jennet helped make supper she told them about Will and Meg. The little girls wanted Ma to let them live with them.

Ma rolled her eyes and laughed. "Find all the orphan kids and bring them here," she said.

"Do! Do!" cried the little girls together.

After supper Marie took Jennet aside and whispered, "Wex should be home next month! But we won't get married for maybe a year."

"Anne told me about his wound."

Marie's face blanched. "I hate this war!"

Jennet thought of all the runaways who had passed through her place, and she nodded. She hated it for more reasons than having Wex hurt.

"I learned something that will make you mad," whispered Marie.

Jennet didn't know if she wanted to hear, but she said, "What?"

"We didn't get the letters you wrote us when you lived with Uncle because Roman picked them up from town and tore them up. He told Pa just a week ago and he apologized, but it still doesn't make it right."

Jennet pressed her lips tightly together as anger rose in her.

"I wasn't going to tell you, but I thought you should know."

Jennet nodded.

"I hope Free doesn't turn into a mean man like Roman was."

Jennet gasped and felt faint. She'd never thought of that. What if that did happen?

CHAPTER

14

♦ Jennet lifted her flushed face to the warm spring breeze. She felt heavy and awkward and out of sorts. "April twenty-fifth! Just a few more days and I'll have this baby and be done with this misery." She'd always wondered why Ma had been so ornery during the last days before delivery. Now she knew.

Calico rubbed against her ankles, and she frowned down at him. "I'm not good company today, Cal." Jennet went outside to the bench and awkwardly, carefully, sat down. Immediately Calico jumped up and tried to find her lap.

"You'll have to settle for my knees, Cal." Jennet tried to laugh but couldn't manage it.

A forsythia bush in Nina's yard gave a pleasant splash of yellow against the tiny-leafed trees. Meg and Will's laughter floated over from Nina's yard. They were working together to ready the flower beds. Will had convinced Nina that they could do just as good a job as the man she usually hired. Nina had quickly agreed because she liked spending time with the kids, even though they were too noisy and rowdy for her at times.

Jennet smiled. Because of Will and Meg, the winter had

passed quickly for her. Both had learned their lessons well,
though Meg was still a bit slower than Will. Jennet watched
Meg twirl around. What a different girl from when she'd
first come! Will yelled at her to get back to work, and she
made a face at him but obeyed.

Jennet glanced up at the bright blue sky, thankful for the
warm sun. She'd received two short letters from Free and
had finally managed to write a short note back. She had not
told him about the property that Lem Azack had purchased
in her name, about the runaways, or about Will and Meg.
She'd only told him that she was doing well and that she'd
spent an enjoyable Christmas with her family. She didn't
tell him that she couldn't find the courage to tell Roman and
Lillian about the baby even though she'd seen them briefly
when she and Marie were out walking.

Next month Free would be back.

Jennet jerked forward. Calico leaped off her legs with a
yowl. What would Free do when he learned of all that she'd
done? Should she say anything about Blue Newmeyer?
She'd considered telling Pa, then decided against it. It was
better that he didn't know. If anyone asked, he could truth-
fully answer that he had no idea about what had happened to
the man.

Jennet had decided to tell Anne, then learned that Anne
was expecting another child and not feeling well, so she had
shared the terrible secret with no one.

Abruptly Jennet pushed herself up, then gasped as another pain shot through her. The pains had been coming
off and on since she went to bed last night, but she'd kept
it to herself. The baby wasn't due yet, and she didn't want
Nina hovering around her, worried over a few false labor
pains.

Just then Nina called out that she and the kids were going
fishing at the river. "Would you like to join us, Jen?"

"No thanks. Go and don't worry about me. I'll be fine,
Nina."

"We'll bring bluegills home for supper," said Will proudly.

"But I won't clean 'em," said Meg with a toss of her head.

Will jabbed her. "You will if Jen says so!"

Meg shrugged and finally agreed.

Jennet sank back on the bench and watched Nina and the kids walk toward the street. They had fishing poles over their shoulders, and Will carried a can of worms. Men had spread another covering of sawdust over the street early that morning, and the smell of freshly cut wood was strong in the air.

Calico settled back on Jennet's legs, and she absently rubbed his soft fur.

"Ma had false labor pains like this before she had Baby Vernon." Jennet gasped as another pain squeezed her. "Heavenly Father, thank You for an easy, quick delivery and a strong healthy baby," she whispered. It had been her prayer for the past two months, once she'd actually accepted that she was carrying her very own baby. She tried not to think about Free's part in her condition, but thoughts of their time together had flashed in her mind when she was least expecting it. Sewing the baby clothes and talking for hours about what he would look like with Meg had helped keep her mind off Free. Jennet and Meg always talked about the baby as a boy. Even though Ma had had seven girls straight in a row, Jennet had a feeling that she was going to have a boy.

"I really don't care if it's a boy or a girl, Cal," she said dreamily. "I'll just be glad when I can hold him."

Would he look like Free?

Jennet pushed the thought aside. This baby was hers! She loved him even though Free was the father.

Jennet eased herself off the bench, waited for another pain to pass, then walked to the back of the barn and leaned against the board fence. Acorn trotted over to her, a week-old foal at her side. Jennet had named her Cherry because her coat was almost as red as a cherry. Jennet rubbed Acorn's face, but the foal was still too skittish to be touched.

Jennet narrowed her eyes against the sun and looked over the pasture. She still could not see where Blue Newmeyer was buried. Maybe Mr. Foringer had buried Newmeyer beyond the pasture. Oh, she wished she'd learned where the body was so she wouldn't keep looking and wondering!

Jennet heard a rider stop at the barn, and she walked around to see who it was. She wasn't expecting anyone. Maybe Anne had sent a messenger to tell her about another runaway.

A man, dressed in a Union army uniform which had seen better days, swung off the horse and stopped short at the sight of her. He pulled off his cap and studied her, his dark brown eyes wide. "Jen?"

"Wex! Oh, Wex, is it you?" She reached for him and clung to him.

Wex hugged her and kissed her cheeks, then stepped back and looked her up and down. "Jen, it's so good to see you!"

Jennet brushed tears from her eyes so she could see him clearly. He had gotten taller and more muscled out across the chest. His face had thinned down, and he had the firm jaw of a man. Love for him rose inside her, but she realized it was the same love she felt for Will.

"Anne told me where I could find you."

Jennet knew Wex saw her condition but was too much of a gentleman to mention it. "How are you, Wex? You look strong and healthy!"

"It took a while, but I'm fit."

"What about your leg?"

"I still have it." He grinned crookedly as he tapped his left leg. "And a limp to go with it."

"Oh, Wex!"

"But I'm alive."

"Yes! And I'm glad! Do you realize that in just a few days it'll be your nineteenth birthday?"

Wex nodded. "Do you still have the hankie you made for my seventeenth birthday?"

"No, I don't," Jennet whispered. She forced back a flush as she remembered Free's anger when he'd seen the hankie and took it from her. She had never learned what he'd done with it.

"It was a very special gift to me, Jen," Wex said softly.

"But that was when we were children," Jennet whispered.

"Yes. Yes, it was. A lifetime ago."

Jennet squeezed his hand, then let it go. His hand was larger but softer than she'd remembered, and she knew the softness came from his weeks in the hospital. "Water your horse and we'll go inside for a cool drink of buttermilk."

Limping, Wex led his horse to water at the horse tank, then tied him to the rail beside the barn.

Jennet hated to see Wex limp. He'd always been so quick on his feet.

A false labor pain squeezed Jennet, and she couldn't move for a minute. Thankfully Wex was looking at his horse and hadn't seen. She managed to smile as he walked beside her into the house.

Jennet poured two glasses of buttermilk and set out a plate of oatmeal raisin cookies. Wex carried them to the front room for her, and they sat side by side on the sofa with the tray of cookies and buttermilk on the low table in front of them.

Wex drank half his glass of buttermilk before setting it back down. He turned to Jennet with a relieved smile. "The war is over at last, Jen."

"I heard rumors that it might be," Jennet said. Before

she could continue, another pain struck. The pains really were getting bothersome! "But I've heard the same thing for four years now."

"This time it's true. The South is defeated and cannot talk further of secession. I've heard that there are still a couple of battles going on, but when they hear that Lee surrendered to Grant at Appomattox, the others will stop fighting. And once again we'll be united."

"What wonderful news!"

As Wex talked, she stared at him as if he was a total stranger. He was not the boy she'd shared secrets with! He talked of places she had never seen and probably would never see. He talked about the politics of war and sounded like his pa.

"You're so grown up!" Jennet exclaimed.

"We both were forced to be," Wex said softly. "I'm sorry for all that happened to you. Marie told me in her letters."

Jennet fought back hot tears. "We both survived."

"Are you happy, Jen?"

Jennet thought of Will and Meg and the baby. "Yes. Yes, I suppose I am."

"It's strange that you married Free."

"And that you'll marry Marie."

Wex flushed. "I'm embarrassed at the way I once spoke to you of marriage."

"Oh, don't be!" Jennet caught his hand and gripped it tightly. She looked into his dark brown eyes that were so much like Free's. "Wex, you were my dearest friend!"

"And now we are brother **and** sister as well as friends." Wex smiled at her, and she felt his love flowing to her. Eagerly she received it and returned her love to him.

Jennet lifted his hand to her cheek and closed her eyes. He was the brother she'd never had! He would always be her brother. She opened her eyes to see Free standing in the doorway. His dark eyes smoldered with anger.

A muscle jumped in Free's jaw. Would Jennet ever look at him with the love that showed on her face for Wex?

Jennet's heart stopped, then thudded so hard she felt the room move. She dropped Wex's hand as if it had burned her.

Wex jumped up. "Freeman!"

Free saw the fear in Jennet's wide blue eyes. He fought against the urge to knock Wex across the county. "I came to talk to you about Grandpa's trees," he said hoarsely, his eyes never leaving Jennet's face. Even in her condition she looked beautiful! He knew he could've waited to see her until next month when he'd be home for the summer, but he'd felt a strong urge to be with her now.

A strong labor pain gripped Jennet. She closed her eyes and struggled not to cry out.

Free saw the pain on her face, and he thought it had to do with his breaking up her meeting with Wexal. Agony writhed inside him and spread until it turned to anger as it surfaced. He strode forward, his eyes boring into hers, and motioned at Wex. "Just how long has he been with you?"

"I just arrived," said Wex, frowning slightly.

Jennet started to speak, but another pain squeezed so hard she almost screamed aloud. When the pain lessened, she awkwardly pushed herself up and faced Free. "You said you'd be here in May. I didn't expect you yet."

"So I see."

Another pain seized Jennet, and she knew she'd been deluding herself. She was not having false labor. This was the real thing, and it was serious. "It seems you're just in time for the birth of the baby," she whispered as yet another pain gripped her.

"What?" cried Wex.

The color drained from Free's face. "I'll get the doctor," he said, starting for the door.

"No!" Wex caught Free's arm. "You stay with Jen, and I'll get the doctor."

Free told him the doctor's name and address, and Wex hurried out to his horse.

Perspiration dotted Jennet's face as another pain started. This one lasted much longer and was more intense. When it was over, she slowly made her way to the bedroom, and Free followed her. "You don't have to stay with me," she said stiffly.

"I won't leave you alone," Free said gruffly. He'd helped birth animals but never a human baby. He hated feeling frightened and helpless. "What can I do to help you?"

"Nothing," Jennet said. At another pain she reached out for the bedpost and gripped it until her knuckles turned white.

"Let me help you into bed."

Jennet shook her head, unable to move. From the pressure of the baby she knew it was time for the birth. She couldn't wait for the doctor or for Nina. She remembered how easily Eve had given birth to Joshua, squatting in the corner of Tait's house. Maybe she could do it the same way instead of in bed as Ma always had.

Jennet had to undress, but she knew she couldn't manage alone. She flushed with embarrassment as she realized Free would have to help her. She didn't want him with her, especially now with the baby coming.

Free saw the pain she was in and he wanted to take it from her and bear it for her, but he couldn't. "Help her, Lord," he whispered, then realized having Jig around all winter had helped him remember to call on God.

Her face red, Jennet swallowed her pride and whispered, "Help . . . me . . . undress."

Free gently helped her undress, then slipped the robe on her that was lying across the bed. He wanted to put his arms around her and hold her and soothe her, but he was afraid she'd push him away.

Jennet picked up the folded quilt from the foot of the bed and dropped it on the floor. A great pressure squeezed her, and she gripped Free's arm tightly. Another great pressure broke her water, then a pain almost took her to her knees. Jennet knew the baby was ready. Just as she had seen Eve do, she squatted down over the quilt and with a loud cry and a mighty push delivered the baby.

To Jennet's surprise, Free caught the baby in his hands and carefully lifted him up by his heels. The baby sputtered, cried a tiny little cry, then cried a lusty cry that made Jennet laugh and cry at the same time.

Free looked at the baby in his hands, and a love welled up inside him like he'd never experienced before. "It's a boy!" he said in awe.

Jennet laughed again as she looked at their wrinkled red son. "A boy!" She glanced at Free, and the love in his eyes for the baby melted her very bones.

Together they cut and tied the cord. Jennet pointed out a soft flannel blanket and Free wrapped the baby in it, laid him in the tiny cradle beside the bed, then carried hot water to Jennet so she could wash the baby and herself.

Much later Jennet lay in bed with the baby at her side. She smiled at Free, and he smiled back.

"A boy," Jen said softly.

"Our boy," Free whispered. He wanted to take Jennet in his arms and hold her close, but he couldn't find the courage. It would hurt too much if she pushed him away or, worse yet, only endured his touch the way she had before.

"What shall we name him?" Jennet asked.

Free hadn't thought about names, hadn't thought about having a baby or being a father. "I don't know."

"How about Clay? After your grandpa?"

A lump lodged in Free's throat, and he couldn't speak. He blinked back tears.

"If you don't want to name him Clay, we could call him Freeman after you."

Free was shocked that she'd even suggest naming the

baby after him. Finally he found his voice. "We could call him Clay Freeman Havlick."

She nodded and smiled down at the tiny baby. "Clay Freeman Havlick."

Free leaned over and kissed Clay's soft cheek, then his eyes locked with Jennet's. He wanted to kiss her, but he saw the sudden panic in her eyes and he stood up and turned away.

Jennet looked at his back. Had she seen pain in his eyes because she hadn't lifted her lips to his? She frowned. She was only imagining it. He had started to kiss her because as her husband he felt he should.

"I'll stay here with you a few days, then get back to camp," Free said in an unsteady voice.

"It's not necessary."

"Why?" He turned to her. Because of Wex?

"Nina will help me. And Will and Meg."

"Will? Meg?" He was puzzled by the names.

Before Jennet could explain, Wex and Doc Mundy rushed in. The doctor's face was red, and his usually well-waxed mustache drooped. He stopped short when he saw Jennet and the baby.

"It took me a while to find the doc," said Wex as he stared in surprise at Jennet and the baby.

"It seems I'm too late," Doc Mundy said, laughing.

"It's a boy," said Jennet. "Clay Freeman."

"He's a real beauty," said the doctor.

Jennet smiled at Wex. "What do you think, Wex?"

He bent over Jennet and the baby and whispered, "He's a keeper, all right."

Jealousy ripped through Free. "We'll get out of here so you can rest, Jen. Come on, Wex."

"Good-bye, Jen," said Wex, smiling. "I'll tell your family the good news."

"I'd appreciate that," she said.

"What good news?" asked Free sharply.

"The baby," said Wex, looking oddly at his brother.

Free flushed and walked toward the door.

"I'll just check on mother and baby," said Doc Mundy.

On his way out Free caught Jennet's eye. She saw his haunted look, and she frowned questioningly. He thought her frown meant she was impatient for him to leave. Abruptly he closed the door and walked to the kitchen with Wex.

"Are you going to the farm now?" asked Free as he tried to push aside his jealousy and remember Wex was his beloved brother.

Wex nodded. "I meant to be on my way before now. I just got into town yesterday."

"I heard talk the war is over."

"That's right." Wex rubbed an unsteady hand over his eyes.

Free leaned against the doorframe between the kitchen and the dining room. "Anne told me you were in Tennessee."

Wex nodded as he sank to a kitchen chair. "In the fall of '63 I was with General William Rosecrans in Tennessee. We were pursuing General Braxton Bragg southward into Georgia after he evacuated Chattanooga. At a place called Chickamauga Bragg's army turned and engaged us." The color drained from Wex's face, and for a minute he couldn't speak.

Free had read about the battle without knowing Wex had been involved. Was this stranger his little brother?

Wex cleared his throat. "We hadn't realized he'd received reinforcements from Virginia. The sounds of rifles and cannons were deafening. All around me were the smells of gunpowder and sweat and blood. I couldn't stand the cries of the wounded or the smells of dying men. But I was there, in the battle, and I couldn't walk away." Wex looked unseeingly across the kitchen. "Our northern right flank crumpled and broke completely. The left flank fought on under General George Thomas. We fought hard, but we had to retreat into Chattanooga." Wex told Free about starving in Chattanooga for about two months because Bragg had them boxed in and cut them off from their food supply in Bridgeport. "All we ate was corn and gruel. Thousands of horses and mules starved to death." Wex's voice broke. "Finally Grant's army came from the west, floated down the Tennessee River, and overtook the Confederate troops guarding the river. Then food and supplies were brought in. Sherman arrived to help, and we took Lookout Mountain. Within days we were free. But not without losing many men."

Free could see the pain on Wex's face. "I'm glad you're back, Wex."

Wex was quiet for a long time, then said "When did you see Pa and Ma last?"

"Not for over a year. Are you home to stay?"

"Yes." Wex grinned and almost looked like his old self. "And I learned that Grandpa left a farm to me. Pa never said a word about it."

Free told Wex about the land and money that Grandpa had left him. He didn't tell Wex that he'd inherited only because of marrying Jennet.

"I hear Pa's changed," said Wex.

"That's hard to believe."

Wex shrugged. "I'll see for myself. If I leave now, I should be there just after dark. Want me to say hello for you?"

"To Ma."

Wex picked up his blue cap and ran his finger around the worn bill. "It doesn't pay to carry a grudge, Free." He kept his eyes on his cap.

Jig had talked to him all winter about forgiveness. Now Wex was trying to say the same thing. Free changed the subject. "Do you want something to eat before you go?"

"I have some food in my pack so I can eat as I ride." He smiled. "I'm anxious to get home."

Free clamped his hand on Wex's shoulder and suddenly realized that Wex had grown since last he'd seen him. "Wex, I'm glad you're back. And that you're in one piece."

Wex grimaced as he tapped his leg. 'I didn't lose it after all. But others did. Too many dead soldiers. I see 'em in my sleep, Free. I hear the screams of agony." His voice broke. "Only a miracle from God kept me alive!"

They talked a while longer as Free walked Wex outside. After they shook hands, Wex mounted his horse.

"Do you plan on coming back to see Jen?" asked Free, forcing his voice to stay light. He couldn't manage to rid himself of jealousy.

Wex nodded. "When I'm in town again."

Free's whole body tensed but he didn't speak.

"Tell Jen I'll see her," said Wex. He smiled down at Free. "Congratulations, Papa!"

Free smiled slightly, then stood in the yard as Wex rode away.

Just then Doc Mundy came out the front door with his hat in one hand and his black bag in the other. "She's doing fine, Free. Both are. I'll look in on them later. In eight days I'll circumcise the baby." Doc walked to his buggy and Free fell into step beside him. "You planning on being here long?"

"I have to get back in a few days. Jen told me she has help."

"So she said." Doc stepped up into the buggy. "That girl has a lot of strength, Free. A lot of strength."

Free didn't agree, but he didn't argue. For the years that he'd known her she'd needed protection and help from someone strong. Like him. "Thanks for coming, Doc. I'll take care of the bill before I leave town."

"No need. Jennet already did. She had it all tucked away and gave it to me just now."

That surprised Free, but he didn't let it show.

As soon as Doc Mundy drove away, Free walked inside. The house seemed very quiet after all the excitement. He peeked into the bedroom. Jennet and the baby were fast asleep. He stood in the doorway and looked at them. His heart swelled with pride and with a feeling he couldn't or wouldn't identify.

Jennet opened her eyes. "I thought you left," she said sleepily.

"I'll be here a few days," Free said stiffly.

"No need. Will and Meg will be home soon."

Free knotted his fists at his sides and a pulse throbbed at his temples. "Who are they?"

Jennet took a deep breath and told him.

When she finished, he said in a dead calm voice that alarmed her, "You mean to tell me you just let those orphan kids take over the house?"

"They lived in a box!"

"I know that's sad, but it's the orphan asylum's problem, not yours."

Jennet tried to sit up but fell back, too weak to move. "I couldn't let them live in a box during the winter!"

"It's not winter now."

Jennet turned her face from him and closed her eyes. He'd be gone in a few days, and she could do what she wanted.

Neither spoke again. Free couldn't stand the awkward silence, so he left the room. He resolved to take care of the orphans since Jennet couldn't bring herself to.

With his hands locked behind his back Free walked through the house. He stopped in the other two bedrooms and frowned. The orphans had really taken over. Why hadn't Nina or Tunis stopped Jen?

Free heard the back door open, and he hurried to the kitchen. Nina and two children walked in with a stringer of fish.

"Freeman!" cried Nina, throwing her arms around him.

Free hugged her and realized just how much he'd missed her. At camp he'd kept so busy that he hadn't realized he missed anyone. "Hello, Nina." He stepped back from her and eyed the children.

"Hi," said Will as he dropped the fish into a pail. "I'm Will, and this is my sister Meg."

"Where's Jen?" asked Meg, suddenly looking frightened.

"She's in bed."

"In bed?" asked Nina in alarm, heading toward the doorway.

Free caught her arm and stopped her. "She had a baby boy about two hours ago."

"No!" cried Nina.

"A boy!" said Meg, her face filled with excitement. "We knew it would be a boy. I want to see him."

"Hold it," snapped Free. "Jen needs to rest."

"But she'd want us to see the baby," said Meg in a small voice as she stepped close to Nina.

"She would," said Nina. "We'll just peek in."

Free gave in with a shrug.

"I'll take the kids home with me."

"That's not necessary, Nina," said Free.

Her brow cocked, Nina looked at Free. "Is something troubling you, Free?"

"You go ahead and look in on Jen and the baby."

"What did Jen name him?" asked Meg.

Free hesitated a second. "Clay Freeman."

Meg clapped her hands. "That's what I suggested!"

Disappointment washed over Free, but he wouldn't let it show. He'd thought Jen had chosen the name herself.

Nina led Meg and Will to the bedroom while Free trailed behind them. They were dirty and smelled of fish. But if Jennet wanted them as badly as Nina said, he'd let them visit her.

Jennet turned her head at the sound of the door. She smiled with delight at the sight of Nina and the kids. "It's a boy," she said. "Free probably already told you."

Nina kissed Jennet's cheek while Meg and Will stared down at the baby in the cradle.

"He's sure little," said Will. "When he's bigger, I bet I could teach him how to fish."

"He's so beautiful I think I might cry," whispered Meg. She turned to Jennet. "He sure looks like his papa."

Jennet saw the pleased look on Free's face. She'd already noticed that the baby did look a lot like Free.

Nina gently lifted the baby into her arms and kissed his soft cheek. "Clay Freeman Havlick, you are blessed of God! May you live your life serving Him and doing good to all mankind." With tears brimming in her eyes Nina looked from Free to Jennet. "May the two of you love and nurture this baby and help him to grow up knowing and loving his heavenly Father."

"I will," whispered Jennet, a promise to Nina, but to God first of all.

Free nodded, unable to speak around the lump in his throat. He'd never realized until just now that Clay Freeman Havlick was his responsibility. His and Jen's. It was up to them to tell Clay about God and to teach him to be honest and upright. It was an awesome, almost frightening duty.

Nina kissed the baby, held him out for Will and Meg to kiss, then gently laid him in the cradle. She bent over and kissed Jennet again, then led the children out.

Free turned to go, but Jennet said, "Free, don't go." She'd struggled with speaking to him but finally knew she had to.

Free walked to her side. "I'm sorry for upsetting you before."

Jennet nodded to acknowledge that she'd heard and accepted his apology. She had something to say to him, and she would say it! "Free, Meg and Will belong here." She would not let her voice quiver! "They are going to stay here with me."

Her forceful words surprised him. He'd never heard her speak that way before.

"I love them and they love me. We help each other."

"They're too much work for you, Jen."

"No. They are not!" Jennet looked Free squarely in the eyes. "Don't send them away and don't do or say anything to hurt them."

Free was too dazed to do anything but agree. Maybe there was more to Jen than he'd thought.

Jennet smiled and closed her eyes to sleep.

CHAPTER

15

♦ Jennet sleepily opened her eyes to see Free slipping into bed. She tensed, but he didn't touch her.

Free could tell she was awake, but suddenly he was tongue-tied. He wanted to turn on his side and lie with his arm across her the way he'd done the two and a half months he'd been home before. But he tucked his hands under his head and stared up at the ceiling. He heard little sounds from the baby in his cradle, and he smiled. Finally he said, "You awake?"

Jennet whispered, "Yes."

"I remember when I first saw you."

She smiled. This was a safe topic. "I was eleven."

"You tried to rob a bee tree, and you were running from a swarm of mad honeybees."

"And you caught my hand and ran with me to the creek and ducked down under the water with me."

"I almost drowned you."

"But I didn't get stung."

Free chuckled. "I did later."

"When we got the honey out." Jennet fingered the tip of

her braid as she watched the shadows dance in the moonlight. "It was good honey."

"That it was. I took some with me when I left." That was the first time he'd left home. Free could still remember his anger and his loneliness. "Even then Pa knew about Grandpa's money. But he didn't say a word."

Jennet heard the bitterness in his voice, and she turned her head to look at him. "Free, you've got to forgive him."

"I can't."

"With God's help you can."

Having her say that surprised him. Free moved but still couldn't find the courage to touch her.

"I remember the first time I saw you," she said softly. It was easier to talk to him in the semidarkness.

"Oh?" He'd thought it was when he'd first seen her.

"You were chopping down a tree. That big old wild cherry that stood next to the granary."

Free said thoughtfully, "Pa told me it had to come down because a branch fell off and wrecked the corner of the roof."

"You swung that ax and you hit the same spot every time. Chips flew right out from it."

"I loved that old tree. I used to climb it when I wanted to get away from Anne and Wex."

"I heard you call, 'TIMBER!' just like in the woods when it was ready to fall."

He grinned, remembering. "I didn't know you were watching."

"I was afraid to speak to you. You were so dashing and so handsome!" Her eyes widened at her admission, and she wanted to grab back the words. They had seemed to slip out on their own.

With a grin Free turned his head to look at her. "Handsome? Dashing?"

Jennet heard the laughter in his voice, and her heart jumped strangely.

They were quiet a long time, listening to the house creaking and the baby making funny little noises.

"Jen, thank you."

"For what?"

"Our son."

"He's beautiful, isn't he?"

"Perfect. He's perfect." Free found her hand, squeezed it, and let it go. "Good night."

"Night," Jennet whispered. The warmth of his hand on hers sent a tingle of awareness over her. She closed her eyes and listened to him breathe, then finally drift into sleep. In his sleep he turned on his side and wrapped his arm around her. Her eyes flew open, and she stiffened. His breath was warm against her face and his arm heavy on her waist. Slowly she relaxed and drifted off to sleep too.

At dawn Jennet awoke to the cry of the baby and slipped from under Free's arm and out of bed. Gently she picked up the baby and sat in the maple rocker beside the cradle to nurse him. Silently she praised God for His goodness and His help just as she did each morning. The only sounds she heard were the faint creak of the rocker, Free's breathing, and the baby's little noises. She burped the baby, kissed his fuzzy cheek, and put him to nurse again.

Jennet closed her eyes and worshiped God, her heart full of love for Him and her baby.

Just then she felt impressed to tell Free all that had occurred since he'd left. She frowned at the frightening thought, then tried to push it away, but it persisted. "Heavenly Father, I will tell him," she whispered.

Maybe she should tell him right now while her courage was high. She shook her head. No, she wouldn't wake him. Later she'd tell him.

When the baby finished nursing, she burped him, changed him, and laid him on his stomach in the cradle. She eased into bed and for one wild minute thought of moving close against Free. The desire was gone almost before the thought was over. She sank into her pillow and fell asleep. When she woke again, he was gone.

Jennet slipped out of bed and stood beside the cradle to admire her son. "You are a beautiful, precious baby," she whispered. Finally she turned away to dress.

Halfway through buttoning the front of her yellow-and-brown calico dress with the loose waist, Jennet stopped to press her hand to her racing heart. What would Free say when he learned about her work with runaways?

"I won't tell him." Yet she knew she had to tell him. He was her husband, and she should not keep secrets from him even if he'd be angry. "I can do it with God's help!"

Jennet glanced in the looking glass. Her stomach was not flat like she'd thought it would be. She felt very slim, but her reflection said different.

She brushed her long chestnut-brown hair, tied a ribbon around it, and left it to hang down her back and over her shoulders. She smiled in the looking glass, then stuck out her tongue and wrinkled her nose at her reflection. "I *will* lose that rounded stomach!"

Clay stirred in his cradle but slept on.

The door opened and Free walked in.

Jennet jumped guiltily.

Free stared at her. He wanted to stroke her shiny hair and kiss her moist lips.

The look in his eyes sent a trembling through Jennet, different from the fear she usually felt.

Free frowned. He wore dark pants and a light blue shirt with wide gray suspenders. "Why are you up?"

Jennet shrugged and managed a smile. Could he hear the unsteady beat of her heart? "It's a beautiful sunny day, and I couldn't stay in bed a minute longer!" She sank to the rocker and slipped on her shoes, unable to look at him without blushing.

Free stood beside the cradle. "Didn't the doctor say to stay in bed more than a day?"

Jennet waved her hand. "Ma was up and about hours after giving birth." Her face clouded. "Except for Baby Vernon."

Free wanted to insist she climb back in bed, but he didn't. "How is your ma now?"

Jennet told him about her family and how thankful she was that Ma was in such good health. Then she thought of Dacia, and that made her think of Blue Newmeyer.

"What's wrong?" asked Free, peering into her suddenly ashen face. "Maybe you should get back into bed."

"No. I'm fine."

Free sighed. She was not the submissive girl he'd left behind!

Jennet struggled against not telling him anything. "Where are the kids?"

He'd wanted to send them to the orphanage, but he didn't mention that. "At Nina's already. I didn't want them to wake you."

"That'll give us a chance to talk."

For some reason that frightened Free. He didn't know what to expect of her any longer. "What about the baby?"

"He'll sleep for a good while." Jennet stepped into the hallway. It felt strange to walk without the weight of the baby. "Let's sit outdoors."

Free didn't speak until they were side by side on the bench near the back door.

Jennet lifted her face to the warm sun. Calico jumped on her lap and curled up against her. She stroked his back and listened to the clip-clop of horses' hooves as two riders rode past.

"What did you want to say?" Free asked, surprised that his voice didn't quiver. He felt her tension, and it made every nerve in his body tighten. Was she going to tell him that she wanted to leave him to marry Wex? Surely she wouldn't do that! Divorce was wrong and she knew it.

"It started the day you left to go to camp," Jennet said in a low voice that she managed to keep steady.

"What started?" Free asked hoarsely.

Haltingly Jennet told him about Dacia and Colin, then about Blue Newmeyer. Free interrupted with questions and angry exclamations, but he was thankful she wasn't talking about going to Wex. She saved the details of Newmeyer's death until last.

"So, he's buried out there somewhere." Jennet couldn't look at Free but kept her eyes on Calico asleep in her lap.

Free groaned. "Jen, I don't know what to say!"

"I thought you should know."

Free looked at her as if he'd never seen her before. She was not the frightened, helpless girl he'd married. "Is there anything else?"

"Not about runaways."

Free stabbed his fingers through his dark hair. Now, was it about Wex? "What then?"

Acorn nickered, and Cherry squealed a funny little squeal.

Jennet took a deep breath and told Free about going to Prickett and about buying the land so the forest could grow again.

Free felt as if he was listening to a stranger. His own mother didn't have the courage to do anything unless Pa told her to.

"I don't want Michigan to be a land without trees," Jennet said.

Free frowned. "That can't happen."

Jennet turned to him in surprise. "How can you say that? It will if all of you keep cutting them down."

"Let us worry about that, Jen."

Jennet brushed back a strand of hair. "I'm not worrying about it, Free. I'm *doing* something about it."

Free lifted his brows questioningly.

Jennet's stomach tightened. "I bought the land, and I

won't let anyone touch it so that forests will grow again."

"Only to be cut down in another eighty years or so."

Jennet hadn't thought of that. "By then other people will know the importance of keeping the forest. Someone else will save tracts of land. I'll teach Clay the importance. I'll make a will that says they can't cut down the trees!"

Free didn't want to argue further with her. She was only a woman and didn't really know how things were. "Why'd you tell me all this now?"

Jennet moistened her lips with the tip of her tongue. For some reason this was even harder to tell. Silently she prayed for help. "This morning when I was praying, I felt I should tell you." Slowly at first, then gaining more confidence as she talked, she told him about rededicating herself to God and about learning to live as He wanted her to. "I had forgotten that God loves me and is always with me. He knows when even a sparrow falls, and He says I am of more value."

"You are," said Free under his breath.

"And so are you."

Free shrugged. At times he didn't think he had any value.

"Tune told me that Grandpa Clay was a strong Christian man the last few years of his life."

Free nodded.

"Did he ever talk to you about Jesus?"

"Yes." Free thought back on the talks and how much he'd enjoyed them. "When I was fourteen, I was born again."

"I didn't know that."

"This winter with Jig around I've been reminded of my promise to God." Last summer Free had told her all about Jig. "It's sure easy to let God fade away into the background of your life." Free laughed. "Except when Jig's around. Or Tune and Nina."

They smiled at each other. He studied the curve of her

pink lips, the line of her fine brows the exact color of her chestnut-brown hair hanging over her slender shoulders, and the depth of her blue eyes, and his gaze felt more intimate to her than a caress. She tried to look away but couldn't. He lowered his head to her, and she lifted her lips to him. Her pulse pounded in her ears, and she could hardly breathe. Before they could touch in a kiss the baby cried.

Flustered, Jennet jumped up, her face red. Her lips tingled at the thought of his kiss, and that sent another wave of crimson up her neck and over her face.

Free abruptly turned away from her, hurt because he thought she was relieved that she wasn't subjected to yet another unwanted kiss from him. Why keep asking for more pain? She loved Wex.

Free strode behind the barn and leaned against the fence to watch Acorn and Cherry and bring his wayward emotions into check.

Trembling with the strange feelings that Free had aroused in her, Jennet picked up Clay, sat in the rocker, and fed him. She touched his tiny fingers, his ears, and the dark hair on his head. "My baby," she whispered in awe. "Mine and Free's." She once again felt Free's eyes on her, and she flushed as she realized that she'd actually wanted his kiss.

Why should that embarrass her? She was Free's wife!

Jennet thought of the looks of love that had passed between Ma and Pa. Was it possible for her and Free to have that kind of love? It would take a miracle.

But God worked miracles. Jennet smiled. Maybe now that she'd gotten rid of her anger toward Free and with him here this summer they could really get to know each other and grow to love each other.

Maybe he isn't interested in love. The thought had never really occurred to her before.

Tears pricked her eyes, and she blinked them quickly away. Would they have to live their lives without love? She'd seen other couples live that way, people who had married for convenience or because the marriage had been arranged by parents.

Clay squirmed, and Jennet lifted him to her shoulder and burped him. She smelled his baby smell and smiled. A picture of Free catching Clay in his hands at the birth flashed across her mind. He easily could've walked away from her when she'd started giving birth. But he'd stayed at her side through it all. Pa could never stay at Ma's side during delivery. He'd always said he didn't want anyone to see a grown man faint dead away.

Jennet kissed the baby's soft cheek. "Clay, your papa's quite a man."

Outdoors Free sighed heavily, then turned away from the fence to walk back to the house. Before he reached the back door Tunis drove up in his buggy.

"Bad news, Free!" called Tunis as he jumped to the ground.

Free strode to Tunis's side. "What's wrong?"

"Your man Link stopped in my office to get a message to you."

"I told him that would be the best way to reach me. What'd he say?"

Tunis pulled off his hat and rubbed his thinning gray hair. "Link heard a couple of men telling about stealing your logs."

"When? Where?"

Tunis told him, and Free smacked his fist into his palm. Pirating logs was big business. All logs were struck on both ends with the heavy marking hammer that carried the lumberman's mark. Free had seen men steal logs two springs ago. The thieves hid along the stream, and as the logs floated past, they'd snake out their long pike poles, gaff a few logs, saw off the ends, and strike their own marks.

Free clamped Tunis on the shoulder. "Thanks for telling me. I better be on my way to check it out."

"Anything I can do to help?"

"Drive me to the stage." When logs were floating, the rivers weren't the safest mode of transportation. "I'll go get a few things and tell Jen."

"I'll be at home. Just give a holler when you're ready."

Free nodded. He walked into the bedroom just as Jennet was about to lay Clay in the cradle.

She turned and smiled at Free. "Would you like to hold the baby?"

Free hesitated, then nodded. A couple of minutes wouldn't hurt.

Jennet held Clay out to him, and their hands brushed as Free took the baby. Free's touch sent sparks flying through her, and she forced back a telltale blush.

Feeling awkward, Free held Clay to him. How he loved this little baby who bore his name! He nuzzled his cheek and whispered softly, "I love you, little Clay."

Jennet smiled at father and son.

Free caught a look of tenderness in Jennet's eyes that surprised him. But then he realized the look was for Clay and not him. "Jen, Tune just told me that someone stole some of my logs."

"Oh, no!"

"I've got to check it out. I hate to leave, but I must."

To her surprise, she realized she didn't want him to go. "When will you be back?"

"I don't know. I'll have to go on to Big Pine from Grand Haven."

"Two weeks?"

"Maybe more." Free peered closely at her. Would she miss him? Didn't she want him to go? His heart leaped at the thought.

He smiled, and the warmth of it wrapped around her heart. He kissed Clay, laid him carefully on his stomach in the cradle just as he'd seen Jennet do, then turned to her. He wanted to pull her close and kiss her, but he was afraid to in case he'd misread her softening toward him. "Tune will drive me to the stage."

"I wish you could be here when my family comes to see the baby."

"I do too."

"Once Wex tells them, they'll come as soon as they can." Jennet knew that would be after spring planting. "Your folks probably will come too."

Free frowned at that. "Don't let Pa boss you around."

"I won't."

Free gathered up his things and stuffed them in his backpack. He'd been home less than twenty-four hours, but he felt as if those hours had changed his life. He didn't want to leave Jen or the baby, but he had to.

"I'll walk you out," Jennet said, smoothing down her dress and buttoning the top button that she'd missed before.

Free gripped his pack tighter just to keep from reaching out to pull her close. With one last look at the baby he walked into the hall, to the kitchen, and out the back door.

Tears stung Jennet's eyes as she followed him. She wanted to put her arms around him and kiss him good-bye, but she couldn't find the courage. "Good-bye, Free," she whispered.

"Bye, Jen." Free stood before her, his hat in his hands, his pack on his arm. "Go back to bed for a while, will you?"

Jennet nodded. "You'll be very careful, won't you?"

Free nodded. He wanted to call to Tunis and walk to the buggy, but he couldn't move away from her.

A door slammed and Tunis called, "Ready to go, Freeman?"

The shout broke the spell, and Free hurried to the buggy.

Jennet sank to the bench, then waved to Tunis as he walked across his yard. Finally she looked at the buggy where Free already sat. She lifted her hand in a wave. He tipped his head toward her and waved as Tunis drove them away.

A great loneliness washed over her, leaving her weak and ready to cry. She forced herself to walk inside and fix something to eat.

Eventually Jennet stretched out on the bed with a quilt over her. She hadn't realized she was so tired. She closed her eyes and Free was there inside her head, imprinted on her eyelids. He smiled at her. She smiled back and then drifted off to sleep.

CHAPTER

16

♦ Jennet clung to Nina as the hot July wind blew against her. "Nina, it's so hard to say good-bye to you."

Nina stepped back and wiped tears from her eyes. "I'm going to miss you, Jen! But you're doing the right thing. You belong with Free."

Jennet nodded as she dabbed her tears with her hankie. She'd miss Tune and the house that had become a wonderful home to her and Clay. And she'd miss Meg and Will. Nina had talked Jennet into letting them live with her and Tunis. Meg and Will had agreed, with the promise that they'd visit her regularly wherever she and Free lived.

Clearing his throat, Tunis stood beside the buggy with his arms around Meg and Will. "We'd best be going, Jen." He was driving her to Big Pine, then he would take a boat back to Grand Rapids. "It's already daylight in the swamp."

Cherry whinnied from the pasture. She was staying behind, too, for Meg and Will to train. Hitched to the buggy, Acorn nickered, bobbing her head.

"Are you sure you have everything you'll need, Jen?" asked Nina as she looked over the bags in the buggy.

"I double-checked," said Jennet.

Tunis chuckled and patted Nina's arm. "We might call Big Pine the wilderness, Nina, but they do have a couple of stores there."

"I survived at Prickett," said Jennet, smiling as she adjusted the light blanket over Clay who lay in a basket in the buggy. "I can survive Big Pine."

"You certainly can," said Nina. "I know you can. God is with you even in the wilderness!"

Once again Jennet hugged Meg and Will and Nina. "I love all of you! And I will write."

"I'll write too," said Meg as tears trickled down her rosy cheeks. That was a big task for her since she hated writing.

Jennet spoke to Will. "I'm glad you decided to work with Tune at the paper."

"I'll work hard," Will said gruffly as he blinked away tears.

Jennet stepped up into the buggy, Tunis flicked the reins, and Acorn walked away from Nina, Meg, and Will and away from the house where Jennet had lived for over a year.

On her birthday in June her family had finally been able to get away from the farm and had come to see Clay. They were all proud of Jennet and pleased with the baby. Marie had whispered to Jennet that she and Wex were getting married right away so Wex could inherit the farm Grandpa Clay had left him. She said she hadn't told Pa yet. Jennet hoped she and Free would be able to make the trip for the wedding.

A week later Roman and Lillian had visited. They were formal but admired the baby and asked after Free. Jennet told them that he'd left home to check on men stealing his logs but had never found them. He had gone on to Big Pine and had been delayed there for one reason and another. She showed his letters to them, and Lillian read them aloud, eager to hear word of Free. Roman listened with interest but scowled until his brows almost touched over his nose.

He had voiced his surprise that Free really did seem to know the lumber business.

"You're sure quiet, Jen," said Tunis, swaying with the motion of the buggy as he drove along the rutted road between miles of ugly black stumps sticking out of the ground. "Are you sorry you're going?"

"Maybe a little."

"It's hard to leave people who love you."

Jennet patted his arm and smiled. "It's a little scary for me to go to Big Pine with Free not expecting me."

"He'll be glad to see you."

Jennet wasn't as sure about that as Tune seemed to be. He had learned that Free was having trouble with Willie Thorne over tracts of land, and that was keeping him in Big Pine, even though he'd planned to return home no later than the middle of June. If things kept going the way they were, it would be September and time for Free to go to the lumbercamp again. Jennet knew she belonged with him, but Nina had to convince her to take action.

"I know where his cabin is, so we'll go there," said Tunis.

The canvas top on the buggy shielded them from the hot sun. The buggy seat grew harder to Jennet as the day stretched on. Without asking Tunis to stop, Jennet changed and nursed Clay several times. She knew they had to keep going so they wouldn't be on the trail after dark.

Shortly before dark Tunis pulled alongside a small cabin tucked among tall white pines just outside Big Pine. "Here we are," Tunis said, sounding tired.

Her heart thudding, Jennet stared at the cabin. The door didn't open. "He must not be home."

Tunis climbed out of the buggy and helped Jennet down. Her legs felt stiff after sitting so long. She slowly approached the cabin while Tunis carried Clay in his basket. She saw a stick leaning against the door. Tunis had told her it was a sign to Indians to pass on because nobody was home. If the stick wasn't there, an Indian could walk right in and expect to be fed.

Tunis moved the stick and pushed open the heavy door. It was neat and clean inside and smelled of coffee.

Butterflies fluttered in Jennet's stomach as she stepped through the door onto the puncheon floor. Free probably had split the floor logs himself, and with a broad ax had cut the faces of them flat. The rounded side lay against the ground, and the smooth finished side was turned up. A trestle table with two chairs pushed up to it stood in the middle of the room. A cast-iron cookstove was against one wall and a bed against another. Light filtered in through two glass-paned windows. Pegs in the wall held clothes that she recognized as Free's.

Tunis quickly unloaded her things. "I'll put Acorn in the barn, then walk on back to Big Pine before dark. I sure don't want to run into a wolf." He grinned, but she knew he was serious. "Will you be all right even if Free doesn't come back tonight?"

"I will." She hugged Tunis and saw him on his way.

Jennet took in every inch of the small cabin. A peace settled over her, making her feel as if she had indeed come home. She closed the door and put the latch in place but did not pull in the latchstring in case Free came home. She lit the lamp in the middle of the table, then started a fire in the stove to keep out the chill of the night and to make supper.

Clay whimpered, and she knew it was time to feed him. She settled into a chair and hummed softly as the baby nursed. After a while her eyes drooped, and she yawned several times.

Jennet changed Clay and settled him in for the night. He'd sleep in his basket beside Free's bed.

I'll share the bed with Free tonight. To her surprise, the thought didn't frighten her as it had before. *After all, he is my husband!*

Just then the door swung open, and a redheaded man burst inside. He wore dark pants, black boots, a big-sleeved gray shirt, and wide black suspenders. He stopped short when he saw Jennet. "Who're you? Where's Free Havlick?"

As sure as she was born, Jennet knew the man was Willie Thorne. Fear pricked her skin, but she said calmly, "He's not here right now. I'm his wife, Jennet."

"Well, well." Willie walked around her, eyeing her and chuckling to himself. "His wife, huh? Well, well."

"Is there something I can do for you?"

"I came to see Free. But this is better."

The look in his eyes sent a chill through her. "He'll be home soon, I'm sure," Jennet said.

"I'm sure too. But he's gonna have a jolt, he is." Willie grabbed her arm and dragged her toward the door.

"Let me go!" Jennet cried, struggling to break his hold, but he was too strong for her.

"We're goin' for a walk. A nice little walk." Willie Thorne grinned, then laughed. "Free won't want to tangle with me once he sees his little wife was wolf bait."

The words turned her blood to ice. She struggled harder, but Willie snaked an arm around her and pulled her backward until she was tight against him. Silently she cried out to God for protection. She darted a look at Clay to make sure he was still asleep. She realized if Willie Thorne knew about Clay, he'd kill him too, so she stopped struggling. She dare not wake Clay!

Willie continued to chuckle as he pushed her out the door and closed it. There was still enough light 'o see several feet away.

"Please, just let me go back inside Please!" Her voice broke.

"Not on your life, girl!" Willie Thorne walked her out of the clearing and into the tall pines. The fragrance of pine was heavy in the air, but over that she could smell Willie's sweat. She felt the heat of his body as he forced her on-ward. "I heard tell Free thinks he's gonna take some tim-ber I want. This'll give him something else to think on."

Jennet bit back a moan. What if Free didn't return to-night? She'd be torn apart by wolves, and Clay would be all alone, maybe starve to death. Pain of losing Clay ripped through her body, and she jerked away from Willie, catching him off guard. She fled from him, but her skirt caught on a blackberry bush, trapping her. She ripped it free and ran as hard as she could.

"You can't get away from me," called Willie, laughing as he chased her.

Jennet ducked behind a pine, dashed to another and ducked behind that, then stopped, her breath coming in gasps. If she stood very still, Willie wouldn't find her. She listened but heard only the usual night sounds. Where was Willie Thorne?

"Gotcha!" cried Willie.

Jennet started to turn, but he struck her on the back of the head. Pain exploded inside her, and she crumpled to the ground. Her mind felt like it was crammed full of cotton, but she could still see Willie's black boots and hear him chuckle.

"Nobody'll ever know you didn't just run out here and get lost," Willie said. "Course I'll tell Free so he'll know I'm somebody to be reckoned with."

Willie mumbled something she couldn't make out as he walked away, leaving her in a heap at the base of a giant white pine. The smell of dirt and old pine needles almost strangled her. With a groan she pushed herself to her knees. Her head spun. Trees loomed over her and around her. Gingerly she touched her head until she found a lump the size of an egg behind her right ear. Her thick hair had given her enough protection to keep the blow from breaking her skin.

Jennet pushed herself up until she stood against the

trunk of the giant pine. She turned her aching head to look around. She couldn't see the light of the cabin. Before long it would be too dark to see anything. She fought against an urge to scream for help. If Willie Thorne heard her, he might come back and hit her again, this time hard enough to kill her.

Jennet pushed away from the tree and waited until the forest stopped spinning, then took a step forward. Which way was the cabin? What if she stumbled deeper into the woods? She'd heard many stories of people walking off the path to get lost and never find their way back. She sniffed back hot tears.

"Heavenly Father, You're with me even in this wilderness," she whispered. "Send help. Send Free to get me!"

Jennet walked forward, stumbled on a fallen limb, and caught herself before she pitched headlong to the pine needle-covered ground.

Suddenly she heard a low, menacing growl, and perspiration popped out all over her body, soaking her. A large gray wolf stood a few yards away, its teeth bared.

"Help!" Jennet cried, suddenly no longer fearful that Willie Thorne would hear. "Help! Help me! Free!"

The wolf sank to its great haunches and edged toward her, growling ominously. Saliva dribbled from the wolf's mouth.

"Free! Help me, Free!"

Muscles tightened in the wolf as it readied to spring. Jennet inched along, trying to put a tree between her and the wolf. The wolf leaped, and she jumped aside, screamed, tripped, and sprawled to the ground. The wolf landed where she had been standing. It turned and sprang again. A shot rang out, and the bullet caught the wolf in midair. It fell with a crash close to her.

She looked up and saw Free lean his rifle against the tree and reach for her. With a glad cry she clung to him, her arms around his waist, her face pushed into his neck. He smelled of sweat and pine and musky skin, and she never wanted to leave the safety of his arms.

"Jen," he said hoarsely, holding her tight, his face buried in her hair.

"Free, you found me. Oh, Free!"

"I saw Tune, and he said you were here. Clay was in his bed, and I looked all over for you." Free rubbed his hands up and down her back. "I knew you wouldn't leave Clay by choice." A shudder passed through Free, and his voice broke.

"I was so scared! But you came for me." Jennet moved so that she could lift her head and look up at him. "Will you always be around to save me?"

"Always," he whispered. He lowered his head and kissed her, a gentle, searching kiss.

She relaxed against him. Her eyelids closed, and she curled her fingers into the thick hair on the back of his head. He molded her body to his and the kiss deepened, igniting a passion in her that she'd never felt before. He lifted his head, but she pulled it down to kiss him again. Their hearts beat together, blocking out the sounds of the forest around them.

Suddenly, reason returned to her, and she tore her mouth from his and cried, "Clay! We must get back to him!"

Free caught her hand and picked up his rifle. They ran through the pines to the cabin.

Jennet rushed to Clay's basket and knelt beside it. He was sleeping soundly, but she touched him to make sure he was all right. She sighed in relief. Slowly she stood and faced Free.

As quickly as she could, Jennet told him what had happened. He leaped to his feet and she caught his arm. "What're you going to do?"

"Go after Willie Thorne," Free said fiercely.

She cupped his face in her hand and felt the hard stubble of his beard. "Please don't go tonight."

"I must."

"He might kill you!"

"He won't. He'll try, but he won't kill me!" Free pulled her close, glorying in the feel of her. Finally he held her from him. "You're taking Clay, and you're going back with Tunis in the morning."

"I'm staying."

Jennet shook her head and pushed away from him several feet. She squared her shoulders and looked directly into his eyes. Dirt streaked the side of her face and dress. "Free, I am going to stay here with you. You can't make me leave."

"We'll see about that." Free picked up the rifle that he'd leaned against the wall. "I'm leaving this for you. Keep it beside the bed with you, and if anybody but me comes, shoot 'em."

"Free, please, don't go!"

"I have to." Free wanted to hold her tight and never let her go again.

A tear spilled down Jennet's cheek, then another, and Free groaned. Once again he set the rifle aside and pulled her close to him. Jennet felt the thud of his heart against her. She wrapped her arms around his neck and lifted her lips to his. Having her willingly kiss him brought tears to his eyes. He'd never expected it to happen. His lips were feather soft against hers, then he kissed her with a passion that had been building between them. She returned his kiss, eager to give to him what she'd never been able to before.

Finally Free pushed her away, his face set. "I have to take care of Willie Thorne. But I'll be back. That's a promise."

Jennet managed not to cry out in fear for him.

"Pull in the latchstring when I leave."

Jennet nodded slightly. She knew she couldn't stop him.

Free closed the door, and Jennet lowered the wooden latch and pulled in the leather latchstring so no one could open the door from the outside. She stood there a long time, then finally walked to the bed and sank to the edge, her head in her hands. Oh, but she wanted to follow Free! But she couldn't with Clay. She clasped her hands tightly together, bowed her head, and prayed for Free.

Several minutes later Free strode into the saloon where he knew he'd find Willie Thorne. The noise rose around him, seeming to be extra loud after the silence of the woods. Men lined the bar, talking and laughing. Saloon girls, their bright skirts flapping about their legs, walked to the tables carrying trays with drinks.

"Willie Thorne!" Free called loudly.

Willie tensed, then slowly turned until his back was pressed against the bar. "Havlick," he said with an easy grin that didn't reach the cold steel of his eyes. "What brings you in here? Thought this was your idea of sin."

Men and girls laughed, but Free ignored them as he took two more steps forward. He smelled cigarette smoke and beer as well as the sweat from the many hardworking men standing around the stained and scarred bar.

"Willie Thorne, you took my wife into the woods, struck her over the head, and left her for wolf bait!"

Men murmured as they turned to stare at Willie. In this neck of the woods women were treated with great care and respect.

Free waited until the hubbub died down. "That's a coward's way to fight this battle we're in."

Willie shot away from the bar, his face as red as his hair. "You calling me a coward?"

Free nodded, the anger so great in him that he wanted to rip Willie limb from limb.

Jas Lotown, the owner of the bar, came around the bar, a

shotgun in his hands. "You boys want to fight, step out-doors."

Free glared at Willie, then stalked out of the saloon. He stopped in the middle of the sawdust-covered street and waited with his booted feet spread, his fists doubled at his sides. He watched men swarm out of the saloon, pushing Willie along with them.

Tunis was just leaving the boarding house, and he caught sight of Free. He hurried to him. "What's going on, Free?"

Never taking his eyes off Willie, Free answered, "Get away, Tune. I got a score to settle with Willie Thorne."

Tunis hesitated, then stepped away. "I'll watch your back."

Free nodded briefly to let Tunis know he'd heard. He'd told Tune about Willie, the lawyer, and George Meeker. They were shady enough to try pulling a fast one even though woodsmen demanded a fair fight.

Willie flexed his great muscles and walked toward Free. "It's not too late to call it off, Havlick."

"It's way too late," snapped Free, squatting slightly with his hands out and his feet spread wide. He knew anything would go in this fight—punching, gouging, kicking. And Willie Thorne was good at fighting dirty.

Willie leaped at Free, but he jumped aside. Willie kicked out, caught Free in the leg, and sent him sprawling to the ground. The roar of the crowd seemed to explode inside Free's ears as he rolled and leaped up just as Willie kicked at his ribs. Free shot out a fist and caught Willie below his left eye, sending his head back with a snap. Free shot out his other fist and caught Willie in the stomach. He stumbled back but didn't fall. Willie lunged again, this time catching him in a bear hug that almost crushed Free's ribs. They fell to the ground, rolling and writhing. Willie grabbed Free's hair, then tried to gouge out his eyes with his thumbs. Free bucked and twisted and sent Willie flying off. Before Willie could move, Free landed on him and pinned him to the ground.

The desire to kill Willie burned inside Free, and he pressed his thumbs against Willie's windpipe. From deep inside Free heard, "Don't kill him."

But Willie deserved to die!

"Don't kill him."

Free struggled but finally obeyed the still, small voice. Although the rage had seeped out of him, he didn't get off Willie. He pushed his face close to Willie and saw the panic in Willie's eyes. "Admit to what you did tonight!"

"No!"

Free pressed harder.

"Okay! Okay!" gasped Willie.

Free lightened his hold. "Talk!" He glanced over his shoulder. "You men listen to this!"

Willie shuddered and closed his eyes. "I took your wife into the forest, knocked her out, and left her."

The men muttered angrily. Tunis stepped closer to Free.

"Now tell about the crooked deals you made for George Meeker."

"George Meeker!" murmured the men who now formed a tight circle around Free and Willie Thorne.

Willie moaned. "Don't make me."

"Tell now!"

Willie muttered the story, but the men were close enough that they heard. They exclaimed in anger, many of them shouting out that they'd been cheated and robbed.

At last Free released Willie and struggled to his feet. Tunis wrapped an arm around him and held him up while they watched the crowd of men take charge of Willie. Several of the men congratulated Free, and he nodded in acknowledgment, too tired to do more.

"I'll take you home," said Tunis.

Free pulled away. "No, I can manage."

"If you say so."

Free weakly brushed dust off himself and gingerly touched a bruise on his cheek. He looked at Tunis. "Tomorrow you are taking Jennet right back where she belongs."

Tunis smiled and spread his hands wide. "She belongs here with you."

"It's not safe."

"With Willie out of the way she'll be all right."

"Maybe. Maybe not. She's going back."

Tunis laughed. "You'll have your hands full convincing her of that. If you haven't noticed, she's one stubborn lady."

Free had just started to notice that. "She said she won't go back."

"She won't."

Free sighed heavily, suddenly too weary to argue. "Will I see you before you leave?"

"I made plans to leave at dawn."

"Then I'll say good-bye now." Free held out his hand and Tunis took it in a firm shake, then Free hugged Tunis and slapped him on the back. "You're a good friend."

"So are you. Clay would be proud of you."

Free smiled through sudden tears. "Tune, I finally understand why Grandpa wanted me to have a wife and family. There's nothing more important."

"That's right, Free. That's sure right!"

Free trudged down the street and into the darkness beyond to where his cabin nestled among the trees. After a while he saw the soft glow of the light in the windows, and his heart quickened. Jennet was waiting for him. He thought of her warm response and her willing kisses, and he walked faster. This time she wouldn't push him aside or freeze him out.

Inside the cabin Jennet settled Clay back in his basket,

softly continuing to pray for Free. He had to come back safely. She heard a sound outside the cabin and she held her breath, her eyes wide and her hand at her throat.

"Open the door, Jen. It's me."

His voice left her almost too weak to move, but she managed to run to the door and swing it open. Free stepped into the lamplight, and she gasped at the bruises. "Oh, Free! Are you all right?"

He caught her arms and pulled her to him. "I'm fine," he said huskily.

Jennet gently touched her lips to his. "Let me clean your wounds," she said against his mouth.

"First take care of my heart," he whispered.

CHAPTER

17

♦ Free stopped the buggy and with a wide, proud smile turned to Jennet beside him. Clay lay sleeping in his basket at her feet. "Here we are!"

Jennet's eyes locked with Free's and she couldn't look away, nor did she want to. The past six weeks had been the happiest time of her life.

Free laughed low in his throat. "Your eyes are shining."

Jennet wanted to fling her arms around him, but she knew it was unseemly to do such a private thing out in public. "You make them shine," she whispered.

Just being with her gave him such pleasure! He'd liked sharing his cabin with her and Clay, and he'd spent most of his time with them. But soon he'd be too busy for them. He leaned toward her slightly. "We're here to look at the camp. Remember?"

Jen laughed, rubbed her hands over her print skirt, pushed back a strand of hair that had come loose from the braid coiled at the nape of her neck, and looked around at the buzz of activity. "So this is a lumbercamp?"

This was where Free would live in just a week. He planned to leave her at the cabin outside Big Pine. Somehow she had to find a way to stay here with him. She'd heard that some of the lumbermen, foremen, and cooks had their wives live at camp with them.

Free had already showed her the banking grounds where soon millions of feet of pine logs would be piled parallel with the river to wait for the spring thaw. Giant skidways were made by clearing off the brush and timber along a riverbank. After the thaw a key log would be dislodged, and the logs would roll down the skidways into the river to float down to the sawmill.

"There's the bunkhouse, home to all the shanty boys," said Free.

Jennet studied the log building. It was low and squat. The walls were chinked with clay and grass, and the roof was covered with tarpaper.

"I spent two winters in one." Free chuckled. "The bunks are spaced just far enough apart to slip in, and they're made of boards covered with spruce boughs. Rather tough on the back, but we were always so tired we didn't care what we slept on. We used our turkeys as pillows."

She laughed. "Turkeys?"

Free grinned. "We each had a grainsack filled with our personal stuff."

"I like my feather pillows."

Free's dark eyes twinkled. "Me too."

"Now that you're the big lumberman you don't sleep in the bunkhouse on spruce boughs with a turkey as your pillow?"

"Nope. See that?" Free pointed to three small wooden shacks standing in a row. "The first one is for me, the second for the foremen, and the third for the cook and his family." He waved his hand. "Over there is the office, there the barn that stables about eighteen teams of horses, and beside it the blacksmith shop, which carries everything from toggle chains to bridle bits. Over there the company store and the cookcamp. Sometime this week the tote teamster will haul in hay, grain, beans, molasses, tea, tobacco, salt pork, salted beef, lard, prunes, potatoes, flour, dried apples, blankets, candles, kerosene, kitchen stoves, and plenty of pots and pans." He thought of the cookies as big as stove lids that he'd eaten, and he told her about them. "I could go for a big mug of coffee and half a dozen cookies about now."

Jennet glanced up at the warm August sun. "It's almost dinnertime. Let's go home, and I'll cook dinner for you." Her stomach growled, and she realized she was hungry too. She knew Clay would awaken soon to be nursed.

Free turned away from Jennet. He hadn't told her yet that he had booked passage on a boat to Grand Rapids for her and Clay and that they'd leave early that afternoon. "We'll leave in a minute." He wanted their short time together to be pleasant. "I was able to hire on one of the best fiddlers in Michigan. One of the best cooks too."

"And will you sing for all of them?" Jennet asked, her eyes twinkling as she smiled. During the past six weeks, she'd learned that Free loved to sing and that he had a very good voice. He'd sung Clay to sleep almost every night.

With a grin Free nodded. "I've brought many a good man to tears with my songs."

Jennet giggled. "I thought they liked your singing!"

Free was always surprised when she teased him, and he laughed in delight.

"I've just had the most wonderful idea, Free!" Jennet said as three kids under eleven years of age ran past. "While I'm here with you I can have school for the kids just like I did for Meg and Will."

"I guess I best tell you."

Jennet had a sinking feeling. "Tell me what?"

"You're going back to Grand Rapids today. Going home."

Jennet's face fell, and it tore at his heart. "But my home is with you!"

"You can't live like this!"

"But I can! I survived living at Uncle Tait's, didn't I? And you'd be here with me. And Clay."

Tears welled up in her eyes. "Why don't you want me?"

"Want you? I can't survive without you!"

"I want to stay. Clay needs you. I need you."

Her words wrapped around his heart, and he suddenly knew he couldn't survive eight long months without her and Clay. "You know a woodsman's day starts about four in the morning and ends at dark."

"Like a farmer's day?" Jennet asked with a grin.

Free nodded and chuckled. "Can Clay take the snow and ice and cold weather?"

"Other babies have before him."

"You don't give up, do you?"

"I hope not."

Free wanted to pull her close, but he squeezed her hand instead. "I want to show you the prime lumber we'll do after this section is finished." He flicked the reins, and Acorn stepped forward and onto the deep trail that led away from camp.

Clay squirmed and whimpered a little but settled back to sleep with the sway of the buggy.

About half an hour later Free stopped the buggy and waved his arm in a wide arc. "All of that, Jen! This'll make me one of the wealthiest lumbermen in Michigan. We'll build a house bigger than the one Witherspoon has. And his house has fifteen bedrooms!"

Jennet clasped her hands, and her eyes sparkled as she looked. White pines reached a hundred and fifty feet in the air and were at least five feet across. "Free, the trees are massive! Oh, the beauty!" She turned to Free with a slight frown. "Don't you hate to cut them all down and leave only ugly stumps behind?" On their drive out to camp from Big Pine they'd passed section after section of stumps where once white pines had stood in all their grand glory.

Free said, "Jen, the country needs lumber. People are going West where there aren't trees for lumber. They need the lumber that I'll send West. Trees will grow again." Free knew it took about eighty years for a white pine to grow big enough to cut, but he couldn't be concerned with that now. "This will make us rich, Jen! Clay can have anything he wants."

Jennet locked her hands in her lap. "Free, Clay needs you and me more than he needs 'things.'"

"I know that."

"If I could choose between saving those trees and cutting them down, I'd choose to save them, no matter what the dollar loss."

"Jen, you're talking crazy."

Jennet shrugged but didn't argue further. She would save the timber that she could save, and Free could lumber out what he wanted. "When can we see the land that your grandpa left to me?"

Free frowned. Didn't she know? He was sure he'd told her. He cleared his throat and tightened the hold on the reins. "This is it," he said in a voice that he forced to sound normal.

Jennet gasped as she looked around at the massive, tall, straight white pines. These were the very trees that Grandpa Clay had left to her! These were the trees that she'd planned to preserve for future generations. Michigan would not become a state without forests! She turned to him, her blue eyes troubled. She must've misunderstood him. "But, Free, you can't cut these trees down."

Free's jaw tightened. "I can."

"But they belong to me!"

Free struggled against his anger and frustration. He'd make her understand the importance of lumbering these giant trees. He could build a house for her with twenty bedrooms! Then she wouldn't complain because he'd gone against her wishes. "Jennet, I *can* cut them and I *will* cut them."

Jennet didn't want to anger him or fight with him, but she couldn't let him cut down these trees. The forest was the heritage of future generations. Once all of Michigan was covered with trees, but no longer, not since the lumbermen had discovered the wealth. She moistened her lips with the tip of her tongue. "Free, please understand. I want Clay to be able to show these white pines to his children and know that Grandpa Clay walked among them, canoed down the stream that runs through them. These trees have stood here for hundreds of years! I want our children to take refuge in the trees like we both have."

Free's dark eyes narrowed as he looked at Jennet. "It's already in my schedule to cut them."

Jennet's face hardened. "Then change your schedule."

A muscle jumped in his cheek. "These trees are some of the finest around, Jennet!"

"All the more reason to keep them!" Jennet looked up, up, up to the tops of the straight-as-an-arrow white pines. The terrible thought of felling the giants and turning the section into stumps upset her more than she could say. She reached for Free's hand but felt him stiffen at her touch. She jerked back and locked her suddenly icy fingers in her lap. She stared straight ahead, her heart heavy. "I talked to Lem Azack about these trees."

"Nothing will change my mind," said Free hoarsely.

"He said under the law not even you can log them out unless I give you written permission." Jennet kept her eyes glued to her clenched hands. "I will not give you written permission."

Free thought he'd explode on the spot. "You're just like Pa!"

"How can you say that?" Jennet cried.

"You're trying to keep me from succeeding in the lumber business!"

"But you've already succeeded!"

"Am I as big as Witherspoon? Driscoll? No!"

"But why do you need to be that big?"

"I want to be," Free said grimly.

"To prove to your pa that you can be?"

Fire shot from Free's eyes, and she knew she'd hit a tender spot.

"Free, you don't have to prove anything to Roman. You know and I know that you're successful."

Without another word Free turned Acorn and drove away. He'd thought he loved her. Yes, loved her! No, he didn't! Right now he hated her with a passion that alarmed him.

Jennet felt his great anger, and she remembered her conversation with Marie at Christmas about Free turning as mean as Roman had been. Maybe it would be better for her to return to Grand Rapids. Hot tears burned her eyes, but she wouldn't let them fall.

Just as they were driving past the camp, Jig stepped out and shouted, "Free! I have a word with you." His Swedish accent made his words almost impossible for Jennet to understand.

Reluctantly Free pulled Acorn up. He did not want to face Jig today. Jig, like Tunis, could see into his heart, and right now he couldn't afford to let anyone see his heart.

Jesus saw his heart. The thought came instinctively now, but Free brushed it aside as he wrapped the reins around the brake handle.

Jennet looked at the tall rugged man carrying a muzzle-loader and smiled. She knew Jig from Free's description of him.

"You are Jennet, Free's little wife!" cried Jig, reaching up a dirty work-roughened hand to her.

"And you're Jig," Jennet said as she placed her hand in his.

Jig nodded as he helped her to the ground. "You are a beauty, Jennet. Is she not a beauty, Free?"

Scowling, Free walked around to join them. "I didn't expect to see you until later in the fall."

"I heard your Jennet was with you, and I had to set my eyes on her."

Jennet laughed. "Would you like to see Clay?"

"That I would like." Jig pulled off his cap and held it close to his heart as Jennet lifted Clay from his basket. "Clay Havlick's great-grandson is blessed of God through Jesus Christ our Lord. May he walk all his days upright toward God."

"Amen," whispered Jennet.

Free nodded, his lips pressed tightly together. He wasn't ready to give up his anger. He had to admit the sight of Jen holding Clay for Jig to admire softened his heart some.

"Watching this little one grow up will make my heart warm," said Jig.

"They are going back to Grand Rapids," Free said sharply.

Jennet shot him a startled look. She'd thought he'd decided they could stay. The icy look in his dark eyes and his aloof manner toward her locked her argument inside. She knew she'd burst into tears if she tried to speak. And she would not cry in front of Jig or Free!

Just then Clay started crying the cry that meant he was hungry and couldn't wait a minute to be fed. She excused herself and climbed in the back seat of the buggy with Clay.

Free led Jig away so that Jennet couldn't overhear them. She saw Free glance at her, and she knew he was talking to Jig about her. But what was he saying?

Free cleared his throat as he looked away from Jennet. "Jig, you said you'd do anything I asked. This is important. I want you to take Jen and the baby back to Grand Rapids tomorrow morning. I was going to send them by boat, but if you'll drive them in the buggy, it'll mean Jen will have the buggy at home. If you leave at dawn, you'll be there before dark."

"You said she does not want to leave here."

"I say she is." Free clenched his fists at his sides. "Either you take her, or they go by boat today."

Jig sighed. "Her I will take. Yes." But he didn't look very happy about it.

"Thanks Jig. You can come back by canoe or boat."

"No worry about that, Free. Jig will get back."

They talked until Free saw Jennet lay Clay back in his basket, then walked back to join her. She looked expectantly at Free.

Enough anger had drained away that Free felt bad for what he was going to do. He couldn't meet Jennet's eyes. "Jig will drive you and Clay back to Grand Rapids at dawn. You'll have the buggy and Acorn with you. Jig will come back by boat."

Tears filled Jennet's eyes, but she refused to let them fall. Without a word she climbed into the front seat of the buggy and sat staring straight ahead.

CHAPTER

18

♦ Jennet scowled at the ugly stumps as Jig drove south of Big Pine on his way to Grand Rapids. She glanced at Jig. "You know I'm right, Jig." For the past hour, since they'd left Big Pine at dawn, she'd tried to convince Jig to turn around and take her to the lumbercamp and Free.

Jig drove around a deep rut and almost struck a rock protruding from the ground. "My girl, Jennet, Free told me what to do with you."

"You know I belong with him! Grandpa Clay, your good friend, made his will to force Free into getting married and having a family. Grandpa Clay would want me with Free. And you know he would, Jig!"

Jig chuckled, reined Acorn around, and drove off the road to turn around among the stumps, then drove back on the road toward Big Pine. "Say no more. Clay Havlick said families are more important than anything. Time after time he said they belong together."

Jennet laughed as she patted Jig's hand. "Thank you."

"Free will be as mad as a bear with a sore tail."

"He'll get over it." But would he? The way things were

right now he wouldn't. Until he forgave Roman and let his anger go, he could not be free to live his life the way God wanted him to. Until then, his relationship with God was blocked, and it left room for Satan to cause trouble.

Silently Jennet prayed for Free. An idea flashed into her mind and she turned to Jig. "Will you do something to help Free?"

"That I will. Clay Havlick I promised. What is this you will ask of me?"

"Jig, Free needs to see his pa. They must have time together to talk." Jennet had remembered her talk with Pa, and she wanted that same thing to happen with Free. She knew he loved Roman but couldn't forgive him or couldn't set aside his anger.

Jig nodded as he slowed Acorn even more to keep the buggy from hitting the ruts too hard. He knocked a mosquito away from his matted hair, which hung down to his broad shoulders. Birds flew up from the branches of scrub pine trees and bushes. The sun glowed brightly just at the eastern horizon as Jig drove north to Big Pine.

"I want you to get a message to Roman to come see Free. You'd have to take it yourself because this is harvest time. A letter wouldn't be enough to make Roman come. If Free could see how much Roman has changed, and that he does want to mend the breach between them, maybe he'll be able to let go of his anger."

Jig shrugged. "I have not been out of the wilderness for a very long time. But for Clay Havlick, and for you, Jennet Havlick, I will go."

Baby Clay sneezed and cried. Jennet turned him in his basket, covered him, and patted his tiny back until he slept again. She looked at Jig. "Drive to the river in Big Pine and you can go yet today."

"And what of you?"

"I'll drive myself and Clay to the lumbercamp."

Jig scratched behind his ear. "Do you know the way?"

"It's a clear road, Jig, between Big Pine and there. I can't get lost."

Jig scratched his head, his arm, and his head again. "Jennet, my brain is working and spinning at your plan. Why would Roman Havlick listen to one like me? Here in these woods I am a part of all. People and animals knows me. But away from the trees . . ." His words trailed off.

With the tip of her finger Jennet tapped her lips and narrowed her eyes in thought as the buggy rolled closer to Big Pine. "You're right, of course, Jig. But he might listen to me."

"Yes. To you he would listen. Probably."

Jennet laughed breathlessly at a new and daring plan. "Jig, I'll go with you! We can go by boat from Big Pine to the farm! It's a lot quicker than by buggy. And we'll come back by boat with Roman, pick up the buggy, and drive to the camp. We'll be back in two days. Three at the most." Her face clouded. "If I can talk Roman into it." Free's pa had changed, but if he still had his bad temper, he just might beat her before anyone could stop him. She tightened her jaw. She would face Roman—no matter how afraid she was!

"This plan of yours will work. I think," said Jig, nodding.

The sun rose higher as they rode in silence the rest of the way to the dock in Big Pine. Jig booked rides for them on a small steamboat that was leaving immediately and left Acorn and the buggy at the nearby livery. Jennet took a change of clothes for herself and the baby from her trunk in back of the buggy, pushed them into a satchel, and handed it to Jig to carry for her. They walked to the crowded dock where the white steamboat was waiting.

Gulls swooped and cried above the calm gray water near the dock. With shouts of anger and loud teasing remarks dock workers loaded and unloaded three small steamboats and several canoes.

Clutching Clay tightly to her, Jennet picked her way along

the dock around coils of rope, barrels, and a tub of smelly fish. Her bonnet felt awkward on her head, and she wanted to push it off, but she knew she'd need its protection from the sun. Jig helped Jennet board the boat, and her stomach rolled as the boat moved in the water. Once she got her sea legs she knew her stomach would settle down. The captain called out to them and pulled the rope that made the whistle blow. Jennet settled into a seat in the stern of the boat and laid the sleeping Clay across her lap on his stomach. Jig joined the captain in the pilot house, and the boat chugged away from the dock.

Jennet smoothed the soft flannel cover over Clay's back. "I will do anything to save your papa, Clay. And if he keeps this anger and resentment inside him, he'll never be happy."

Much later Clay awoke and Jennet fed him, then made a pallet from blankets for him beside her feet on the deck.

Jennet watched two men outside the pilot house playing cards on an upturned wooden crate. They argued good-naturedly. Jig stayed with the captain, and at times Jennet could hear the sound of his voice. A yellow cat, its tail high, walked along the deck of the boat as if it owned the world. Jennet called to it, but it ignored her as well as the men playing cards.

The warm sun, the chug of the engine, and the gentle sway of the boat lulled Jennet to sleep. Last night she'd slept fitfully, always aware that Free lay cold and distant beside her.

A loud voice jarred her awake. The two men who had been playing cards were arguing and would've come to blows if the captain hadn't stepped in to stop them.

She noticed the sun was gone and dark clouds covered the once-bright blue sky. Wind whipped the river into small waves, rocking the boat slightly. Fear trickled over Jennet. She knew the waves couldn't sink the boat, but there was a real danger of the boat's running aground on a sandbar, hitting submerged logs, or catching fire. Just last month she'd heard the *J. W. Montrose* had caught fire and burned to the water line. No one had died, but several people had suffered injuries.

Jennet shook her head hard. No! They would not run aground or hit logs or burn! God was with them, watching over them! He had angels surrounding them to keep them safe. She let the Bible verse, "For God has not given us a spirit of fear, but of power and of love and of a sound mind," play over and over in her mind until she truly felt the words. *I will not be afraid!* she thought.

Jig sat beside her, his face pale under the dirt and whiskers. "My insides seem to be rolling like the water."

Jennet reached for his hand and clasped it tightly. "Tell me more about Clay Havlick." She knew that would take Jig's mind off his seasickness.

As Jig talked, Jennet had to listen closely to hear and understand because of his accent and the noise of the engine.

"When I first joined up with Clay Havlick, I spoke no English. He taught me while we canoed to the Indian villages to trade for the beaver pelts. The first word he taught me was *beaver*." Jig laughed. "Beaver was important to Clay Havlick. He was an honest man with hair and eyes as dark as his grandson, Free. Clay could talk to the Indians in their own language. He taught me a few words of Ojibwa and Pottawatomie. But English I learned the most."

By midafternoon the wind died down, and the river was calm again. Jig joined the captain to leave Jennet free to nurse the baby. When they reached Grand Rapids, Jig hired a canoe to take them down the Thornapple River to the landing near the farm where Tait had first taken Jennet. Jig rented a one-seater buggy with a black canvas top and drove them to the Havlick farm just as the sun set. Across the road from the main house a pig squealed and ran after other pigs. Horses and cattle were grazing in the pasture

behind the barn. Flowers bloomed brightly along the front
of the huge white farmhouse.

"What a grand place," said Jig as he stopped on the road
and pulled off his cap to scratch his matted hair. "But no
trees, Jennet. No trees!" He pointed at the cornfields
stretching on and on. "What became of all the trees?"

Jennet shrugged. "Roman cut them to make room to
plant. There's still a woodlot beyond the barns."

"A shame, a crying shame! But I will sleep in the woodlot
and be happy." Jig slapped the reins on the bay mare's back
and drove into the drive.

"There's plenty of room in Roman's house or Pa's. Even
the barn," said Jennet.

"Can't sleep in the confines of walls."

She wanted to ask him why not, but she didn't. She
looked longingly down the lane that led to her family's
house, but she knew she must face Roman before seeing
them. "Stop here, Jig."

Jig stopped in front of the big house. "Want me at your
side when you speak to Clay Havlick's son?"

Jennet hesitated. She needed all the support she could
get, but she shook her head. "Thanks anyway, Jig." Just
then she spotted Tim at the barn. "Take the horse to the
barn." She pointed. "Tim's inside. He'll show you where to
park the buggy and where to water the horse."

Jig nodded and drove away as Jennet pushed open the
gate and followed the walk to the huge house. Should she
go to the front door or the back? Finally she decided on
the back because she knew Kit or maybe even Marie would
be in the kitchen making supper.

Baby Clay whimpered and wriggled, then settled back in
her arms. Butterflies fluttered wildly in her stomach. She
looked back toward Pa's house and longed to run to Ma's
comforting arms.

Jennet hesitated, then knocked on the big white door.

Her legs felt almost too weak to hold her. To her surprise, Free's mother opened the door.

Lillian's face turned white, and she stared at Jennet with her mouth open. She plucked at the white apron covering her gray dress. Suddenly she burst into tears and tugged Jennet inside. "What's wrong? Why are you here? Is Freeman dead?"

"He's fine, Lillian. I promise, he's well. I came to speak with Roman."

Lillian's dark eyes widened fearfully. "Oh, my!"

Jennet realized she'd made a terrible mistake. She wasn't brave enough to speak to Roman. One harsh word from him and she'd turn tail and run.

"He'll be in for supper soon," said Lillian weakly.

Clay whimpered, and Jennet slipped the cover off him.

Lillian gasped in delight, looked around as if she were afraid her husband would walk in and see her, then held her hands out. "Could I hold the baby?"

Jennet laid Clay in her arms, and Lillian looked down at him with love like Jennet had never seen on her face.

"We'll go in the front room and sit," said Lillian, leading the way.

In the front room Jennet glanced around at the massive dark green leather sofas, walnut end tables, and a large walnut table covered with potted ivy, red geraniums, and pink begonias. Everything looked new, as if no one ever used the room. Jennet draped Clay's multicolored quilt over the arm of a dark green leather chair. Maybe she should leave now, go to her Grand Rapids home, and forget what she'd planned. The idea appealed to her more and more as she waited for Roman.

Lillian cooed softly to Clay but didn't speak to Jennet. Smells of frying chicken drifted in from the kitchen.

Jennet moved restlessly. Would she want to spend her life in fear of her husband as Lillian had? Jennet shook her head. But if Free couldn't forgive Roman, he might turn into a mean-tempered, money-hungry man she couldn't love or respect.

Jennet frowned slightly. Did she love Free as a wife was to love a husband? She had enjoyed being with him, but she hadn't thought about the change in her feelings toward him. She hadn't understood why she couldn't abide living eight months without him.

Indeed, she was in love with Free! Why hadn't she realized sooner that she was in love with Free like Ma was in love with Pa? She obeyed God and forgave Free, told him things she'd done even when she'd not wanted to, then went to Big Pine to live, but loving him hadn't occurred to her.

Did Free love her the way Pa loved Ma?

Jennet's heart gave a funny little jerk. He always took such good care of her, and he seemed to like to have her around. She frowned. Except now. And not just because he thought camp life was too rough for her but because she wouldn't allow him to lumber out the white pines that belonged to her.

Maybe she should give in to him, let him chop down the giants. Jennet shook her head. Loving him didn't mean giving him his own way, especially over such an important issue.

Just then Jennet caught Lillian's eye.

"You were deep in thought, Jen," said Lillian nervously. "I said I heard Roman come in."

Jennet trembled but jumped to her feet, leaving her dark blue bonnet beside Clay's quilt. Silently she called out to God for special strength to face Roman.

Lillian looked ready to run away as she stood with Clay in her arms. "I'll take Clay to the kitchen to show him to Marie while you talk with Roman."

"It's all right if you stay."

Lillian shook her head. "I couldn't! No. No, I couldn't do that!"

"Then take Clay to the kitchen."

Jennet heard footsteps coming toward the front room, but instead of feeling nervous a great calm settled over her.

Roman filled the doorway as he stopped to pierce Jennet with his dark eyes. He smelled of animals and outdoors. His graying hair was pressed down where his hat had been. A few pieces of straw stuck to his brown pants. "Why'd you come?" he barked.

"I'll tell you after you see Clay," said Jennet, proud of her calm voice.

Lillian held Clay out, and Roman looked at him, his face softening a fraction. Then he looked back at Jennet with a scowl. Lillian scurried from the room, the baby clutched to her.

Jennet walked closer to Roman, then stopped.

"You come to see Wexal?" he asked bluntly.

"No. You."

His brow shot up in surprise. "Me?"

"About Free."

Roman stiffened. "Is he hurt?"

"No." Jennet nervously fingered the top button of her dress. "He needs to talk to you. Get things settled between you. So he can get on with his life."

"Is he such a coward that he sent you to do his talking?"

"No!" Jennet's eyes flashed. "He doesn't know I came."

Roman looped one hand around his wide suspender. "I have nothing to say to you. What's between my son and me is no concern of yours."

"But it is!" Jennet doubled her fists at her sides, and her breast rose and fell. "You did Free wrong, and you know you did. But he must forgive you for it. He's all knotted up inside because of anger toward you." She brushed a strand of chestnut-brown hair off her cheek. "You could talk to him, tell him you care about him."

"He knows I do!"

"No, he doesn't. He believes you think he's worthless, a failure because he's not farming with you. He thinks you hate him because you kept his grandpa's inheritance from him."

Roman sank to a chair, his head bowed.

"Talk to him! Tell him how you feel!"

"How can I? He won't come to see me."

Jennet hesitated, then knelt at Roman's knee and looked into his face. She saw the fine lines that fanned from the corners of his dark eyes to his graying temples. Suddenly she caught a glimpse of how Free would look in twenty years. Jennet smelled Roman's sweat and dust from the fields. "Then you go see him," she whispered.

Roman frowned. "How can I?"

"Let Pa take care of things here, and you go back with Jig and me."

Roman shook his head. "I can't."

"You can! You know you want to see Free."

"But I got work here! I've never left during harvest."

"You can't wait until after harvest because of winter coming on." Jennet stood up and sat in the chair across from him. "Free needs you." She told him how obsessed Free was about succeeding as a lumberman because he wanted to prove to Roman that he could. She reminded him that Free loved God, but the sin of unforgiveness blocked his relationship with God. "I've been praying for him, and I think you have been too. I know God works miracles. I think you can help this miracle happen."

Roman sat in silence a long time. Finally he lifted his haggard face. "When do we go?"

Jennet's heart leaped, but she didn't let it show. "At dawn."

"How?"

"A buggy to the Thornapple, a canoe to Grand Rapids, and a small steamboat to Big Pine. From there we'll take my buggy to camp. It'll take the whole day if all goes well. You'd only be gone three or four days. I'm sure you'd want to stay a bit with Free to see his work." Jennet held her breath for his answer.

"I'll go. Me and Wex."

Jennet said, "Very well. I'll take Clay to see my family and be here at dawn."

Roman nodded but didn't get up.

Jennet hurried down the wide hall toward the kitchen to get the baby. Outside the kitchen door Wex stopped her with a glad cry. He caught her hands and squeezed them tightly.

"This is a great surprise," Wex said, grinning. His hair was damp from just washing up, and he was wearing clean clothes. "You see Marie yet?"

"Just on my way."

"We're getting married after harvest."

"That's wonderful!"

"Can you come? You and Free?"

"I'll talk to him and see." Jennet looked back toward the front room. "Your pa has something to tell you." Jennet touched Wex's arm. "How are things between you and Roman?"

Wex pushed back a strand of dark hair that fell over his forehead, a gesture she'd seen Free do many times. "There're still times we fight, but he doesn't even try to beat me and sometimes he even listens to my ideas." He lowered his voice. "I think he even cares about me. He never says so, though."

"What does he say about you leaving here for your own farm?"

Wex shrugged. "He didn't like the idea, but he's getting used to it. Your pa's here to take care of a lot of the work.

And it helps to have Tim around. He and Pa get on well together."

"How're things between Anne and your pa?"

"Right as rain! Pa even let Ma stay with her when she had her baby girl a couple of weeks ago."

Jennet leaned forward with a giggle. "If he's not careful, he's going to have folks complain because he's so perfect."

Wex laughed. "It's good to see you again, Jen. You have a glow in your eyes I never saw before."

Jennet flushed. "Do I?"

"Did Free put it there?"

"Yes," she said softly.

"You always did have a soft spot for him."

"I guess I did, come to think of it." Jennet laughed and wrinkled her nose. "I better go see about Clay and let you go talk to your pa."

Wex grinned at her and walked away.

Jennet smiled. So, she'd always had a soft spot for Free, and Wex had noticed! Had Free noticed? Maybe he'd rescued her so many times because of it. Or maybe he'd had a soft spot for her and had rescued her because of that!

Maybe God had planned for them to be husband and wife. Tunis had said that Grandpa Clay had prayed often for the wives of his grandsons and the husband of his granddaughter. When Clay had gone to be with the Lord, Tunis and Nina had taken over for Clay and had prayed for them, in fact, still continued to pray. Who would've thought that the little girl Free had saved from the honeybees would someday be his wife?

With a low laugh Jennet entered the kitchen.

CHAPTER

19

♦ Free walked inside his empty shack and sank
to a chair with his head in his hands. The ring of the hammers as the men finished the last of the bookkeeper's
shack along with the shouts of the men drifted in the open
door. The smell of wood smoke from the cookcamp and the
blacksmith's shop hung in the air.

A great loneliness filled Free. Jennet had been gone only
two days, but it had felt like forever. Could he survive without Jennet now that he was used to having her around? He
never should've taken her out to see Grandpa's trees! He
should've lumbered them out, then told her what he'd
done. But could she forgive him if he'd done that?

What difference did it make? She'd never forgive him for
lumbering them now, permission or no.

What a mess he'd made of things. The past weeks
they'd been happier than he'd thought possible.

Free closed his eyes and heard Jennet's laughter and
smelled the soap she used and saw the twinkle of her blue
eyes and felt the softness of her beautiful hair.

Why hadn't he let her stay? She'd wanted to, even
though it'd be a hard life. Why had she wanted to? Was it

possible that she'd grown to love him the way Nina loved Tune?

The thought knocked Free back, and he sprang to his feet to pace the tiny area. She had joined him because it was the proper action for a wife to take. When first they'd married, she'd been a *proper* wife. But the past weeks she'd acted as if she enjoyed being with him. She'd been warm and passionate and had told him her thoughts and feelings.

Did she love him with the deep, passionate commitment he'd always wanted?

Free stopped stock-still. Maybe he should go to her to learn the truth and leave Glory Be in charge. He was a good foreman and knew the business well.

Free stopped in the open door and rammed his fingers through his thick dark hair. What about Grandpa's pines? "They have nothing to do with love," he muttered. The giant pines were business, nothing more.

But Jennet called them their heritage. She wanted them left for all times. They were not *business* or *money* to her.

Free groaned from deep within. He wanted to lumber the trees, but he also wanted Jennet. Was it possible to have both?

Impatiently Free strode to the barns, saddled a horse, and rode through the tree-covered hills to Grandpa's white pines. "Jen's white pines," he muttered as he leaned low to miss a branch.

He tied his horse to a branch, then followed the stream several feet into the woods. Ground squirrels scurried under the layer of needles. Hundreds of birds rose with loud cries and flew away. A brown bear dropped to his haunches, and lumbered out of sight.

Free picked up a pine cone and tossed it as far as he could. It landed without a sound.

As a young man, Grandpa had walked here and had canoed down the stream to trade with the Indians. He'd been angry about the law that forbade the Indians to speak their own language and practice their native religion. They had taken Clay Havlick to their hearts because he had respected them for who they were.

Free stopped and watched a beaver swimming near its dam.

"From the beaver I made my money, Freeman," Grandpa Clay had said the first time he'd taken Free to the woods with him. Free was nine then.

"I thought there'd always be beaver, Freeman. They were everywhere. The beaver hat was the craze in Europe and so the craze spread here, and all the men wanted the tall beaver hat to show their importance." Clay spread his hands wide and shrugged. "Why not take advantage of it? I traded for all the beaver pelts I could get from the Indians and the French trappers. Soon the beaver were gone. Sure, some are around, but not like they used to be." Clay rubbed a hand over his stubbled face. "I was wrong, Freeman. The beaver didn't last forever like I thought. You can't keep killing off animals and expect them to survive."

"I want to be a fur trader just like you, Grandpa." Free had gripped Clay's hand as he looked up into his lined face. "How can I be if all the animals are gone?"

"You can't make it a big business, Freeman, but you can make a fair living at it. Me and John Jacob Astor and a few others made our fortunes off fur, but that's history. There were plenty of beaver, bear, mink, marten, fox, otter, deer, elk, raccoon, wolves, lynx. And there's more to be had, but not for a fortune like I made. No, not no more." Clay patted the trunk of a giant pine. "Here's the big money of your future, Freeman. Lumbering. It's already started, but in a few years it'll be bigger than beaver hats. But the trees won't last forever. Just like the beaver. Lumber out the forests, and the farmer will come in and plow the land. Your children might never see the forests of Michigan."

Free laughed. "Grandpa, I won't have no children. I won't never get married."

"Don't let your pa hear that poor grammar or you won't never grow up big enough to get married." Clay laughed and clamped Free's shoulder with his big hand.

"Grandpa, why don't Pa love you like I do?"

Clay brushed a hand over his eyes. "I was off trading when your pa was growing up. When I was with him, I took no mind of him."

"You take mind of me and Anne and even Wex."

"I do that. But I learned the hard way, Freeman. I love your pa, but he won't never believe it."

"I love you enough for me and Pa both, Grandpa."

"I love you, Freeman. Don't you never forget that! I love you more'n fur trading, more'n walking them woods, more'n sleeping between pine boughs under the stars at night."

Free's heart almost burst. Nobody else loved him that much. Ma loved him some, but not enough to take his side against Pa when he got mad and whipped the daylights out of him.

"You make me proud, Freeman. Just being you," Grandpa Clay had said with a firm nod.

Suddenly the beaver slapped its tail against the water and dived out of sight. The sound brought Free back to the present. He brushed moisture from his eyes and cleared his throat. Grandpa had loved him and had taught him many things.

Slowly Free walked on. He heard wild pigeons in the tops of the trees and looked up to watch them.

"Free, wake up," Grandpa Clay had whispered one morning when Free was ten. "The wild pigeons are back."

Free had rolled out of bed, still sleepy, but excited to go with Grandpa to see the pigeons. The spring morning was frosty but not cold like wintertime.

Together they walked away from the clearing to the trees. Thousands of wild pigeons filled the air and the tops of the trees.

"When I first walked these woods, pigeon droppings was about a foot deep," said Clay. "I aimed up in the air and shot and always got a few birds with each shot."

"Really, Grandpa?" Free knew there were times when Grandpa exaggerated a story to make it better or teased him to see how he would respond.

"Sure is. It don't take much to kill them birds. I'd feed 'em to the pigs." Clay laughed. "You should've seen them pigs fight over them pigeons." Clay leaned down to Free. "Tonight we'll come out and knock 'em out of the trees and give 'em to the pigs for breakfast."

That night just as Grandpa had promised they knocked the wild pigeons out of the trees and they fed them to the pigs. Then Grandpa Clay had gotten real quiet. "Freeman, there'll come a time when even them pigeons will be gone. In the future men'll look back and make fun of a person who says once the sky was full of wild pigeons."

Grandpa's prediction had come true. Free nodded. The wild pigeons were dying out because of the farmers and the lumbering.

Free sank down on the thick cushion of dried pine needles and leaned against the rough black bark. Had Jennet seen the wild pigeons when she was young? Maybe she'd knocked them out of trees too. He smiled at the thought, then a great loneliness swept over him.

Was Jennet at home now, visiting with Tune and Nina or catching up on all the news from Meg and Will? Maybe when she was settled at home she'd not even miss him. He groaned at the terrible thought.

If he wasn't too busy, maybe he could leave Glory Be in charge at least once a month and make a trip home to see her.

Free rubbed his face with an unsteady hand. His whiskers felt rough. If he kept thinking of Jen, he just might go home now and leave Glory Be in charge. No, he couldn't do that. He had to be here to see that everything got under way.

Free thought of his first visit to Fordham's lumbercamp just to see the setup. He and Grandpa had eaten in the cookcamp with the shanty boys. To Free's surprise, no one spoke during the meal. No talking was allowed, Grandpa had said. Free had yearned to own a wide red sash like each wore and be big and strong and swing an ax to hit the same mark each time.

Free smiled. He did get the wide red sash, and he'd worn it two winters. Now it was tucked away in a drawer in his cabin. Someday he'd show it to Baby Clay and tell him about his life as a woodsman. He'd already shown it to Jennet. Laughing, she'd slipped it on, picked up the ax, and gone to the woodpile to split a stack of wood.

"There," she'd said when she'd returned, handing it back to him, "I can say that I'm a shanty boy!"

Free had hugged her so tight she'd squealed, then they'd laughed together and he'd kissed her. "Grandpa would've loved her," Free muttered as he brushed off pine needles and walked further along the crystal clear stream.

The trees were full of thoughts of Grandpa Clay, full of the love they'd had for each other and the experiences and the memories.

Seven years Grandpa had been gone now. Free knew that Grandpa had gone to heaven and only his body remained to be buried beside Grandma in the special spot in the woods, but still at times the loss was great. Tunis had been there to fill the gap that Grandpa had left, but it wasn't quite the same.

Free kicked a stone in the water, listened to the splash and watched the whirlpool it made. It hadn't been a good idea to come here when he was feeling so low.

Free looked up at the trees around him. Would Grandpa

care if he lumbered out these white pines? It didn't matter. He was going to do it. Besides Grandpa had said lumbering was the way for him to make his fortune.

Abruptly Free turned and walked back down the stream to where his horse was tied. He let the horse drink, then mounted, and rode slowly back toward camp.

Maybe he'd change his mind if Jennet came back and begged him to leave the trees standing. He frowned. What a dumb thought. She wouldn't be back. She'd get so busy with her life in Grand Rapids that she wouldn't give him or the white pines a second thought.

CHAPTER

20

♦ Jennet stood beside the buggy and looked all around the lumbercamp. Was Free in his little shack on the other side of the cookcamp or off in the woods? Her hands shook as she reached to take Clay from Wex.

"Are you all right?" Wex asked.

"I think so." Jennet saw Jig talking to the blacksmith and heard his laughter. The cook's children peeked out from behind the cookcamp to stare at her. Hammers thudded against nails as men finished the roof on the bookkeeper's shack. Where was Free?

Wex patted Jennet's arm. "Relax, Jen. Pa will find Free and talk to him and get everything settled. You'll see."

"It all sounds so simple, and I know it's not. It was really a foolish idea!"

"It was a good idea," said Wex. "Don't give up so soon."

She held Clay close to her heart and looked around, then frowned. "Where did Roman go?"

"In the cookcamp where Jig suggested he start."

Jennet turned. As she did, her ankle twisted, and she started to fall.

Wex caught her and held her. "Are you all right?"

Before Jennet could answer, she heard a loud, angry bellow. Suddenly Free grabbed Wex and hauled him away from Jennet. He socked Wex in the jaw, sending him sprawling to the ground. His hat flew off his head and landed near Jennet's booted feet.

"Don't touch her!" roared Free, fire shooting from his dark eyes. His gray shirt tightened across the bunched muscles of his back and arms.

In shock Wex stared up at Free towering over him.

"What are you doing?" cried Jennet, tugging at Free's arm before he could hit Wex again.

"Stay away from my wife!" Free reached to haul Wex to his feet so he could knock him down again.

Wex rolled away and jumped up, his fists ready, his face red. "Don't do that again, Free!"

"I should've put a stop to this a long time ago," growled Free.

Jennet stared at them in growing alarm. Clay whimpered in her arms, then was quiet.

"You always wanted her, didn't you, Wex?" Free narrowed his dark eyes as he circled Wex, his fists ready, his temper rising even more.

Before they could attack each other, Roman grabbed Free from behind and held him in such a tight hold that Free couldn't break loose. "Stop it, boys!" barked Roman. "What's the meaning of this?"

Jennet glanced around to find the few people at camp watching. A red-hot flush crept up her neck and over her face. "Take Free inside his shack where we can talk in private," she said in a low, tight voice.

"Let me go!" snapped Free. He wanted to tear Wex into little pieces and feed him to the wildcats.

Roman twisted Free's arm harder. "You get that temper in check, and I'll let you go."

Wex brushed dust and pine needles off his pants, scooped up his hat, and dropped it in place. "You don't have anything to be mad at, Free," he said sharply. "What's got into you anyway?"

"Get in the shack," said Jennet in a low, angry voice. "We don't need everybody here to know our family business."

Free struggled, embarrassed that his workers witnessed the event. "Let me go, Pa," he said hoarsely. "I won't attack Wex. Just let me go!"

Roman released him, and Free strode to the shack and held the door wide for the others to crowd in. Jennet laid the baby on the narrow bunk and turned to face the men. Her blue eyes flashed, and her breast rose and fell. The high neck of her blue dress suddenly felt hot and tight.

"What're you doing back here, Jen?" Free stood with his hands on his hips.

Jennet faced him bravely, her chin high. "I said I intended to stay here with you. And I meant it."

"You're not staying."

"I am."

"No!"

"And I brought your pa so you could talk to him and settle this fight between the two of you."

"You think this will keep me from lumbering those trees?" Free's voice was cold.

"I want you to talk to your pa," she repeated.

Free realized that Pa *was* there, even though it was harvest time. His words died in his throat, and he numbly shook his head.

Roman pulled off his hat and tossed it on a peg beside the door. "Vern and Tim are taking care of things at home." He cleared his throat. "I thought it was time I saw what kind of work you do around here."

Jennet knotted her fists at her sides. "You did not come for that reason, Roman Havlick, and you know it! You came to tell Free you love and respect him and are proud of him."

Roman flushed and couldn't look at Free.

"Don't back down now, Pa," said Wex.

Free shot a look at Pa.

Roman cleared his throat and rubbed a hand over his red face. "It's time you hear me say I'm sorry about not telling you about your grandpa's will. I'm sorry for trying to keep you on the farm when you wanted to do this." He waved his hand and looked uncomfortable. The tiny space suddenly seemed even smaller. "This is hard for me, Free, but I'm doing it anyway."

"You ruined my life, Pa!" cried Free.

"He did not!" blurted Jennet.

Free pointed his finger at her. "You stay out of this!"

Jennet locked her trembling fingers together in front of her. "You have me."

He narrowed his eyes. "Not another word!"

"And Clay."

"Quiet!"

"And your lumber business!"

"Jennet!"

The color drained from her cheeks, but she wouldn't back down. "And God is on your side."

Free plucked at his suspenders as he stared at Jennet.

"Will you forgive me, Free?" asked Roman gruffly.

Free turned his head to look at Pa. Was that really Pa looking so sorry and so humble? A strange feeling rose inside Free. He thought of all the times both Tune and Jig had talked to him about this very thing. He thought he'd carry his anger toward Pa for all his days, but suddenly he knew he didn't want to. He was tired of being angry, tired of struggling over his guilt for not forgiving Pa, and sorry that he'd put a wedge between himself and God. It took him a long time to find his voice. "I do, Pa," he whispered.

Jennet almost burst into tears.

Roman brushed a tear off his cheek.

"I need *you* to forgive me, Pa," said Free.

"Said and done," replied Roman.

Free felt a load lift and he smiled broadly.

Roman took a deep breath. "Now, how about showing me and Wex around your place here?"

Jennet sank to the bunk, her legs shaking so badly she couldn't stand another minute.

"Sure thing, Pa." Free held open the door and waited for them to walk out.

"I'll come too," said Jennet, jumping up.

"Stay here," snapped Free.

His look and his voice sent a cold dart through her heart. She would *not* allow her lip to quiver. "I have to feed Clay anyway, so I will stay here." She'd expected him to give her a quick hug and kiss for what she'd done for him, but he was still upset with her.

Free walked out, closing the door after him.

Jennet sighed and pressed her trembling hands to her flushed cheeks. She'd expected a long fight between Free and Roman, a great struggle, then a loud scene where they finally cleared the air. But it was settled at long last!

"Thank You, heavenly Father!" Jennet said fervently. "You worked another miracle today!"

But it wasn't over yet! Not until Free loved her the way a husband was to love his wife.

Outdoors Free forced back thoughts of Jennet and showed off the cookcamp where they had coffee and raisin cookies, the stable, the blacksmith shop, the company store, and the other buildings, telling them about each one. Free introduced Pa and Wex to his workers and made arrangements for them to have a place to sleep for the night. He felt like a little boy who had trapped his first beaver.

"You got quite a place here," said Roman, looking at Free proudly as they stopped at the rise of a hill overlooking the large camp. "I never knew it'd be like this. It takes brains and brawn to be a lumberman."

Pa's look and his words healed something inside Free that had been an open sore for a long time.

"It suits me," said Free.

"Like farming suits me," said Wex.

Free slapped Wex on the back. "I'm sure sorry about that punch. I saw red when you put your arms around Jen."

"She tripped and I caught her."

Relief swept through Free and he laughed.

"He's got eyes only for Marie," said Roman, pushing his hat to the back of his head.

"Is that right?"

Wex nodded. "We're getting married in November. We'd like you and Jen to be there."

"Jen will be home so she can be there, but I don't think I can make it."

"Jen's planning on staying here," said Wex.

"She is, is she?" The excitement that flashed through Free quickly turned to anger. He didn't know what to make of Jen with the change in her. "We'll see about that," he said gruffly.

"She told us about your grandpa's trees," said Roman.

Free stiffened. Had she brought Roman just to stop him from lumbering the trees?

"She's got a point, Free," said Wex.

"There's plenty of white pines," said Free with a shrug.

Roman pulled off his hat, wiped his forehead, and dropped his hat back in place. "I know your grandpa wanted the trees left standing."

"How do you know that?" asked Free sharply.

"We talked about it. He tried to get me to keep a stand of hardwood trees, but I was too pigheaded and wouldn't. He said it was important to keep at least part of the land the way we had found it."

Free remembered the talks he and Grandpa had had about that. Suddenly logging the trees didn't matter, having the money didn't matter, and not even being as big as Witherspoon mattered. "I can't fight you and Grandpa . . . and Jen too." Laughing, Free spread his arms wide. "I can see I'd better back down on this one."

"I'm proud of you, son."

A lump lodged in Free's throat and he couldn't speak.

"Jen plans to stay here with you, Free, and I think you should let her," said Roman.

"I can't give in on everything, Pa."

"She deserves to be happy." Roman looked uncomfortable. "And you make her happy."

He did? Free shrugged. "I'll talk it out with her," he said. Would he have the heart to send her away?

At dark after the men were settled in for the night, Free stood in his shack with Clay in his arms while Jen sat at the table. A wildcat screeched and a horse nickered, then all was quiet except for Clay's gurgles, Free's cooing, and the distant lament of a fiddle. The lamp on the table flickered, sending out a smell of kerosene. Jennet locked her hands in her lap as she waited for Free to lay Clay in his basket. Finally he did, then turned to her. She tried to read his expression.

"You went to a lot of trouble to get your own way," Free said. Just looking at her sent his pulse racing.

Jennet's heart sank, but she wouldn't give up. "We will have to get a bigger bed in here and a bed for Clay. He's getting too big for his basket."

"You think so?"

She met his eyes squarely. "I'm staying, Freeman Havlick!"

Free almost laughed aloud at seeing the stubborn set of her jaw. What a fighter she'd turned out to be! "Oh, all right! Have it your way!"

"But I want you to be glad!"

"You can't have everything," he said hoarsely

She bit her lip.

"I can arrange for a bigger bed." Free sat on the chair across the tiny table from her. The night was warm enough that he hadn't started a fire in the small stove. A moth dived at the lamp. "What else will you need?"

She needed him! "A place to have school for the cook's three kids."

Free had expected her to say something different. "You can use one of the offices for now until we can figure something else out. Anything else?"

"No."

Free frowned. "You could ask for a bigger place to live."

"I said I'd be able to live here."

"So you did."

He wanted to take her in his arms and tell her he was glad she was there, but he couldn't.

Jennet stared at the flickering flame. She'd planned to fling her arms around him and tell him she loved him as soon as they were alone, but she couldn't find the courage.

Free stood up. "I'll be going now."

Jennet's heart froze. "Going?"

"You and Clay sleep here, and I'll bunk in with Pa and Wex."

Jennet struggled to hold back tears.

"See you tomorrow then. Right after breakfast I'm taking Pa and Wex out to the trees we'll be chopping first."

Jennet wanted to go along, but she didn't say so. "I'll get acquainted with the kids."

"Fine."

She moved restlessly. "Are you mad because I brought your pa and Wex here?"

"No."

She lifted her eyes to his. "Are you mad that I came back?"

"Yes. But I'll get over it." Free stood at the door and

watched the lamplight play over her. "Good night."

"Good night," she whispered.

He opened the door and closed it quickly to keep the moths out. He stood there a long time.

Inside Jennet covered her face with her hands and burst into tears.

For the next two days each time she was alone she cried, even though she'd try not to. If she couldn't see Free or even talk to him, why stay? Maybe she should return with Roman and Wex.

But Jennet couldn't leave Free, couldn't stand the thought of being so far away from him for such a long time.

The day after Roman and Wex left, Free pulled up in the buggy just outside the open door of the shack. "Jennet, bring Clay and take a ride with me," he called.

Jennet's heart leaped, and she scooped up Clay in his basket and walked to the buggy. She set the basket on the buggy floor and climbed in with a hand from Free. Her skin tingled from his touch, but she couldn't look at him.

Love for her rose inside him so strong it almost knocked him off his seat. When had he fallen so deeply in love with her? Did she know she was essential to his very being?

"Where're you off to?" called Jig from the outside of the cookcamp where he stood with a large mug of coffee in his hand.

"For a ride," said Free, so excited about having time alone with Jennet that he wanted to shout at the top of his lungs.

"You want me to keep Clay with me?" Jig asked.

Jennet giggled at the thought of Jig changing Clay. "No thanks, Jig," she called. She waved to him and he lifted a gnarled dirty hand to her.

"You sure stole his heart," said Free. *And mine,* he thought.

"I love him too."

Frowning, Free clucked to Acorn and flicked the reins. Would Jen ever say those words to him?

When they left the camp clearing, Free said, "I told Wex we'd try to make it to his wedding."

Jennet turned to Free with a cry of joy. "Oh, that's wonderful! Marie would be so happy!"

"I was pretty jealous of Wex and you."

Jennet flushed. "You had no reason."

"I know that now." Free watched an eagle fly high in the bright blue sky. How could he tell her he loved her? "You haven't asked me about Pa."

"I wanted to. But I figured I'd better let you tell me when you wanted to."

"It's fine between us now."

"Good." She'd already known it was by the way they'd acted together, but it was good to hear him say so. She wanted to ask how it was between her and him.

"I was wrong to hold a grudge. I told him so."

"I'm glad."

Free wanted to say so much more, but he couldn't get past the wall he felt between them. Had he built it—or had she?

They didn't speak again until Free stopped Acorn at Jennet's white pines. Her heart sank. Would they have to fight over the trees again?

Jennet jumped to the ground before Free could reach her side and help her out. Clay was sound asleep in his basket, so she left him in the buggy. She draped a light blanket over the basket to keep out the mosquitoes. When she turned around, she almost bumped into Free. Her pulse leaped and she couldn't speak.

"I have something else to tell you," Free said as he took her hand and led her away from the buggy to stand at the base of a nearby pine. He liked the way the soft blue of her dress matched her eyes. He wanted to touch the strands of hair that had fallen down her neck.

Just then Clay cried and Free ran to him and carried him to Jennet, talking to make him laugh.

Jennet's heart almost burst at the beauty of the two together.

When Free reached Jennet's side, he held Clay up high in both his hands. "Clay, you won't see the wild pigeons or the beavers in great numbers, but I promise you that you will see these white pines. They'll be here for your children and their children and their children."

Tears slipped down Jennet's cheeks.

Free looked down at Jennet and gently brushed away her tears with his thumb. "Jen, you were right and I was wrong. Grandpa felt the same as you. I remembered some of the things he told me. And Pa said they'd talked about it. Pa said he was too stubborn to save some of the hardwood trees around his farm, but he didn't want me to be too stubborn to save the white pines."

"Oh, Free," she whispered. A gentle wind blew the pine boughs, sending the clean smell of pine whirling around them.

"I've already sent out my timber walker to find more property for me. I can't quit being a lumberman, but I can let these trees stand forever."

Clay squirmed and started crying his hungry cry. Jennet took him and sat on the ground under the tree to feed him while Free talked to her about what the time with his pa had meant to him.

"I never thought I'd love Pa like I did Grandpa Clay, but I do. It's strange. A real miracle. I know God did it, Jen."

"I know too," she said with a catch in her voice. Silently she thanked God for answering her prayers. He had another one to answer, that Free love her as a husband should love a wife. It would happen because God was faithful to perform His Word. He never broke His promises!

Several minutes later Jennet laid Clay on his stomach in

his basket and walked back to join Free beside the stream. She heard the water rushing over the stones. Minnows darted in and out around the weeds and rocks. A frog croaked and hopped in the water with a tiny splash.

"I'm having a bigger place built for us," Free said without looking at her.

"You are?"

"It's behind my old shack. I'll show you when we return. The men are working hard on it, and they said it'll be done by tonight."

"It will?"

"Yes."

Just then white-tailed deer ran into sight, spotted them and leaped away, their tails high and waving like white flags.

She mustered up all of the courage in her and said, "I didn't want another night without you."

Her words curled around his heart. Slowly he turned to face her. A squirrel chattered at them from a tree. "I've missed you, Jen."

"You have?"

"I have." Free looked deep in her blue eyes, and the message in them sent his blood pounding. But he had to hear the words before he was satisfied. "Jen, do you . . . love me?"

Without hesitation Jennet said, "Yes. I do love you!"

He pulled her against his heart. "I don't know when it happened, but I fell in love with you." He held her away enough to look into her face. "I love you more than I've ever loved anyone." He cupped her face in his hands. "I love you with a love that will never end. All that I have belongs to you. I will love you and keep you and protect you all the days of my life."

Jennet slid her arms around his neck. "Freeman Havlick, I love you with a love that will never end. All that I have belongs to you. I will love you and keep you and protect you all the days of my life."

Free lowered his lips to hers, and she met his kiss with a passion that matched his own. He crushed her close, and she pushed her fingers through the dark thickness of his hair. The time for talking was over.

ABOUT THE AUTHOR

Hilda Stahl is a writer, teacher, and speaker, who offers writers seminars and lectures both to schools and organizations across the country.

Born in the Nebraska Sandhills, Hilda grew up telling stories to her five sisters and three brothers. Yet she never once thought of becoming a writer. Instead, she wanted to be a rancher and raise horses and cattle.

After she had her first three children, Hilda began to write, and has since published 62 fiction titles, 450 short stories, a radio script for "Children's Bible Hour," and a one-hour Christmas play. Hilda writes stories of mystery, romance, and adventure and portrays God as the answer to the sensitive and difficult issues of our lives.

The author is mother of seven children, grandmother of two, and lives with her husband, Norman, in Michigan.